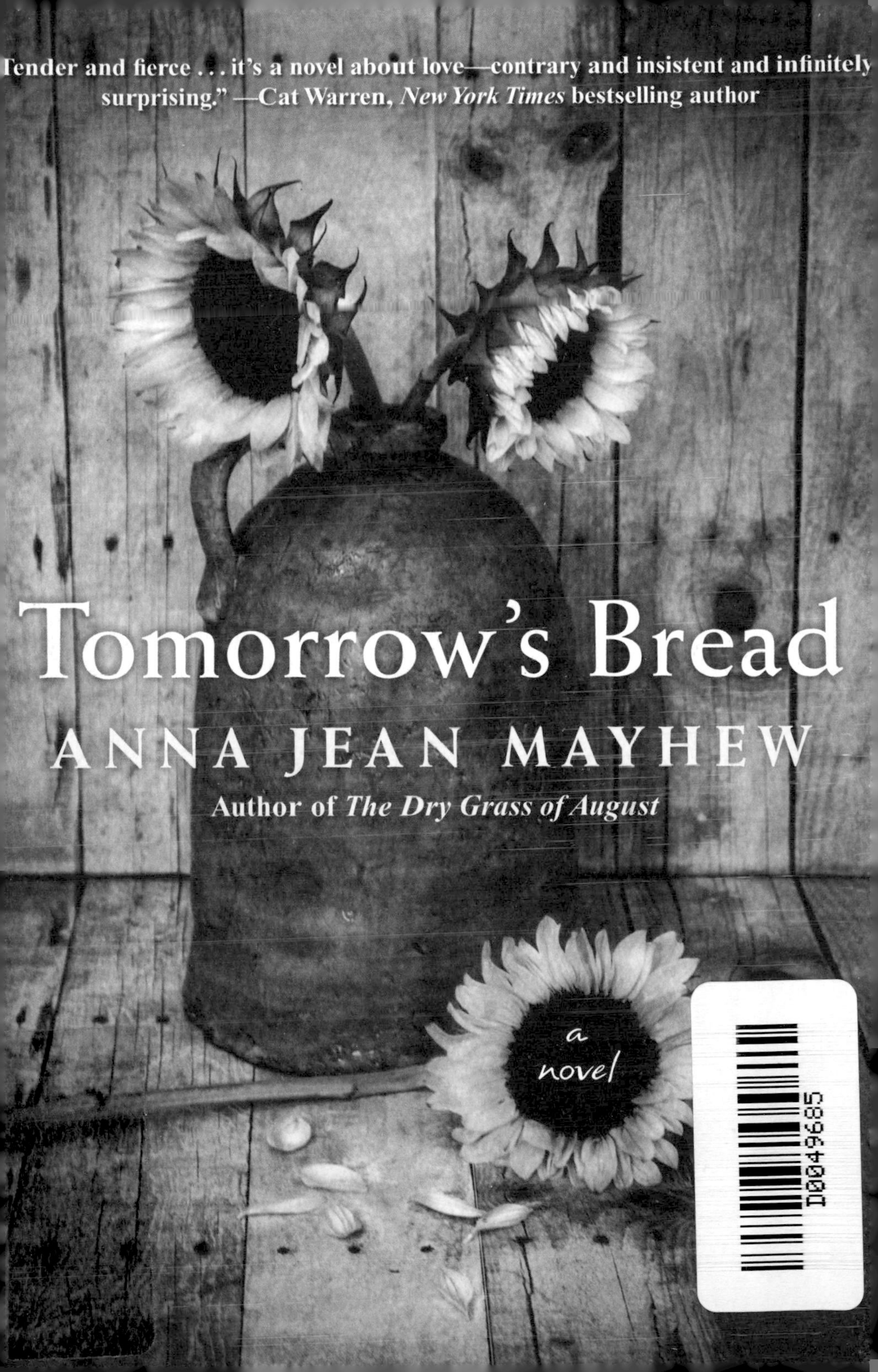

"Tender and fierce . . . it's a novel about love—contrary and insistent and infinitely surprising." —Cat Warren, *New York Times* bestselling author

Tomorrow's Bread

ANNA JEAN MAYHEW

Author of *The Dry Grass of August*

a novel

U.S. $15.95
CAN $21.95

From the author of the acclaimed **The Dry Grass of August** *comes a richly researched yet lyrical Southern-set novel that explores the conflicts of gentrification—a moving story of loss, love, and resilience.*

In 1961 Charlotte, North Carolina, the predominantly black neighborhood of Brooklyn is a bustling city within a city. Self-contained and vibrant, it has its own restaurants, schools, theaters, churches, and night clubs. There are shotgun shacks and poverty, along with well-maintained houses like the one Loraylee Hawkins shares with her young son, Hawk, her Uncle Ray, and her grandmother, Bibi. Loraylee's love for Archibald Griffin, Hawk's white father and manager of the cafeteria where she works, must be kept secret in the segregated South.

Loraylee has heard rumors that the city plans to bulldoze her neighborhood, claiming it's dilapidated and dangerous. The government promises to provide new housing and relocate businesses. But locals like Pastor Ebenezer Polk, who's facing the demolition of his church, know the value of Brooklyn does not lie in bricks and mortar. Generations have lived, loved, and died here, supporting and strengthening each other. Yet street by street, longtime residents are being forced out. And Loraylee, searching for a way to keep her family together, will form new alliances—and find an unexpected path that may yet lead her home.

Praise for Anna Jean Mayhew and *Tomorrow's Bread*

"In her wise and empathic new novel, Anna Jean Mayhew returns to Jim Crow–era Charlotte, North Carolina, where the vibrant black community of Brooklyn is about to be demolished. Richly drawn and deeply felt, *Tomorrow's Bread* is a haunting story of irreparable loss. It is also a testament to the sustaining power of resistance and the unexpected satisfactions of sheer endurance. This is a story for our time."
—Kim Church, author of *Byrd*

"This is a moving, vivid story—historical fiction that's both instructive and entertaining."
—Pam Kelley, author of *Money Rock*

"A marvelous job re-creating the day-to-day life of a lost era and a vanished place. Mayhew's careful historical sleuthing calls up the human and physical landscape of Charlotte's old Brooklyn. But even more, she captures the flavor of daily life, especially the small details that may seem "off subject" but are true to how all of us think, feel and act."
—Thomas W. Hanchett, author of *Sorting Out the New South City: Race, Class, and Urban Development in Charlotte, 1875–1975*

"In prose as gentle as falling snow, Anna Jean Mayhew spins a tale of two communities, one black, one white, adjacent and interdependent but worlds apart. Characters from each appear, drawn with remarkable sensitivity, and intersect with each other in ways that will leave them forever altered. Larger in scope even than her *Dry Grass of August*, the novel is an honest but affectionate account of a time long gone—not with the wind but with the dramatic changes the last fifty years have wrought in the racial landscape of American society. The story is at times lyrical, at times thrilling, but inherently important: a must-read for those who remember it and those for whom it is history."
—Thomas Grant, author of *Lake Pontchartrain*

"Over 150 black neighborhoods were destroyed by the urban renewal program of the 1960s. Anna Jean Mayhew makes that loss personal in *Tomorrow's Bread* through her empathy, her specificity, and her clean, vivid prose. It's an important and sadly relevant story, one that I found deeply moving."
—Lewis Shiner, author of *Black & White*

And praise for *The Dry Grass of August*

"Anna Jean Mayhew has a true ear for Southern speech . . . *The Dry Grass of August* is a carefully researched, beautifully written, quietly told tale of love and despair and a look backward at the way it was back then in the South."
—*The Pilot* (Southern Pines, North Carolina)

"Once you've experienced *The Dry Grass of August,* you'll swiftly see that Anna Jean Mayhew's debut novel deserves all the early praise it's getting . . . the power, bravery and beauty of Mayhew's narrative is beyond contestation and well-deserving of a wide readership."
—*BookPage*

"An extraordinary, absorbing novel."
—*Historical Novel Reviews*

"If you liked *The Help,* you must read *The Dry Grass of August.*"
—*Ahwatukee Foothills News* (Phoenix, Arizona)

"With her look back at a racial and cultural society in transition, Mayhew also delivers a coming of age novel that will touch readers' hearts. Then she serves up a tragic moment that will give those same hearts a hurt that will be long remembered."
—*The Enquirer-Journal*

"A superior book to *The Help.*"
—Christina Bucher, *North Carolina Literary Review*

Tomorrow's Bread

Books by Anna Jean Mayhew

THE DRY GRASS OF AUGUST

TOMORROW'S BREAD

Published by Kensington Publishing Corporation

Tomorrow's Bread

ANNA JEAN MAYHEW

KENSINGTON BOOKS
www.kensingtonbooks.com

KENSINGTON BOOKS are published by

Kensington Publishing Corp.
119 West 40th Street
New York, NY 10018

All Kensington titles, imprints, and distributed lines are available at special quantity discounts for bulk purchases for sales promotion, premiums, fund-raising, educational, or institutional use.

Special book excerpts or customized printings can also be created to fit specific needs. For details, write or phone the office of the Kensington Sales Manager: Kensington Publishing Corp., 119 West 40th Street, New York, NY 10018. Attn. Sales Department. Phone: 1-800-221-2647.

Kensington and the K logo Reg. U.S. Pat. & TM Off.

ISBN-13: 978-1-4967-2056-6 (ebook)
ISBN-10: 1-4967-2056-3 (ebook)
Kensington Electronic Edition: April 2019

ISBN-13: 978-0-7582-5410-8
ISBN-10: 0-7582-5410-5
First Kensington Trade Paperback Printing: April 2019

10 9 8 7 6 5 4 3 2 1

Printed in the United States of America

For Jackson, Reese, and Scott

Democracy

By Langston Hughes

Democracy will not come
Today, this year
        Nor ever
Through compromise and fear.

I have as much right
As the other fellow has
        To stand
On my two feet
And own the land.

I tire so of hearing people say,
Let things take their course.
Tomorrow is another day.
I do not need my freedom when I'm dead.
I cannot live on tomorrow's bread.

        Freedom
        Is a strong seed
        Planted
        In a great need.
        I live here, too.
        I want freedom
        Just as you.

Retitled "Freedom" by 1967, and appearing this way in THE COLLECTED POEMS (1994), this poem was originally known as "Democracy."

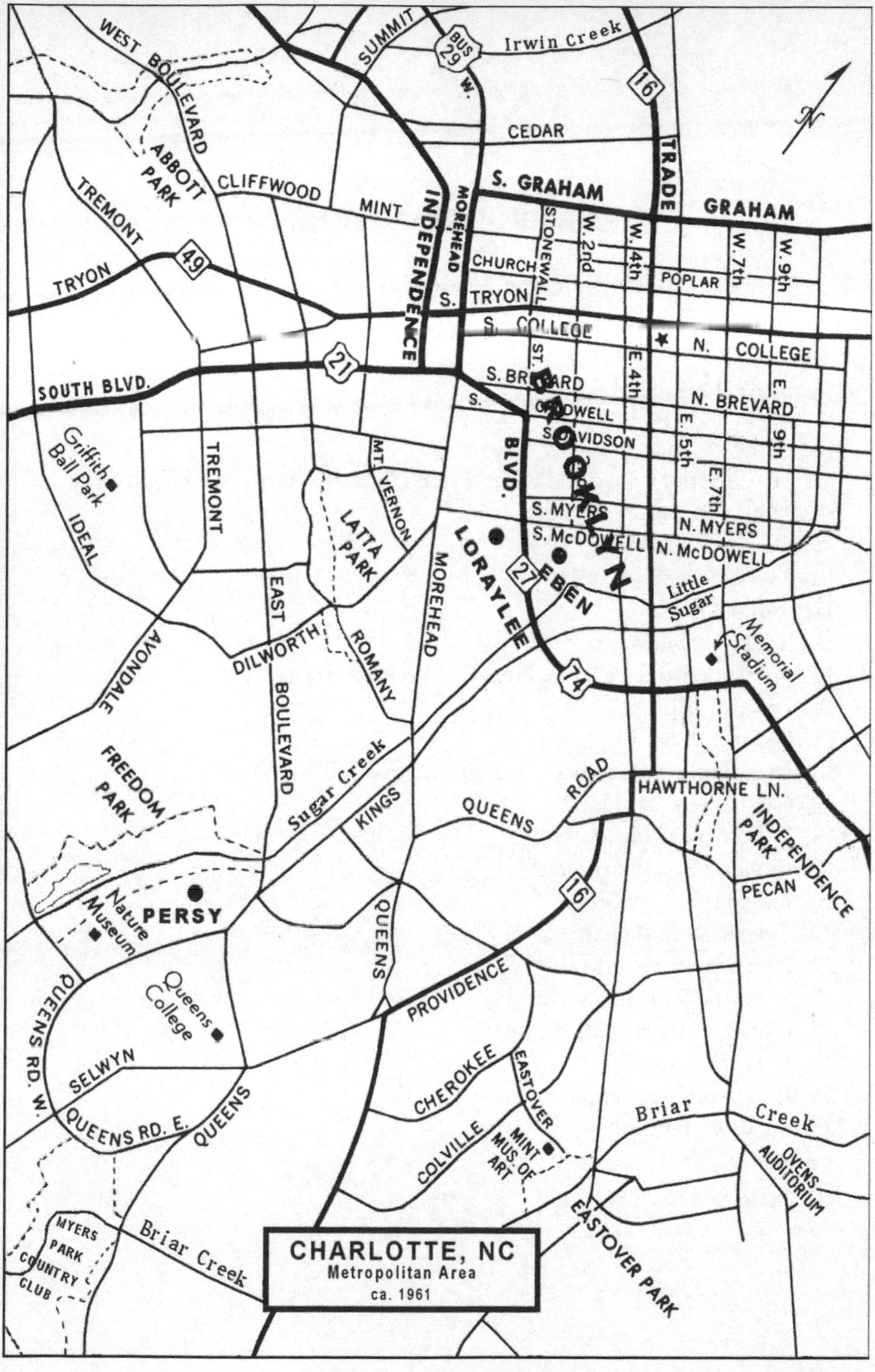

⋆Independence Square

THE BROOKLYN AREA

1. Loraylee, Hawk, Bibi, and Uncle Ray
2. Boyce, Veola, and Desmond Whitin
3. Dooby Franklin
4. Tunnel Under Independence Blvd.*
5. Savoy Movie Theatre*
6. Stone's Grocery
7. St. Timothy's Second Presbyterian Church, Manse, and Cemetery
8. House of Prayer for All People*
9. Stirewalt Flowers
10. Myers Street School*
11. Talford Park
12. Tocky's Nightclub
13. Roberta Stokes ("Blue Heaven" Neighborhood*)
14. Law Building*
15. Second Ward High School*
16. Mecklenburg County Courthouse and Jail*
17. Charlotte City Hall*
18. Wholesale Auto Parts*
19. Queen City Pharmacy*
20. Lamarr Beauty Shop*
21. Tyler's Shoe Repair
22. Brevard Street Library*
23. Edward Wilkins, MD
24. College Street Parking Lot*
25. S. H. Kress & Co.*
26. Independence Square*
27. S&W Cafeteria*

*In existence in 1961

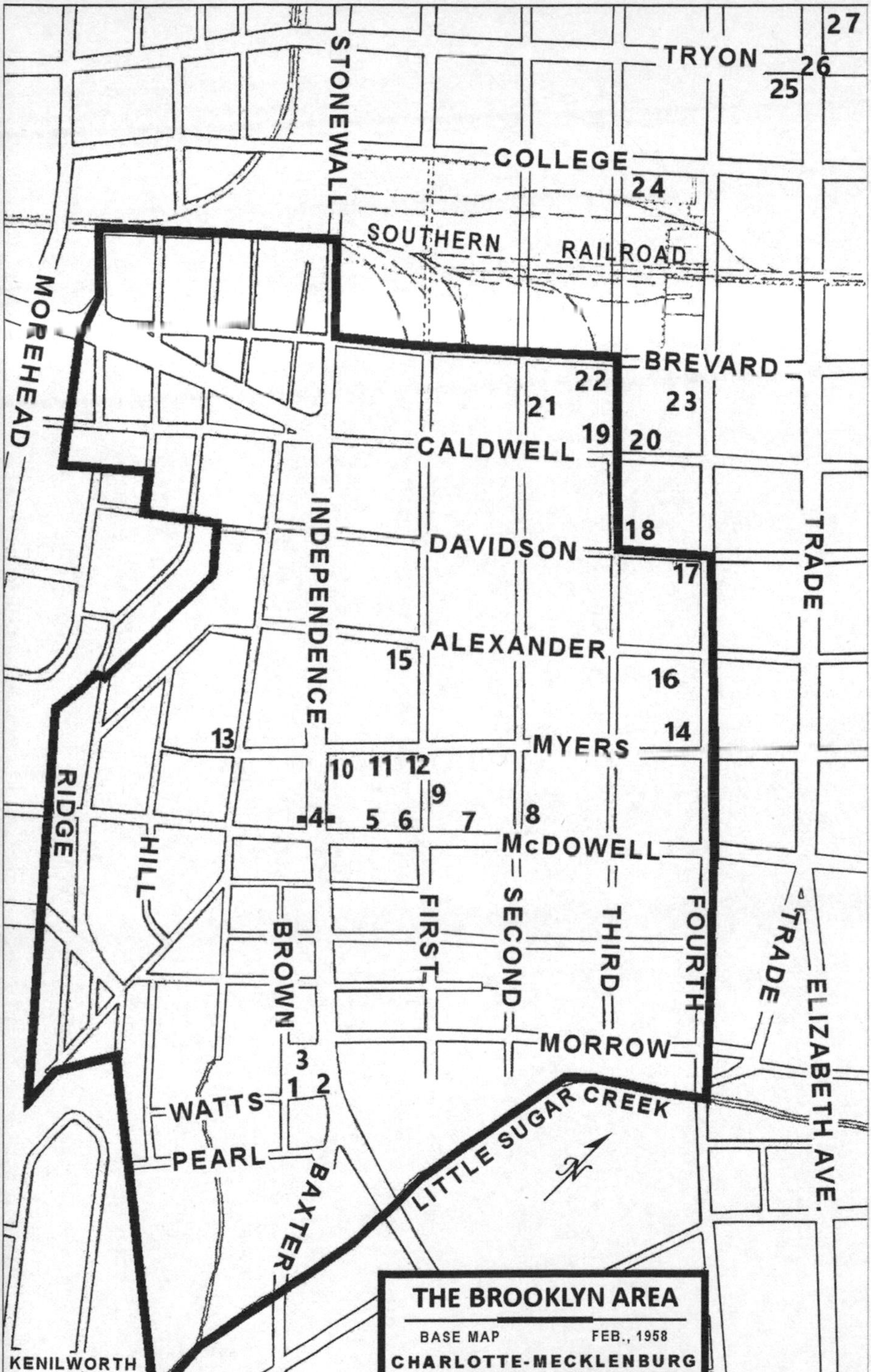
TRYON
COLLEGE
SOUTHERN RAILROAD
STONEWALL
MOREHEAD
BREVARD
CALDWELL
DAVIDSON
ALEXANDER
MYERS
McDOWELL
MORROW
INDEPENDENCE
TRADE
RIDGE
HILL
BROWN
FIRST
SECOND
THIRD
FOURTH
ELIZABETH AVE.
WATTS
PEARL
BAXTER
LITTLE SUGAR CREEK
KENILWORTH
N
1 2 3 4 5 6 7 8 9 10 11 12 13 14 15 16 17 18 19 20 21 22 23 24 25 26 27
THE BROOKLYN AREA
BASE MAP FEB., 1958
CHARLOTTE-MECKLENBURG PLANNING COMMISSION

CHAPTER 1

Down in the gully Little Sugar whispers, sliding through the night like a ghost. On a pretty day it calls my boy to it. If I don't catch Hawk first, he'll be halfway to Pearl Street, a bucket in one hand, a net made from a stocking in the other, bent on frogs or crawdads or whatever pulls him down to where that creek lives. He's breathing steady in his bed across the room, not knowing how slippery the mudbank gets in early March, how quick the water could drag him under.

Uncle Ray's chickens clucking in their coop. Day coming on. Got to rouse Hawk soon, get him fed and dressed. Bibi, my grand, say when he was born, "Enjoy him being a baby, Raylee. It won't last." He's six now, long legs, knobby knees, in first grade.

I walked to Myers Street School with him for a week last September to be sure he knows the way. I tell him about traffic lights, got to look up and down the street before he crosses, use the tunnel under the boulevard. We leave the house and he takes my hand—his small in mine—tugging on me to stop so he can holler, "Hey!" to Dooby Franklin next door or Jonny No Age, waving to us from his delivery van, or Mayrese Hemphill, heading downtown in a new coat and hat.

At the corner of South Myers, Hawk tilts back his head to stare at the school building, two stories, chimneys on top. We go inside, down a rackety hall to a room that's different day to day because Miss Madison keeps changing the maps and pictures she hangs on the walls, sets the desks in rows one day, a circle the next. She is short and full built, in dresses that hug her waist and stretch tight across her backside. Hawk say she smells good. She calls me Mrs. Hawkins, thinking a mother must be married.

The day I drop in to take Hawk his lunch he forgot, I see him leaning against Miss Madison, her hand on his back, like he's special to her.

Now he gets to school on his own, with Desmond, his friend that lives behind us. I stand out front and watch him going away from me. Slim, like his daddy, his round head bobbing while he talks to himself the way he does, then around the corner and out of sight.

I'm with a bunch of people under the awning on the Square, trying to stay out of the rain. Most days I walk home from my job at the S&W, saving the bus fare. Unless it's a drencher like today. I got a paper bag tucked under my arm for when I have to get off the other side of the boulevard.

A white man in the crowd say, "No justice in that," in a loud voice. He wants people to hear him, making me glad I don't know what he means so I won't get riled. I board behind him and speak to Gus, been driving for the city most of his life, always say, "Hey, Loraylee," when I drop my dime in the box, his blue eyes shining beneath the bill of his cap.

The noisy man is on the bench seat next to the door, with a bunch of men going home from work. I walk on by. The mat that runs down the middle of the bus use to have a line on it and coloreds had to stay behind that line, like we wouldn't still be breathing the same air as the whites up front. All that changed when the lines disappeared four-five years ago. But I like the back of the bus, the long seat under the big window, even if I am allowed to ride up front now with those stiff-necked men in their hats and suits.

My stop is four blocks from home in the chilly rain. I hold the bag over my head, running from alley to alley through backyards, getting mud on my shoes, my legs, my uniform. I step over the magnolia branches that cover our front walk. Uncle Ray planted that tree when I was born and he say it's the prettiest one in Second Ward. I go up the sagging steps, drip on the mat, toss the wet bag on the rocker.

In the living room I call out, "Hey, y'all." Nobody home, not even Bibi. No telling where she is. Uncle Ray must of taken the umbrella and gone to meet Hawk, the kind sort of thing he does. Nice being alone in the house so I can shuck my uniform to the kitchen floor. Even my slip is soaked, my cold nipples showing through.

I get the percolator going for a cup of hot coffee, head for the room I share with Hawk, and there is Bibi, in Hawk's bed, under his plaid spread, snoring. If she sleeps all day, she'll be up all night, a problem for me or Uncle Ray, but I leave her be, put on dry clothes, empty the hamper to start a load before I fix supper. I toss the dirty clothes in the washer on the back porch, get it going. I like smelling soap powder instead of mildew or ashes, or the coal bucket by the door.

At the sink, popping leaves off a cabbage, I'm glad I have a clean uniform for tomorrow; that load of wash not gon dry in this damp house overnight. All us who work at the S&W wear uniforms, except Mr. Griffin. Retta Lawrence, my friend girl there, say uniforms save wear and tear. They sure save time, and S&W pays for them.

Bibi complains she always had to buy her own uniforms.

Last lady she worked for docked her pay four dollars if she needed a new one. Bibi talks about that like it's yesterday, not two-three years ago. "Miz Easterling misplace something and she fire me, say, 'Girl, you stealing.' Then she kep those uniforms I paid for, like she gon get another maid same size."

Bibi's the one misplacing stuff, same as she does here. Without a reference from the Easterlings she couldn't find another job, but I come to like having her here with Hawk when he's not at school. Before she got so bad off I was afraid what she might forget next. Don't know what I'd do without Uncle Ray, Bibi's younger brother, keeping an eye on things when I'm at work.

The screen door scrapes the front porch. "Raylee!" Bibi shouts. How'd she get through the living room without me hearing her?

"Raylee!" She never say Loraylee, won't put the Lo in my name, which is for my Auntie Lorena. The way Bibi's mind is bent, a little bit sticking and a little bit not, maybe someday she'll forget she's mad at her sister.

I find her standing in the yard in the drizzling rain, stupid from not remembering why she's there. "Bibi, c'mon back inside. You getting soaked."

She grins like I've promised her ice cream. "Okay." I hate seeing her lose her sense, makes me want to take her shoulders and shake her and tell her try, you're not trying. But that would do no good.

I bring her up from the yard, onto the porch, and before I can get her through the door she settles into the rocking chair. "I loves to rock on a summer afternoon." I don't bother saying it's March and almost sundown, leave her rocking so I can get supper ready before Hawk gets home. He is fierce about food, like he'll never get another meal. Fast as he puts it down, he works it off running in the yard or making a fort under the magnolia or feeding Uncle Ray's chickens. Gon be tall like his daddy, judging by his feet. But except for his gray eyes and rusty hair, that boy is me, my high cheeks, my wide flat nose, my mouth.

I hear Uncle Ray and Hawk talking to Bibi, glad they're home, out of the rain.

We having hot dogs, which Uncle Ray favors. I make slaw and baked beans, chop onions, heat a can of Bunker Hill chili. The trick is opening the bottom of the can; all the fat rises to the top while it's been sitting on the shelf, and that grease tastes bad. Last thing is steaming the buns. Bibi likes a soft bun for her hot dogs, and Hawk wants everything exactly the way she does. I watch him next to her at the table, leaning on her arm, looking up at her to ask a question. She has got a temper since she started forgetting, but she's always gentle with Hawk.

I sit on the porch with Uncle Ray while Hawk helps Bibi do the dishes. The air is clean, cool, when the rain stops. Even the muddy street looks washed. Uncle Ray sets his glass of tea on the rail. His seventy-two years show in the wrinkles on his face, the skin hanging under his chin like a rooster. Bibi pushes food at him, trying to put some fat on his bones. But he's fit, can clear the yard after a storm if his lumbago isn't acting up.

The setting sun flows through the magnolia branches, making the ice in his glass sparkle. "Would you look at that?" He runs a hand over the top of his head where his scalp shows through, shiny walnut under a light snow. "Reminds me of when I saw the light." I know what's coming. I sit back in the rocker, stare down toward the creek.

"After I took that bad fall, I left this world, saw something like that sunbeam."

His tobacco sack, a box of wooden matches, and his pipe sit on a barrel between us. He tamps his pipe, puts it in his mouth, fires it up. "Dr. Wilkins brought me back and the light faded." He flicks the match over the rail to see how far it'll fly before it lands in the wet grass. "I was dead, don't you doubt it, but St. Peter wasn't calling yet." Puff, puff, smoke rising. "The light is what a baby sees when it squeals out from its mama. Souls get to start all over in a newborn child, don't you see?" He looks at me. "Death. Is. Birth." He gets up, goes down the steps toward the street, stopping to pick up the match.

"Mm-hmm," I say. "Maybe you're right."

Uncle Ray folds his long legs into a squat beside the walk, poking at the ground, smoke drifting from his pipe.

I look past him toward Watts Street, pulling the letter from my pocket.

Uncle Ray stands, stretches. "What you got there?"

"A notice from the City of Charlotte. We knew it was coming and here it is." I hold out the envelope.

He reaches for it, reads the front. "Mrs. Livinia Hawkins. Did you show it to Livvie?" Uncle Ray always calls Bibi by the nickname he's used since they were children.

"She wouldn't understand it."

"Dated February 28, 1961. Why have you been carrying it around for close to a month?"

I don't answer, just stare into the dusk. Out in the road a pole lamp comes on, glistening in puddles.

He sits careful on the steps, touches my foot. "We can't know how a thing's gon turn out."

CHAPTER 2

The Reverend Ebenezer Gabriel Polk sat by his dining room window, staring at motes of dust in a sunbeam that fell across his Bible. He preferred the Revised Standard Version for his personal worship, felt it was the clearest word of God, though he had not convinced his flock of that.

The church's worn King James stayed at the pulpit, so he could read from it during sermons, as the congregation expected. The opening pages of the old Bible recorded the history of the church. St. Timothy's Second Presbyterian was Second Presbyterian Church Colored when it was founded in 1842. After the Civil War the elders elected to drop "Colored" and add St. Timothy. Why, he often wondered, with that pale saint's Catholic connections?

As he had done most of his life, he closed his eyes, wandered through the Bible, flipping pages. In his previous reading, he'd opened to Isaiah, where he was reminded to exalt the Lord and praise His name throughout all the earth. Such commands bothered him. Why would a deity need blatant worship that approached flattery? He varied his readings as much as possible, hoping for spiritual guidance. With his finger sliding down the inside column of the left page toward the end of the Bible, he opened his eyes enough to be sure he wasn't in Revelation, which he didn't like or trust or understand. At I Peter 4:7, he focused and began to read, "The end of all things is at hand; therefore keep sane and sober for your prayers."

The end of all things. Those graves. The sacred resting places that would now be uprooted, with him unable to stop the looming desecration. The oldest plots in the cemetery distressed him the most. Unmarked or poorly so, often only by a rock at head and foot, where several bodies might be in one site, given the way folks disposed of slave remains. But every one of them had souls that went on to heaven, according to what he'd been taught.

He flexed his right leg before standing, bracing himself on the mahogany table Nettie had brought to their marriage, waiting for the fiery throbbing in his knee to ease enough for him to fix lunch. "Arthritis has got me, dear girl," he said to the framed photo on the buffet. He loved that image of Nettie. They'd gone to the state fair, where a roving photographer caught her laughing at something he couldn't remember. Her mouth slightly open, sunlight on her curls.

Her death three years earlier still bewildered him. One day she didn't feel well and the next she was moaning in pain. Then she passed. That's how the progression of her illness felt to him. Dead at diagnosis, he'd overheard someone say at the hospital, and felt again that mix of grief and powerlessness. "Palliative care," her doctor had told him, adding, as if there were no way he could have understood, "she won't suffer." How could they know, those doctors with their needles and pills, whether his Nettie suffered? He'd sat by her bed for a month, held her, talked to her as if she could hear him, while she slipped away into . . . what? His concept of heaven shifted during her final days and he could never again say with certainty that there was anything after this life.

Through the window he saw the backhoe sitting out on McDowell. Reason told him that even the greediest of developers wouldn't take such a machine into the graveyard to eat away at it, but the metal hulk sat there in an attitude of threat. At the last appointment with the city they'd said he had to decide on the options for moving the church. No, not options. The church had to move and there was no choice in that, but he could decide how it would be accomplished. They'd given him that much. He took their recommendations to the elders and the women's circle, which so far hadn't agreed on anything.

The phone rang. He limped around the dining table to answer it. His brother's voice rang out, "Hey, Neezer, whus up?"

Neezer, the childhood nickname that had once been his brand—back when a boy from his gang challenged, "Hey, man, whus yo brand?" and he proudly sang out, "Neezer!" His brother never called him anything else.

"I'm well, Oscar. You?"

"I found a man gon help you."

He was used to his older brother's sudden shifts. "What man, help me how?"

"He gon look at the graveyard for you."

"All right."

"A white man."

"Who is this fellow?"

"He do annapology, some such, digging around where folks has lived a long time, seeing what's left."

"An anthropologist?"

"Sound about right."

"And where did you come on an anthropologist?"

"He hanging around Stone's, axing whus coming down in Brooklyn. Benjy and Hildie told him about the church, that the city gon move them graves. The man lit up like he know about such stuff. I tell him my brother's the preacher." He sniffed loudly. "Can't hurt to talk to him, even if he white."

"No, can't hurt."

"Catch you later, Neezer." And as suddenly as the conversation had begun, it ended.

Neezer. The nickname made him feel like a boy again, the same as when certain smells brought back memories. Wet pine boards after a long rain. Smoke from a coal fire. Oatmeal boiled with cinnamon, a frequent supper when he was a child. The iron tang of blood and a whiff of Clorox from the Dutch Cleanser his mother used, trying to scrub away the stains. But the faint brown splotches were still there, the last time he'd seen the floor of the front hall in their shotgun house on East Second Street.

"Oscar? Ebenezer? Supper!" He crawled out of the culvert, his head cocked, listening. "C'mon, Oscar, she mean it!" His brother's skin was the color of midnight, making him invisible in the depths of the concrete runoff drain for Little Sugar. Their favorite hiding place during games of hoods and pigs, even if the other boys knew it and would find them there eventually. He ran up East Second toward home, calling back to his brother, "I ain't gon catch no whupping like you is."

At the house, he crouched and jumped over the three front steps, landing flat on both feet on the stoop, which shook under his tennis shoes. "I'm home, Mama!" He opened the screen door wide, let it slam against the unpainted siding. "I'm home!"

His mother called from the kitchen, "Any fool could hear that. Get on in here."

In the kitchen, Mama stirred something on the hotplate. He said, "Oscar ain't with me, he in the—" He stopped short. His brother sat at the kitchen table, grinning.

"Hey, Neezer. You seed a ghost?"

"How you do that, get home before me? You was still in the pipe."

Mama cuffed his head. "Y'all don't mess around in that creek. I tole you."

Behind her back, his brother stuck out his tongue.

"We didn't go much in the pipe, Mama, only the mouth of it."

She took a steaming pot off the two-burner hotplate. "Y'all remember the Cookley boys, last year? Both of 'em lost in that creek."

"Shouldna gone in it with rain coming," said Oscar. "We not stupid like no drownded Cookley boys."

"Broke Elna Cookley's heart," she said. "Y'all wash up. Eben, get your sister and come eat."

He stepped into the hallway that ran the depth of the house. "Mary Day? Supper!"

Oscar shoved past him. "Me first! You hasta pump."

Outside the brothers elbowed each other until Oscar—taller, heavier, stronger—won. Neezer pumped while Oscar washed up in the cold water.

Mary Day called from the back door, "Y'all hurry or ain't gon be no supper left."

Eben shook his dripping hands, ran into the kitchen. "What we having, Mama?"

"Mashed potatoes, beans cooked with ham bone, apples."

"Just bone, no meat?" Oscar wedged his long legs under the table. He wore his hair parted high on the right and combed into a kinky wave he called his New York look. He was the darkest of the children, a startling ebony. Mary Day's smooth skin was golden, her copper-colored curls coiled on her neck. Already as tall as their mother and only twelve. He'd heard Mama say more than once that Mary Day would be bringing boys home soon enough.

He was Mama's favorite, something he felt, even if she

tried not to show it. She'd told him once that God had blessed him with milk chocolate skin and almost straight brown hair, serious hazel eyes. She always added that he thought about things too much. But he was the one she trusted to watch after Mary Day.

"You too skinny, boy," Mama nudged him. "Nothing but knees and elbows."

Oscar reached for a heaping bowl. "Hey, Mama, pass me some them beans with no ham just bone."

"Seem to me if you eat like a man, you could get a man's job."

"I'm trying, Mama, I tole you that." Oscar handed Mary Day the mashed potatoes. "How's my favorite little sister?"

"I'm your onliest sister, Carman." Mary Day frowned at the familiar joke.

Oscar laughed. "You the onliest one use my brand, little sister. I'm Carman now, y'all, I keep telling you."

Mama said, "Carman? Not gon get you a car till you get you a job."

"He been doing what a man do," Mary Day said. "I seen him."

Oscar's hand shot out, but Mary Day dodged it.

Mama looked at Oscar. "What you been doing?"

"She don't know nothing." Oscar frowned at Mary Day.

"Uh-huh," said Mary Day. "You ax Lulu about dat."

Oscar stood and Mary Day ducked under the table.

"Elmore Clarkson's girl?" his mother asked.

Nobody said anything.

"What you been doing with her?"

From under the table Mary Day said, "What a man do."

Lulu turned up pregnant and named Oscar as the father. Elmore Clarkson came looking for Oscar with a loaded pistol to get him to the altar, as he put it, "in a necktie or a coffin, however he want it." Elmore's pistol wasn't the only thing loaded. He'd had so much to drink he couldn't see straight, and when he got to 1024 East Second, he pulled out the pistol and aimed at the screen door. Something moved inside and he bellowed, "Oscar Polk, you gon marry my daughter, you hear me?"

Whatever moved called out, "What you saying?"

Elmore took that for a denial and pulled the trigger.

Mary Day bled to death in the front hall as Neezer ran for the doctor, who said later that even if he'd been standing beside the girl when the bullet entered her chest, he couldn't have saved her.

Lulu's baby came out mostly white—not likely a child of black Oscar's. Elmore hung himself in jail, and Neezer made a vow to his mother. "I'm gon get us off Second Street."

CHAPTER 3

On that steamy afternoon in July 1955, when Persy Marshall first went into Brooklyn, she left her home on Sterling Road feeling in charge of her life. No one knew where she was headed.

On East Hill Street she was startled by what she saw: a block of unpainted shacks hugging the curb, no more than six feet of alley between them. Wooden chairs on tiny stoops, garbage cans curbside. A cloud of dust rose in her rearview mirror. She turned onto Myers Street and passed several pastel bungalows with picket fences.

In the front yard of 704 South Myers was a sign: MRS. ROBERTA STOKES, SEAMSTRESS. She sat and looked at the blue house with its white shutters and tidy lawn, azaleas to each side of a stone walk leading to a porch with a rocker, potted begonias, hanging ferns. *What would it be like to live by myself in a cozy house like this?* She got out awkwardly, sliding her swollen belly from under the steering wheel and locking the car. Her heels thumped hollowly on the front porch. A note above a brass button said, "Please ring bell." She stood for a moment by the rocker before pressing the bell.

The woman who came to the door was at least six feet tall and fair-skinned, with the doe-colored hair of blond going silver. If Persy had seen her from the back on a city street, she would have taken her for white. Mulatto. The woman looked at her directly. "Yes?"

"I called you several days ago. Mrs. Blaire Marshall?"

"Yes, ma'am, you're wanting a christening gown. I'm Roberta Stokes. Come on in." The woman opened the screen and gestured to a chintz sofa. Angled beside the couch was a green corduroy easy chair. Starched curtains in the windows. Beaded flowers in a vase beneath a wall of photos. *This could be a neighbor's house in Myers Park.*

"Have a seat. I'll go get my pictures. Oh, you want a Coke or a glass of water? I could make ice tea but that'd take a while."

"Water, please." Persy sat on the sofa.

She smelled something familiar, pleasant. Gardenias in a bowl on an end table by her elbow. Not a hint of brown, they must have been picked that morning.

The woman returned with a glass of water and a photo album, sat down next to her. "This book shows what I can do."

Persy turned several pages. "Mrs. Stokes, your work is elegant."

"You call me Roberta."

"Thank you, and I'm Persy."

"No, ma'am, you're Mrs. Marshall. That's the way it is."

"All right, Mrs. Stokes." *That's the way it should be.*

Mrs. Stokes smiled, pointed to a dividing tab in the black three-ring binder. "That section is baby clothes, christening gowns. What are you folks, Episcopal?"

"Mostly Presbyterian."

"Mostly?"

"A few Baptists and Methodists along the way. At least two Unitarians I know of."

"I've not heard of that one."

Persy turned a page and there it was, exactly what she'd dreamed of. Lace around the neck. Smocking created tiny gathers that spilled into the length of the gown. Long sleeves ended in cuffs with satin ribbons to tie around a baby's wrists. At the hem, another ribbon wove in and out of the white cotton. She touched the photo. "Exquisite. Do you do all this work yourself?"

"I do. Learned from my grand when I was a girl." Mrs. Stokes pointed to the hem of the dress. "That's my own touch. Can make that ribbon blue or pink, or I could leave it white."

She felt a kick below her breastbone. *Is the baby voting for white?* "How long will it take you to do this one for me?"

Mrs. Stokes looked at Persy's belly. "You're what, about seven months gone?"

"I'm due the middle of September."

"Shame you have to go through the heat of summer carrying a baby."

"I'm glad to be this far along. I lost two early on." The words slipped out. She rarely talked about what the doctor called spontaneous abortions.

"That's a heartbreaking thing. Yes, ma'am. We get all excited, then bang, it's over."

"You've miscarried?"

"Twice, same as you. Never did get a baby that lived." Mrs. Stokes pushed back a stray hair. "That's maybe why I make these gowns. Started in with them after I lost number two."

Number two, what an odd way to put it. "Did you find out what went wrong?"

"Midwife say it was the way of God that we can't know. Dr. Wilkins—he's in that blue house on Brevard—say my womb is tipped and the seed planted wrong. Something like that. Then Dennis, my husband, he passed. I reckon I weren't meant to have children."

She sounded as if she had accepted her inability to be a mother. Persy envied that.

Mrs. Stokes said, "But you could even have another one after this, young as you are."

"I'm forty-four."

"You sure don't look it." Mrs. Stokes took a small pad from her pocket. "That one's fifteen dollars for the sewing. Some ladies like to bring me the fabric they want, or I can get it, which will be two dollars extra, and fifty cents for thread and ribbons. I like to buy them myself."

"That's so little for such a fine piece."

"I make out. Don't like to ask too much."

Persy opened her purse and took out a twenty-dollar bill. "Why don't we make it twenty even, and you buy what you choose."

"It'll be seventeen-fifty, and you don't pay me till you see it. You won't be obliged. I can always sell it." The phone rang and she held up a finger, listening. "That's me. Be right back."

Persy heard her say, "Hey there. No, got a lady here seeing about a baby gown." A pause. "I sure enough be there. Wouldn't miss a party." A laugh. "You do that. Say hey to you folks for me." Silence. "Helen, you on the line? If you listening, Helen, you not going to learn a thing." A click.

She came back to the living room. "That's a party line for you. Some folks can't help listening in."

She sat back down next to Persy, made a note on her pad. "So it's number eight, the christening special, seventeen-fifty. I got your phone number. You mind standing up? I'm going to tell you something."

Persy struggled to push herself up off the sofa.

A long look. "Now turn sideways. Um-hmm. It's a boy. Anybody told you that?"

She laughed and touched her stomach. "How do you know?"

"The way you carrying. A boy, sure thing. I've never been wrong, even my own, I knew. . . ." She stopped. "Where do you live?"

"Near Freedom Park." *Blaire always says, "On Sterling Road in Myers Park. Off Queens Road West."*

"Sugar Creek must be close by."

"Yes, behind our house." She gave her address.

"We call it Little Sugar here." Mrs. Stokes put the pad back in her pocket. "I can get to you easy on the Number Three bus."

"I'll repay you for the fare."

"That'd be all right." Mrs. Stokes stood. "I can have it for you in a week or two."

As she was leaving she said, "Your gardenias are lovely. I didn't see the bush."

"It was by the fence out front but folks passing by kept picking it clean, so I moved it to the back."

"Oh, my." She couldn't imagine her neighbors taking her flowers without asking, but there was something enviable, something in the nature of a village that made folks think they could pick one another's gardenias.

On her way to run other errands downtown she passed a large blue house on Brevard. A wooden sign between two posts said, EDWARD WILKINS, MD. What would it be like to be attended by a midwife, and only have a doctor if something went wrong? She thought about her obstetrician's modern offices on Hawthorne.

Ten days after she met Roberta Stokes, she and Blaire were at the kitchen table, supper dishes pushed aside. A front-page story in the *Charlotte News* caught her eye: ONE DEAD IN SHOOTOUT.

> A colored man was killed Saturday night and a Charlotte policeman injured in a shootout in Brooklyn at McDowell and First Streets, the notorious Murder Corner. Two policemen were called to the scene where a fistfight had accelerated. Sgt. Richard Bridges, 34, was rushed to Memorial Hospital with a gunshot wound to the abdomen. His condition is stable. Lew McCreedy, 47, a Negro, was killed while resisting arrest. Oscar Polk, 52, another Negro involved in the brawl, is being held pending investigation.

She showed Blaire the story. "This happened a couple of blocks from Roberta Stokes' house."

"Roberta Stokes?"

"A seamstress in Second Ward. I went to see her about a christening gown. She's bringing it to us next week."

A muscle in his jaw twitched. "For Christ's sake, Persephone! It's dangerous down there."

"Where I went was perfectly safe. I wish you could see Mrs. Stokes' house, a charming cottage on Myers Street."

"Myers? That's on the list for tear-downs."

"Have you been there?"

He went to the kitchen, got a beer from the refrigerator. "I've seen plenty of pictures, horrible shanties up on pilings, dirt roads, garbage."

"The part of Myers she lives on is paved. And her doctor lives nearby in a handsome home on Brevard."

Blaire took a chilled mug from the freezer, filled it, drank deeply. "Persy, I want you to promise me you won't go into those slums again."

Why don't I just salute him? "Yes, sir."

CHAPTER 4

Me and Hawk share a room on the back corner where the sun comes in at a slant through one window in the morning and full tilt through the other in the afternoon. Last thing I do at night is pull the shades down. We only six feet from Dooby's house next door and I can hear him if he sneezes. First thing in the morning, after we dress, I pull the shades up, let the sunshine in. Two single beds, oak chest of drawers between them—tall, golden brown, five drawers with brass pulls I keep polished. Belonged to my daddy, a piece Bibi bought him when he graduated high school, before he joined the navy. He asked Bibi to keep it for him when he got shipped overseas. He never came home, so now it's mine, the only furniture I have from either of my parents.

Bibi say my daddy took care of me. But he left for good when I was five, and try as hard as I can, I only remember he smelled like starch. All I have is that chest and the photo of him that's sitting on top of it. He's young in the picture, maybe twenty-five, same age as I am now, stiff and tall in his navy uniform. Three white stripes on his sleeve. The words at the bottom say, "Seaman Ronald Alexander Hawkins, San Diego, Cal., Dec. 1936." The year I was born. Bibi believes he was married to Shushu—my mother—but has no paper to prove it. Shushu said something about Chicago, according to Pap Shumaker, her father, and that she'd write. He say she never did. I don't think Pap and Grand would keep that from me. I think about her, wondering if she thinks about me. I look at Hawk, see myself in him, and believe she must.

I can also see me in Bibi, in her eyes, hooded like mine. She'll touch my face and say, "You got Hawkins eyes. I want to remember my boy, I look at you." We both got big feet which is another thing the Hawkins women run to, and we the same five feet four inches tall. She's slim, though, where I am heavy in the hips. Her legs are skinny, where my thighs are full, and my calves plump but with small ankles, so I don't mind. Bibi's breasts are way down, almost to her waist, which she say is from never wearing a bra. "Didn't have no such thing when I was a girl coming up, getting shapely. One day Lorena say we should put brassieres on to see what we look like." She throws back her head, laughing with her mouth open, showing her upper plate. "Lord knows, I say once and never again. Pinch me here. Pinch me there. Rub my shoulders. How could any woman get use to it?"

She ask me only one question when I tell her I'm gon have a baby. "You getting married?"

"No, ma'am. That's not happening."

"Well, they'll be talk, but we'll get along. Ain't first baby born to a mama not married."

For seven years now I've had a help wanted ad from the *Charlotte News* tucked into the frame of Daddy's picture on my dresser. Bibi has asked me more than once, "Why you hanging on to that scrap of paper?"

"Leave it be. Something I want to keep for now." I'm not gon tell her it reminds me of how I met Mr. Griffin.

Most of the jobs in the paper said, "Must have experience," and they didn't mean how to unpack boxes, stock shelves, sweep floors. I wanted something more than working in the grocery store, and the ad looked right for me: "Kitchen help. S&W Cafeteria. 6 days/wk, $1.15/hr. Benefits. Will train. 112 W. Trade. Interviews 9 A.M., Mon. Sep. 14, 1953."

I shower, wind my braids into a smooth bun, and get out a dress use to belong to Auntie Roselle, one of her things Uncle Ray gave me. She was built stocky, wide in the hips same as me, and her clothes fit me well.

I tell Bibi I'm ready to leave my job at Stone's Grocery, show her the ad that's now in my daddy's picture. She say, "Um-hm. Let's go to Sears Roebuck. You got to have shoes that show you take care of yourself."

What I want is a pair of leopard skin high heels that'd be so right for going out on Saturday night, but wrong for getting a job. Instead I get black leather pumps that'll do for an interview or going to church. Bibi lets me borrow her small hat with pink flowers on it, same color as Auntie Roselle's dress, and she inspects my gloves, the ones Shushu left behind.

I get up on the edge of the tub in my stocking feet to see as much of myself as I can in the medicine cabinet mirror, and what I see looks so fine. I tip Bibi's hat over my right eye and jump to the floor. She stands in the doorway buttoning her uniform. "You gon get that job." She gives me a dime. "For luck and for taking the bus. You don't want to get sweaty walking to the S&W."

We start out together on that mild fall day, getting to McDowell right before the Number Three bus for downtown that will take me to the Square. She'll catch the Number Three going south to take her to the Easterlings' in Myers

Park. I put one foot on the step of the bus and say, over my left shoulder, "Bye, Bibi, cross your fingers." I drop her dime in the glass box beside the driver, pleased I'm gon be early, and sit on the long seat in the back, waving to Bibi out the window, watching her get smaller as we roll away.

I get off at the Square and walk to the S&W. All my life I've been passing it, wondering what it's like inside. Three stories of windows on Trade Street, with red velvet curtains floor to ceiling, pulled tight today. I've stared through the windows, wishing I could go inside, sit at one of those glossy tables, eat a delicious Sunday dinner, but as Uncle Ray reminds me, "That'll happen someday, but not this day."

A black man steps from the shadows of the doorway. "You here for the job? You mighty young."

I'm thinking he's mighty old to be looking for work in a cafeteria, but I keep that to myself. "I'm seventeen."

He has on what I reckon is his best suit, wide shoulders, shiny pants. We both wearing clothes we'd never wear to work. He touches the knot of his tie. "This your first job?"

I shake my head, not wanting to go into my history with him.

Another man and a girl walk up, both colored. The girl say, "Y'all know what time it is?"

The second man checks his watch. "Ten to nine."

A white man turns off Church Street onto Trade, strides toward us. Tall, wearing a navy suit that shows bony ankles in black socks. He's got on a plaid bowtie, a hat with the brim tipped over his forehead. "I'll open up," he say with a smile, key ring jangling. Can't be more than twenty-five, which makes me feel better about being young myself. "Be right back," he closes the door behind him.

The other girl say to me, "You done kitchen work?"

"Not for pay. You?"

"Huh-uh. What you think it means, benefits?"

"My uncle say health insurance, they pay your bill if you get sick."

"My, my, wouldn't that be something?"

She's about my age, dressed up, with patent leather heels I admire.

The men talk to each other, ignoring me and the girl. The man with the wristwatch is dressed first-rate, like he doesn't need a job. He winks when he catches my eye. I look away. Might be some jackleg winking at me.

The front door opens. The white man has taken off his hat. Wavy red hair, friendly gray eyes, a scrap of tissue near his left sideburn, where he must of cut himself shaving. "Y'all come on in."

Inside, I make myself not show the wonder I'm feeling about what I'm doing in such a place. Ceiling so high it could have clouds. Rows of tables stretching all the way to a serving counter in the back.

"Have a seat," the man say, waving to a plush sofa and easy chairs, like in some living room. I'm feeling jumpy thinking I might work here, but the other girl sits down, crosses her legs, and jiggles her foot like she's having a high time. She lights a cigarette, drops the match in an ashtray.

"I'm Archibald Griffin, manager of the S&W Cafeteria, which has been here twenty-six years. We seat well over two hundred folks for Sunday lunch, when we use all the tables, upstairs, too." He points to a balcony hanging over the rear of the dining room. "We're closed on Mondays except for special parties." He leans on a brass rail that separates the lobby from the dining room. "What I'm looking for is someone willing to go the extra mile." He wants a worker. That's me.

"Any questions before we start the interviews?"

The girl say, "So the job is six days a week. Is that all day, and starting when?"

"We work two shifts. First is six a.m. to two p.m.; second

is two to ten. First shift opens, does breakfast and lunch. Second does supper, cleans and closes."

The girl looks at her jiggling shoe, squashes out her cigarette in the ashtray. "Can we choose?"

"I like new people to start on first, for training."

"I'm glad," she say. "I got somebody to look after my baby mornings."

"Who was the first one here?" Mr. Griffin ask.

"That's me," the older man say.

They shake hands and walk together toward the back.

"My, my," say the girl. "Fancy, isn't it."

"Yes," I say, "Be nice to work here."

"It's gonna be, that's for sure."

Does she think she's already hired? "How old is your baby?"

She looks pleased I asked. "Six months. I've been keeping him and two others, but one of the mamas moved away and the other baby is in nursery school, now she's outta diapers."

We sit there quiet till the first man comes back, tells us goodbye, and Mr. Griffin say, "I'll let you know in a week or so."

"Yes, sir, I be waiting to hear."

"Who's next?"

I stand.

"This way." We start toward the back. He ask, "What's your name?"

"Loraylee Hawkins." I walk fast to keep up, my new pumps making a pleasant sound on the red-and-tan tile floor.

We go through the dining room and stop near the serving counter along the back wall. He say, "We have twenty-eight four tops—that's a table for four—and a dozen two tops on this floor, can seat another seventy upstairs." He points to a wide staircase in the corner, an elevator beside it. "The kitchen downstairs serves all our patrons, using dumbwaiters to get food to the lines on both floors."

Dumbwaiters? He can't mean stupid people, but I don't ask.

"Let's go to the kitchen first." He leads me into an elevator, punches a button to take us down. "We turned this into an automatic about six months ago. The elevator boy now works in the kitchen."

I get a whiff of aftershave. He's removed the speck of tissue below his neat sideburn and I see the nick it was covering. We walk out into a huge room. *Gleaming,* that's the word for it. A row of ovens, shelves of dishes and glasses.

"Even as large as it is, people bump into each other," he say, "so everybody needs to know who's doing what. I'm looking for someone who can work in a hot steamy room, and get along with the rest of the staff." He taps a counter. "I try to find folks who fit in, so we'll have a happy kitchen."

He's proud of what he does. I say, "Yes, sir," even if a lot of it doesn't make sense. Everything's clean, not a speck of dirt on the floor. A whiff of something in the air makes me think of sugar cookies. Stored under a cooktop are pots large enough to do our laundry in. Metal counters. Sinks like bathtubs.

He stops at a row of steel doors along one wall. "Walk-in cold storage, one for vegetables and fruit, one for meat. Part of the job is to track the food in the fridges and freezers so the last thing in is the last thing out." I follow him back to the elevator and we return to the first floor where we go through a door with a brass plaque, ARCHIBALD C. GRIFFIN, MANAGER. Inside is a small room with a desk and two chairs. Through one window is a parking lot. Another one behind the desk overlooks an alley. He points to it. "That's used by delivery vans for several businesses, runs off Church Street. The vendors who serve us have access to a dumbwaiter that takes food down to the kitchen."

I'm feeling easy enough to ask, "I don't know that word, *dumbwaiter.*"

"No reason you would. We have three. They're elevators—but for stuff, not people—from the balcony upstairs to the basement below, carrying food for the serving line, dirty dishes, deliveries." A calendar hangs on the wall, a pencil on a string dangling beside it. "Shift schedule. Changes every week." We sit, him behind the desk, me in the other chair.

"Loraylee, is that right?"

"Yes, sir."

His hair is even redder under the overhead light. "Would this be your first job?" His whole face smiles, his eyes kind.

"I've been working in the grocery for a year and a half, shelving stock when products come in, helping with inventory. Mr. Stone—he's my boss—has been teaching me the cash register so I can work up front, but when I saw your ad in the *News* . . ." I stop, feel like I'm saying too much.

He makes another note. "How old are you, Loraylee?"

"I turned seventeen in August."

"Are you married, any children?"

"No, sir. No, sir."

The phone on his desk rings. "Hello? Oh, hey, Kevin. Sure." He muffles the receiver. "Excuse me, this'll only take a second." He speaks back into the phone. "No, eighty pounds yellow onions, ninety of russets. Y'all got it wrong last order. If there's an overage this delivery, I'm sending it back." The hand on the phone is strong, with blunt fingers, blond hair on the back.

I like how confident he sounds, and wish I could ask him how old he is, if he's married, has children.

He hangs up the phone, takes a pen from his pocket, writes something on a pad. "Are you prompt, punctual?"

"Yes, sir, never late." Not the whole truth, but close.

"Does Mr. Stone know you're looking for another job?"

I nod. "He say he doesn't want to lose me but he doesn't want to stand in my way, either. You can call him for a reference."

"Can you work weekends? Would that be a problem?"

I think about how upset Bibi would be if I didn't go with her to St. Tim's. "No, sir."

"We start serving at twelve-thirty on Sundays, so our diners can get here after church. The staff has to come in at nine."

"Everybody?"

"We shift people around. Those who want to can go to church every couple of weeks."

"That's what I was wondering."

Mr. Griffin stands. "Any questions?"

"No, sir."

As we leave his office, he holds out his hand. Big, warm, like his smile. "You'll be hearing from me, don't worry."

We walk back through the dining room. It's easy to be quiet with him.

So that's how I met my Mr. Griffin, all those years ago. After the interview I decided to walk home. I liked strolling through my neighborhood all dressed up, saying hey to people going to and from work or sitting on porches. I went down East Second Street, which has several places to stop for a Coke: Queen City Pharmacy, where I had my first job, or the Royal Snack Bar across from the record store. Before people started moving away, Brooklyn had everything anybody could need. You could get your shoes shined or your dress hemmed, a tooth filled or a baby delivered. A lawyer could draw up a will, knowing the preacher and the undertaker would be there when it came your time. But even back then we were hearing rumors of the city forcing us out. I thought about that as I headed home.

At an empty lot where somebody use to live, I watched kids play hidey-seek in cardboard boxes from Stone's Grocery, swinging on ropes hanging from the one tree still standing. They'd made rings of rocks, broken bricks, and dirt to squat behind, playing Tom Mix and the Indians, popping each other with sling shots or pea shooters. Everybody knew whose kid was whose, and if a strange one showed up, there'd be questions. That field went from a torn-down house to a playground full of children whose mamas knew where to find them come suppertime.

I stopped at the grocery, thinking I might go in and tell Mr. Stone about the interview, but his GONE TO LUNCH sign was out.

I've been working at the S&W for over seven years now, and we're getting official notices about the redevelopment that's coming, making proof of all the rumors. The second letter we get from the city is addressed to "Owner." That means Bibi, but there's no way she can understand what they say. I take it to the kitchen, where Uncle Ray's at the sink, peeling potatoes.

"We got another one." I rip it open. "From the Redevelopment Commission of the City of Charlotte, like the first one. 'Dear Resident . . .' "

Uncle Ray snorts. "Resident? That doesn't sound good."

"That's the best part. 'A representative from the Office of Urban Renewal will visit you on Monday, March 27, 1961—' " I rattle the paper. "The day after tomorrow. How they know we gon be here?"

"Read it to me, girl."

" '. . . regarding the redevelopment of downtown Charlotte. The deteriorating dwellings along the McDowell Street corridor between East Fourth and Morehead are being assessed for damage to determine if the structures are substandard.' That's the word they're using about St. Timothy's, 'substandard.'"

"Does it say when they're coming?"

"Between ten and noon. Gives a number to call if we need to change it."

"Monday morning I'm taking Bibi to see Dr. Wilkins, get her sugar checked. But you'll be here, won't you? Putting it off won't change anything."

I don't like it, but he's right.

I'm ready when the man from the city drives up, parks in front of our house, gets out of his car carrying a satchel. I'm in the living room peeping from behind the curtain. He comes up the steps, smiling, smiling, like he knows I'm watching him, raps on the door. I let him wait.

He say, "Hello?" I don't want him to see the drooping sofa, the tired rug, the cracked lampshade. Bibi's knitting she's never gon finish.

The man calls out, "Anybody home?"

I'm glad I'm not in my uniform, might make me look like a maid. I grab my sweater from the coat stand that came down from Bibi's grandmother, check myself in the mirror on the key rack.

He's knocking again when I yank open the door. He steps back. "Hello. Mrs. Livinia Hawkins?"

"Miss Loraylee Hawkins. My grandmother's not home."

Shoes polished, white shirt starched, face shining like he just took a bath. He looks past me into the house, fidgeting.

If I make him nervous, I'm glad.

"May I have a few minutes?"

I come through the screen door, wave him to the rocker. Put myself in the straight chair. I feel mean, making him sit on the porch, chilly as it is today.

"Here." He sets down his satchel, pulls a card from his pocket.

It say: "Stewart Menafee, Development Coordinator . . ."

I stick it in my skirt pocket. "What you want, Mr. Menafee?" He's one of those white men jittery around coloreds. His slick brown hair is combed across the top of his head to hide the bald that's coming, but it's coming. Got on a suit that doesn't quite fit. He flips open his case, takes out a small hammer he rubs with his thumb as he stands and walks over to the rail.

"Do you mind?" Not waiting for an answer, he tap, tap on the post that goes from the floor to the ceiling. Dust flies.

I have never cleaned that post, but am bothered it's dirty. I mumble something foolish like, "Should of dusted that, I reckon."

He shakes his head. "You can't whisk away termites."

"Termites?"

"Yes, eating up your house." Tap, tap, tap again, up the post to the top. One place the hammer sinks in. "This support beam is rotting from the inside out."

I feel sick.

"Miss Hawkins?" Mr. Menafee sits back down, his case on his lap. "We have cause for serious concern about the suitability of this structure for continued domestic use." He takes papers from his case. "These documents explain the purpose of the Redevelopment Commission of the City of Charlotte."

"Redevelopment?"

"The commission was established to improve our inner city." He shuts the case, clicks the latches. "Our records show that the owner, Mrs. Livinia Hawkins, has no mortgage, but when this property is appraised and reevaluated, the taxes will likely increase. We understand that might create a financial burden for your family, and we are willing to offer you alternatives. The commission will assist your relocation, in accordance with these documents. There are forms you must complete so we'll have up-to-date information on your property."

I take the papers he pushes at me.

"If you need help filling them out, we can send someone. . . ."

"I read. I write." I want to shove him and his big square head off the porch.

"Read the documents, Miss, and you'll see that we have a plan in place for your welfare. Several of your neighbors have already—"

"Go away!" I shout at him. He jumps, grabbing up his satchel and clutching it to his chest before taking off across the yard to his car.

CHAPTER 5

Eben rolled to a stop in front of St. Timothy's, sat and studied the white cross centered beneath the gable peak, the uneven stones of the walk, the two rocking chairs on the porch set at precise angles. The building needed paint, but that could wait. There was a crack along the foundation to the left of the steps; a bricklayer in the congregation was going to tend to that next week.

He locked his car—*no point in tempting anyone*—went up the steps, and was surprised to find the door open an inch or two, heat drifting out. He pushed it, feeling as much as hearing the squeaky hinges, peered into the dusky foyer and beyond to the sanctuary, where smoke rose from between the two back pews. A sweet smell. Unmistakable.

He approached the haze, making no effort to be quiet. Stretched out in the last row was Oscar, holding a smoking reefer, his dark face lost against the shadowed wood. "Hey there, Neezer."

Oscar took a long draw, holding the dope in, offered the roach, his eyes heavy-lidded, red-rimmed. "Want some?"

Incensed at this violation of his church and alarmed by his brother's emaciated appearance, he said, "That's not for me. Get up, put your feet on the floor. What if one of the deacons walked in?"

Oscar sat up, grinning. "Cool it, brother. Paranoia's supposed to be my thing."

"Why are you doing this in a holy place?"

Oscar pulled on the joint, holding the remaining half-inch between two fingernails, sucking in a deep lungful. He spoke haltingly, letting out a bit of smoke with each word. "Safe . . . my . . . brother. Yo . . . church . . . is . . . safe." He sighed out the last of the smoke, snuffed the joint on the floor, and put what was left into a matchbox he took from his shirt pocket. "Waste not, want not, ain't that right, Pastor Polk?"

He controlled his voice. "Out, Oscar. Now."

His brother got to his feet, stumbled into the aisle, pulled him into a reluctant embrace. "Ease off, Neezer."

He gave in, hugged his brother in return. "How's Noah doing?"

"He fine. More like you than me." Oscar pulled a knit hat from his pocket, settled it on his head. "Has him a job washing cars after school."

"Good for Noah."

"You gotta take him for a while."

He'd known Oscar's visit wasn't casual. "What's going on?"

"Jail again. I made bail, but I'm gon go to court tomorrow."

"A sentence?"

"Probably."

He had to force himself not to lecture. "I'm happy to have Noah."

"Sometime this evening, all right, Neezer?" His brother swayed and hummed as he left the church.

Oscar was just one of many wayward members of St. Tim's Eben had to deal with. Maybe on a Saturday night a man got drunk, picked a fight, and hurt somebody. Families dragged the sorry ones into church, and heads nodded when Eben's sermon included the consequences of sinning, drinking, and fighting in the street, most folks thinking, "Glad it's not me."

He sighed, and headed through the nave to the choir benches, crossing the stage to a door that led to the hallway behind the sanctuary. As he climbed the stairs to his office on the second floor, he thought again of his nephew Noah, tall, lean, ebony like his father, left alone far too much for a boy of twelve. But he seemed to blossom in spite of his father's repeated clashes with the law, which had landed Oscar behind bars too often. On those occasions, Noah came to live with his uncle Eben. He hoped he added stability to the boy's life.

Late that afternoon he opened the back door of the manse to a biting wind that burned his cheeks, one of those twists of weather that turned spring back into winter. He retreated inside to grab the coat he'd bought when he came home from the war and found he'd outgrown his civvies. It smelled of the mothballs his Nettie had hung in their closets. He should have it cleaned, which is what he thought each winter when the cold forced him back into it. Each winter since her death.

He left the parsonage with a bag of trash that he put in the backyard bin, bothered as always by the necessity of hauling it out to the street. The city garbage trucks sent men to carry cans from behind houses in Myers Park, Eastover, Dilworth, while folks in Second Ward had to get theirs to the curb. When he'd called the sanitation department about this inequity, he'd been told that the garbagemen didn't feel safe going behind houses in Brooklyn. Eben had to hold his tongue to keep from pointing out that Brooklyn was home to most of those men.

The can was full and he half dragged, half carried it out to the street. He'd heard about a trash can on wheels, and every Wednesday he vowed he'd look into that. On his walk back to the parsonage, he saw a lanky man in the cemetery, leaning over a headstone, studying the face of it. So blond he looked like he was wearing a white hat. The man straightened and scanned the tombstones, stepped behind a memorial that rose twice as high as most. Eben didn't like such shows of money. *Folks shouldn't overspend on death when others were in such great need.* He called out, "Hello?" as he opened the rusty gate in the low wall that bordered the graveyard.

The man turned, walked toward him. "I'm Marion Lipscomb." He shook Eben's hand. "You must be Reverend Polk, Oscar's brother. I met him at Stone's Grocery. Hope you don't mind if I walk around."

"No, sir, a cemetery is public, maybe the most public place there is." He touched the marker Lipscomb had been examining. "What brings you here?"

Lipscomb waved, encompassing the cemetery. "I'm a grave robber."

Eben laughed. "The City of Charlotte already has that job."

"Have they given you a date?"

"We've got a while yet." He pointed at the backhoe parked on the street. "But that's a strong reminder of what's coming."

"I'm a social anthropologist and an amateur archaeologist," Lipscomb said. "Interested in burial places with some history to them."

"Our oldest stone is 1845."

"And the remains there will be few. At best slaves got a wooden box, but many were buried in shrouds, sheets sewn together." Lipscomb looked at the grave they stood beside. "What interests me is what they took with them."

"To heaven?"

"Or wherever. I'd like to make a record of what's there."

"You mean when we have to move the graves," Eben said.

"If it comes to that."

"Will you be documenting the details for anyone in particular?"

"The descendants of those buried here," Lipscomb said. "Shame on the ones who are forcing this. Why not leave the cemetery, even if they take everything else?"

Eben sat on the iron bench beside his Nettie's grave. "That's exactly what I've been asking myself."

The time was coming when he would have to confront the city about the graveyard, find someone to help him fight what felt insurmountable. When he'd become pastor of St. Tim's upon the death of Reverend Younger Tilley, he'd inherited intriguing mysteries that he first learned of on an August evening, thirteen years ago.

He'd sat at the old man's bedside, breathing in the sour dry smell of the sickroom. The top of a chest of drawers was covered with pill bottles. *Who managed them for Reverend Tilley?* At eighty-five, wasted by cancer, his mind murky, the ailing preacher hadn't been able to name anyone who should be notified of his coming demise, other than his congregation.

"You tell Sister Monroe, she'll get the word out."

"I already did. Everyone's praying for you, Reverend Tilley."

With a wheezing laugh, the preacher replied, "Tell 'em to save dey prayers for dem what need 'em. I'm ready to go, ready to go."

Eben believed him. He'd never known anyone as genuinely pious as Younger Tilley, had grown under the guidance of this devout man who'd led St. Tim's for forty-six years. Now the time had come for Eben to take over as pastor.

Reverend Tilley lifted a crooked finger, growled out a

word: "Important." He hesitated, spoke again. "Got to tell you sumpin important 'bout de sank-cherry." Sanctuary. Eben had grown accustomed to the man's Gullah dialect from the South Carolina coast, had come to love the sound of it. "Dey's peppers I'se not showed you."

"Papers?"

"De register. It was kep secret, den forgot about. Sumpin seem vital, den folks die or forget. Come enough years, what was worth keepin' secret don't matter no more."

He had learned to sit quietly while Tilley rambled. He never knew quite how far gone the old man was.

"Slaves ran off, you know. Kin might say dey was dead, and point to a new grave." Tilley smoothed the covers over his chest. "Weren't dead, jest ran off, but who wants to dig up a grave? Happened. Not often."

He began to understand. "You mean the cemetery."

"Uh-huh. Not all de markers tell de whole truth." Reverend Tilley stared at the wall behind Eben's head, his eyes—his awful yellow eyes—moving left to right as if he were reading a message written there. "Dey's a marker, JTQ."

Eben remembered that pock-marked rock near the back of the cemetery. Lichen covered, the initials carved deep, still readable. He'd sat down beside it one bright day and rubbed it to see if there was anything else besides the two-inch-high letters: *JTQ*. He'd found a date, but didn't know if it marked birth or death or—as was too often true of infants a hundred years ago—both. His best guess was 1856, although the eight might have been a nine. He spoke aloud. "JTQ, eighteen fifty-six."

"Dat right, you seen it. John Thomas Quarry, but it nineteen and twenty-six." Tilley made a grunting, coughing sound, clearing his throat as he did often. "Wonder what came of him."

"You mean how he died?"

"Oh. Yeah, I reckon he is dead now, more'n twenty years ago. He a good man, a friend."

"But the man's grave—"

"Not his grave, jest his marker." Tilley rolled away from him, grunting, spoke slowly. "De register's got everything. All about de cemetery. In de cellar, back of de coal bin. Church history. You'll see why when you find it." He sighed as if weary from the exchange, and was asleep within seconds.

Eben walked from the manse to the church that hot summer evening, went straight to the basement, and stood facing the coal storage bin. He managed to maneuver it a few inches out from the furnace, enough to see the solid brick wall behind it. No room for anything thicker than a sheet of paper. After pushing the bin back under the delivery chute, he brushed off his shirt, looking down at the black smears. He had coal dust in his hair and mouth, on his trousers. He should have changed clothes before tackling the job. Why had he paid attention to the memories of a sick old man?

Reverend Younger Tilley died that night, never having said another word.

CHAPTER 6

Persy was up early, packed to be on the road by seven-thirty. Blaire checked to make sure her luggage was stowed properly in the back of her new '61 Plymouth wagon. She turned in the driver's seat to watch him shifting the luggage until he was satisfied. Wide shoulders, strong arms. At fifty-five, he was graying, with wrinkles around his eyes and mouth; she still found him vital, appealing. She'd seen how women reacted to him, though it amazed her that he didn't seem to notice.

Blaire closed the tailgate and thumped the fender. "Shipshape." He leaned in the driver's window, kissed her cheek. "I wish I could go with you. You know that, right?"

"Sure." What she knew was that they were both lying. He knew it, too, but they'd played these games far past a time when they could change the rules.

"Call me," he said. She released the brake, backed away.

Traffic was light as she drove out of Charlotte on that day in late May, a balmy Saturday that promised a sunny beach. Halfway to Monroe, she felt a twinge of guilt about leaving

Blaire. Again. He wasn't in the least upset, of that she was sure. No doubt he'd already settled down to work at his desk at home, or was on the phone arranging a golf game. He'd drawn quietly into himself after Whitney's death, but lately there'd been a spark about him, a zeal for his work she hadn't seen in years.

Across the South Carolina line, she got stuck in a column of cars and trucks behind a green tractor in a no-passing zone. The man driving it was slouched at the wheel as if unaware of the traffic jam he'd caused. Or maybe inconveniencing people was the only thing that gave him a sense of control. A teenager stood on the dusty shoulder of the road, a cardboard sign against his chest, ANY BEACH. He held a thumb in the air, moved it in a slow arc, a duffel bag and guitar case at his feet. He smiled as cars crawled past, expecting something good to happen.

She decided to stop, offer him a ride.

What will that boy think when a woman alone, almost old enough to be his grandmother, offers him a ride to the beach? She glanced at herself in the rearview mirror and imagined her eyes blue and clear behind her large sunglasses, that she was more blond than silver, that her laugh lines implied maturity and mystery, a woman who took chances.

The pickup in front of her pulled over and the boy said something through the open window. He threw his duffel into the truck bed, added his guitar case with great care before climbing into the cab. She'd missed her chance. The tractor turned off the highway and the pickup gunned it, disappearing around a curve.

She punched on the radio. Static. Twisted the dial, caught one line of Patsy Cline singing "Crazy," a fragment of jazz, a preacher promising, in a deep baritone, ". . . everlasting life for those who believe, truly and deeply that God—" more static. At that moment, with the highway leveling out, red clay fading to sand, an endless stretch of scrub pines bordering newly plowed fields, she couldn't imagine anything less appealing than eternity. Blaire called this area the doldrums: "How can people stand to live with no radio or TV, no movies, no museums or concerts? It'd drive me crazy." Even as he made such observations she wondered what it would be like to live in a farmhouse set back off the highway under sheltering oaks, smoke spiraling from the chimney on a spring morning. And when had she and Blaire last been to a museum or the symphony anyway?

She passed fallow fields, unlimited flat land that stretched to a faint horizon, houses set far apart, an appealing distance between them. She gave up on the radio, grateful for a solitary silence broken only by an occasional truck flying by, rocking her car. She was happy cruising below the speed limit, no deadline, no one waiting.

At the new Winn-Dixie, the last stop for groceries before the waterway, she sat in the parking lot with the windows down, breathing in the salt air. Twenty minutes later she was on the drawbridge, two paper bags on the back seat—bread, fruit, eggs, milk, beer. The center sections began to rise as the switchman, in his glass-enclosed station, moved levers to allow passage of a sleek sailboat. *A couple on a romantic getaway? A lone sailor out for the day?* The water shimmered in the late morning sun.

When it was built in 1880, her grandparents named the house "Zander's Shanty." The two-story gray box sat in the valley of the dunes. The siding of cedar shakes battled the constant wind, but the weathered look was worth the trouble of replacing a few shingles every season.

As always the storage door resisted her, not wanting to give up the treasures in the cave under the house. The rusty lock finally yielded to her persistent key. Sunshine flooded the storeroom. One by one, leaving double-grooved ruts in her wake, she dragged the rockers to the porch where they swayed in the wind. Ghosts rocking, Grandmother had told her when she was a child.

The groaning of the front door welcomed her into the musty, closed-up parlor. When Blaire was with her, he started the three window A/C units as soon as they arrived, even though he knew how much she disliked that. Her way was to raise all the shades, tie back the curtains, open the windows, and prop dowels in those that tended to bang shut. Feel the wind.

Soon everything was in its place, the bed made, her towel hanging by itself, her clothes in the wardrobe. *A luxury of space for my things. For me.*

The pleasant lack of clutter was a testimony to Mother's spare touches, the way she acknowledged the house, let it speak for itself. Unlike the cluttered mess in which Persy had grown up. Bleached pink-throated conchs as doorstops, clamshells as ashtrays. Pictures on the mantel went back ninety years, her favorite in the center: her grandparents standing on the dunes, their daughter and son in front of them, faces somber in the style of the day. Mother was young, sweet-faced, before she grew into her nasty temper. Her bathing costume was probably a vibrant blue, her favorite color. The matting was warped, faded—as in most of the snapshots—but Persy was reluctant to replace frames that dated back to when photographs were a novelty. Then there were the pictures she'd added of herself and Blaire at their wedding, of their honeymoon here. Blaire standing in his office, confident, leaning casually against a shelf of law books. An empty space where a snapshot of her, grandly pregnant, once hung.

The refrigerator jolted to life. The pilot light on the stove responded to a match, the familiar heavy odor of the gas marked her settling in. While faucets ran to clear out the sediment of winter, she swept sand through the front door, the floor gritty under her feet. *How does the sand get in when the house is closed up tight?*

Lunch was a peanut butter sandwich, milk, an apple, a delicious meal eaten on the porch where she was queen of all she surveyed: the sun, wind, dunes, sea oats. The unending green of the ocean.

"Zander's Shanty" was painted in bold black letters on a shake that hung from a hook over the front steps, having survived Mother's ownership and whim of renaming it. When she deeded it over in the fall of 1955, Mother asked if Persy would change the name to something more modern.

"No," Persy had told her. "This stately old place will remain a shanty." She liked the implication of her family's casual wealth when they built the house.

"Stately?" Mother had said. "I suppose it is, compared to the shoddy bungalows they're building today." Mother was concerned about the cost of upkeep to the house, given the damage done by Hurricane Hazel a year earlier, and more storms to come. At least that's what she said. When angry, Mother could be viciously direct, but when she tried to be kind, she became awkward. Persy knew that the gift of the cottage was directly connected to Whitney's death, to Mother's unacknowledged attempt to assuage her daughter's grief. But talking about that would lead someplace Persy was not ready to go.

Two months after the funeral, Mother persuaded her to go to Windy Hill, showed her the quirks of the house, gave her the deed without ceremony.

"Oh, Mother. Really?"

"Yes, really. We'll execute it when we get home. It's yours. If you're smart, you'll put it in your name only."

★ ★ ★

In late afternoon, past the sunburn hour, she stood atop the dunes, gazing at the mostly deserted strand. A steady wind whistled past her ears. Seclusion, a connection to where her family history went back a century. The cottage had withstood all nature could throw at it. As had she, it occurred to her.

Did Grandmother stand in this same spot, pregnant with Mother, her last child, wearing all the clothes women had to wear in 1885? Did she go into the ocean? Persy hoped so.

To the north a new groin began at the dunes, crossed the beach, and continued out into the water beyond the breakers. A rope barrier had been in place for as long as Persy could remember, running from the street to the high tide line, suspended through grommets atop four-foot poles to separate Windy Hill from Atlantic Beach. Three years earlier the town had announced a plan to retard erosion, but a hidden agenda now seemed clear—more distinct separation of the two townships. Blaire had persuaded her of the ecology of the groins—low walls made of boulders brought in from the mountains. "They're a geological necessity," he'd told her.

They joined their neighbors in voting to fund three such structures. Thus far only the one was in place.

When they took over the cottage, scattered houses with empty stretches between them dotted the oceanfront of Windy Hill. She'd foolishly hoped it would stay that way, accepting Mother's gift knowing that Atlantic Beach to the north was for Negroes. The two lots between their place and the groin had been on the market for many years, the FOR SALE signs faded and battered. Blaire told the Realtors to let them know if they got a serious offer. "When that happens, we'll buy the land ourselves; it'll give us a buffer," he'd said, believing that the vacant lots would remain a no-man's-land between the white and colored beaches. At least as of now, he was right.

Laughter drifted to her from beyond the new groin. A man, woman, and little girl were running up the beach. A kite in the child's hand bumped along behind them. Persy doubted it would get airborne. The girl tripped, fell, righted herself, gave the kite to the man. He turned, ran back toward Persy, and the kite took off into the air, soaring above the water. He bent, spoke into the girl's ear, handed her the string. She darted away, the bright kite swooping back and forth behind her. The man and woman stood, holding hands, watching the child run with the kite.

The child looked to be about six. *The age Whitney would have been.* She turned away.

After a long, pounding shower she put on a turquoise blouse, and wrapped a bright print skirt around her waist, feeling like a Gauguin woman. She put white sandals on her bare feet, thinking of Grandmother, who never wore white before Memorial Day. Gold hoop earrings set off her glowing skin, and gold and silver bangles gave her a touch of defiance for breaking Mother's rule about not mixing precious metals.

She bent over, face to knees, her hair flying and snapping as she brushed it with a fury. Persy loved the feel of her hair hanging free, and wished Blaire liked her to wear it down. Age had brought more gray than blond, a change that was less noticeable when she hid it in a French twist or under a hat. Blaire had asked recently, "Why don't you put a little color in?"

Grandmother's mirror stand, angled in a corner between two windows, was tilted at exactly the correct degree for a head-to-foot reflection. What looked back at her was a middle-aged woman—full breasts filling out the turquoise blouse, ample hips and thighs under the bright skirt. She imagined Grandmother's reflection at the turn of the century, dressed for dinner.

With dabs of My Sin at her pulse points Persy headed out, leaving the front door open.

She took Highway 17 down to Myrtle Beach, hoping not to bump into anyone she knew, wanting to enjoy her solitude. With the mild weather, people they'd known for years would soon arrive in Windy Hill and notice that the house was open. Until then, she wouldn't seek company.

She stopped at one of many fish houses dotting the highway. The interior was decorated with nets, seashells, and Spanish moss. Did whoever selected the moss consider the bug life it supported before it became a wall hanging?

The waiter frowned when she said she was alone, leaving her to "check for a table," although the place was half-empty. He returned clutching one menu and led her to the last booth, where she sat facing the restaurant, to entertain herself by looking at anyone else who came in. She ordered her dinner and asked for a beer. For some reason the waiter nodded, as if to say, "Excellent choice, ma'am," though she was clueless about his change of attitude. Maybe Blaire was right, that she was too sensitive. He never seemed to notice the attitudes of clerks or waiters. Then again, maybe Blaire wasn't sensitive enough. She smiled. A man seated by himself at a booth across the room lifted his beer to her.

She went back to her dinner, pleased, feeling attractive for the first time in ages. As she was writing a check at the front counter, she couldn't help glancing to see if the man was still there. He tipped his mug in her direction. She grinned in spite of herself, and laughed in the car as she headed home.

CHAPTER 7

At Belk's, where I go to buy underpants on sale, a pretty skirt catches my eye. It would catch Mr. Griffin's eye, too, and that makes me happy, the way thinking about him always does. I'm so busy deciding if I could spend four dollars on a cotton skirt that I'm already zipping it up when I remember I don't have to be in the back dressing room where the letters COLORED ONLY are faint on the door. Habit's a funny thing. Now I can change where the white ladies do, and here I am, at the end of the hall, in this room smaller than a closet, no mirror, no place to sit. At least it's private.

I open the door to step out to look at myself in the three-way mirror and hear a white lady in another changing room, talking loud.

"Ooh, I like this one, fits well. How's yours?" In the space at the bottom of her dressing room door I see high heels turning this way and that. Admiring her reflection.

From the next room, "A bit tight, but I'm reducing, you know."

"Yes, I know, dear."

The skirt I have on is real pretty, but it's gon go back to the rack. Four dollars buys eight gallons of milk.

The first woman say, "Harold's on the commission, working on that mess in Second Ward. Getting rid of the blight."

I take off the skirt, put it back on the hanger, listening. They don't say anything else about my neighborhood.

Blight. I say the word to myself as I walk home, looking around me to see what it could mean. Got to be bad, but it sounds like *bright* or *light*. Maybe it means outhouses. There's one or two down by the creek, mostly because a sewer line is four-fifty a month. About the same price as a pretty skirt, and worth every penny. When we got city water, we got the wringer-washer, never had to go to the laundry-mat again. The money we saved on that paid for the sewer. But some folks don't see it that way.

I walk by Mabel Morrison's house. She owns it outright, like Bibi, and got it painted last spring, pink with white around the windows and doors.

At home I get Uncle Ray's dictionary from the shelf over the TV. It's almost worn out we've used it so much, the cover torn, pages coming loose. Nothing under "b-l-i-t-e," and "b-l-i-g-h-t" is about a disease that makes plants sick and die. Then I see it: "That which frustrates one's plans or withers one's hopes." That's what the ladies in Belk's meant. I look up "withers." They're even taking hope from us.

Mr. Griffin is the reason I can stand unhappy thoughts like we might have to move, or Bibi heading downhill now. Thinking about Mr. Griffin gets me through everything.

I like the way the skin crinkles around his gray eyes when he smiles, the way his cheeks get flushed in the heat of the kitchen. He's not pasty-faced like some white men. I'd been at the S&W maybe a month when all of a sudden

I saw what a good-looking man he is. After that there was no going back to thinking of him as only my boss. Seeing him at work I get jittery. If he's anywhere around I can't say a thing. But I find myself watching him when he comes into the kitchen, see the way he straightens his bowtie, how he brushes his hair off his forehead. He's well over six feet, but when we stand in the alley talking, if we on break, he slouches some so I don't have to strain my neck looking up at him. Maybe tall men get use to bowing down a little, the nice ones like Mr. Griffin.

At work, we never talk in the kitchen, not even looking at each other too much on break in the alley. Retta looks sideways at me when she's slicing onions or changing the oil in the deep fryer, thinking something's going on with me and Mr. Griffin, but she doesn't know for sure. Someday I'm gon tell her, maybe.

Now I ache for him, like at night when I'm in bed touching myself, wondering if he's thinking about me, having to be quiet, not moving, with Hawk asleep across the room.

The whole thing started over a crate of apples that was borderline mealy, and Mr. Griffin gave some to Retta, some to me, some to the boy who mops up. I imagined applesauce with a slice of ham, a hot fried pie, a batch of Bibi's apple butter on toast. Not thinking about how I was going to carry two bags of apples to the bus stop, until I stood by the back door in my heavy coat, already punched out. I stared at the bulging sacks. I wasn't going to leave them no matter what.

"Loraylee?" Mr. Griffin comes up behind me. "You need some help?"

"Got to figure a way to get these to the bus."

"I could give you a ride. You live downtown, right?"

I wanted that ride, wanted those apples, but when I said

yes, it was for more than two bags of Red Delicious. I walked out the door with him, down the alley to the parking lot on Church Street.

He helped me into his blue four-door Chevy, neat and clean like he is.

Alone in his car, we rode a couple of blocks without a word, the air heavy with the smell of the ripe fruit. Then he asked me what I was gon do with them.

"First I'll get Bibi to stew some for supper tonight. My uncle Ray loves him some stewed apples."

"Who's Bibi?"

"My grand. She does most of the cooking." Back then that was true. Bibi could cook, didn't leave a pot of water on the stove till it boiled dry, or burn the cornbread or boil collards to mush. "What you gon do with yours?"

"I'm not sure, but I couldn't see throwing them out, though I can tell you I won't buy from that supplier again. Twice they've brought us produce that was overripe." He clicked his blinker, turned onto McDowell. "I don't know, maybe some pies. Apples don't freeze, do they?"

"I reckon if you cooked them first, but when they thaw they'd not do for anything but sauce."

We got quiet again. You can only say so much about apples. When he stopped in front of our house, I jumped out and grabbed the bags, saying, "Bye," and heading across the yard, dropping a couple of apples as I went. I didn't want Bibi or Uncle Ray to see me in a white man's car, or Dooby Franklin, either.

A week or two later, we act like Mr. Griffin is giving me a ride because it's cold, fall coming on. But we both know what I'm doing in his car. We wind up in the deserted lot behind Park Center, carrying on in the back seat till the windows fog. Not a word said all the way back to Brown Street, both of us pretending that's a one-time thing.

From then on, whenever we can, we do it in his car, then talk, then do it again. We talk and talk, and in all our talking he calls me Loraylee and I call him Mr. Griffin. He say I should call him Archie when it's the two of us, but I am quick to answer, "No, sir, you're my boss, and if I call you Archie in your car then one day I'll slip and call you Archie in the kitchen of the S&W, and that will be that. No more Loraylee and Mr. Griffin. No, sir."

"Okay." He sighs. He wishes things could be different, too.

One advantage about being what Uncle Ray calls substantial and Bibi say is plump: My belly didn't show till I was almost seven months along, and even if other people at the S&W noticed, nobody said anything besides Retta, who tells me she's glad they didn't make me leave. By then I'd been promoted to the serving line, but Mr. Griffin put me back to work in the kitchen, in charge of the dishwasher, messy work but easy. I missed the line, missed greeting people, asking them would they like a roll and don't forget your butter, or the chocolate pie is real good today.

Just eighteen, I'd never been much of anywhere except downtown Charlotte and the S&W. I knew the bus routes and the neighborhood. Belk's on Trade Street and Ivey's on Tryon. The soda fountain at Queen City Pharmacy where I worked before the grocery store. I'd been around some, had been in another back seat with a boy who didn't know a lot more than I did, but I wasn't ready to have a baby. Then it happened. Soon as I missed my monthly, I knew, and for weeks all I could think about was having a baby to myself, someone to love and love. Didn't tell Mr. Griffin till I had to. Bibi guessed soon enough. She and Uncle Ray asked me and asked me who was the father, but after a while they stopped. I wasn't going to say, not to anybody. I learned something: If you don't want to tell a thing, you don't have to.

Hawk was born October 26, 1954. The pains started on my day off, and I had two weeks of vacation and four days of sick leave before I had to go back.

Bibi and Uncle Ray came to visit us at Good Samaritan. Uncle Ray took one look at Hawk and say, "They's been some milk spilt in the coal bin."

We got home when Hawk was three days old to find Pap and Grand Shumaker waiting for us. Grand studied Hawk, ran her fat brown finger down his cheek. "Humph." That's all she had to say.

A week later I was in the living room, nursing Hawk, when the phone rang. I'd never talked to Mr. Griffin on the phone, but I knew the voice soon as he said, "Hey, Loraylee."

"Hey."

"Are you all right?"

"Yeah. Hurting some, but yeah."

"Do you need anything?"

A daddy for my baby. I said, "I'm okay."

"We miss you down here." So I knew he was calling me from the S&W.

"Okay." Silence hung there on the phone while Hawk sucked my titty, holding onto my finger and grunting the way babies do.

"Well, then, I'll see you soon."

"Yeah, soon." Then click. Tears rolled down my cheeks while I watched Hawk nurse on me.

I wished I could get one of Miss Roberta's gowns for Hawk being baptized, but I made do with a white shirt of Uncle Ray's that Bibi cut down, embroidered with lace for the christening. Couldn't tell it wasn't the real deal unless you looked close and saw where she'd sewed the buttonholes shut. But Miss Roberta's needle makes magic in cotton you can see through. Tiny tucks held with spider thread, rumor is. Tatting and smocking, no two alike.

Of course, Mr. Griffin couldn't go to the christening, which bothered us both. He keeps up with Hawk, asks me about him, saying all casual like, when I'm stocking shelves in the back and everybody else is talking in the kitchen. "How's your baby?"

"He's okay."

"Healthy?"

"Had the rosy-ola, scared me he got so hot. But he's over it."

"Has he got much hair?"

"A whole head full. Curly. Not kinky." I didn't look at Mr. Griffin's wavy red-brown hair.

"Eyes?"

"Yeah, he's got eyes."

Mr. Griffin laughs. "What color?"

"Gray like my grandmother's. Not brown. Not blue." I turn away. Mr. Griffin gets the message. I'm through talking about Hawk that day. But our boy is there, between us, and I feel Mr. Griffin listening whenever I mention Hawk to one of the other girls at the S&W.

We didn't try much to take up with each other again; it just happens, sooner or later, like both of us knew it would.

We careful not to be together in public, but that happens, too, like the July afternoon I'm on the corner, waiting for the bus, and here comes Mr. Griffin, leaving Liggett Drugs. We don't say anything, stand there side by side on that hot yellow day, not even looking at each other. But I feel the back of his right hand touch the back of my left, and one finger of his links one finger of mine, squeezes, lets go. I watch him walk away. Minute or two, a woman hisses in my ear, "Be ashamed." I turn to see who it is, but she's stomping up the street on her fat black legs and her clicking heels.

Hawk ask me once, "Who is my daddy?"

And I say, "He's gone." Give him a look that say not to ask me anymore.

Mr. Griffin and I, in all our talking and all our loving, even if we don't say much about Hawk, he's always there in the warm air of that back seat. Often I get home and find a twenty-dollar bill somewhere, in my purse or my coat pocket. How he does that, I don't know, but it's from Mr. Griffin, doing what he can. I reckon he waits till I'm not watching or maybe when I'm getting my shoes back on, and slips it in my bag, every couple of weeks. I never say anything to him about the money. It's for Hawk, which we both know.

Mr. Griffin jokes about me never doing it with my shoes on, how I won't let him touch me till my feet are bare. Even that first time we crawled into the back seat, both of us knowing why we going there, then getting shy for a few minutes. But he kisses me and I laugh while I take off my shoes. He say, "Why did you do that?"

"I never wear my shoes to bed."

He kisses me again and that's that.

After we do it a few times he starts pestering me about what I like.

I say, "I like everything you do, every single thing."

He touches my titty that's sticking out the front of my blouse. "You like that?"

"Um-hmm," I say.

He moves his hand down. "And that?"

"I like everything except talking about it."

He hugs me, his chest rumbling against me. He has a tummy you'd never notice when he's got his clothes on. First time I see it hanging down when he's on top of me I say, "I like your belly."

"Hush. You don't," but he laughs that laugh.

I haven't told him about the man from the city, how the

commission's gon take our house no matter what. And not telling Mr. Griffin makes me feel like I'm living a lie, but he's my boss, might think I'm asking him to do something or that I want a raise because it's tough at home. One day I tell Retta about Mr. Menafee and what he calls redevelopment.

"Have you told Mr. Griffin?" First thing she say, getting right to the heart of the matter the way she does.

"Why would I do that?"

She turns away, making herself busy loading the dishwasher. "You'll tell me someday, girl, when you're ready."

My days off, I get groceries, take care of whatever needs doing, mostly stuff Bibi can't handle now. Sweep out the whole house, take the broom to the floors, run the vacuum cleaner over the rugs. Couple hours there, if it's done right, with Bibi tracking behind me.

"You get that corner there, girl, I see dirt you missed." Or, "Grandma Alexander carpet that one, won't never wear out." Or, when I start dusting, "You got no oil on the cloth, Raylee. How you gon do it proper with no oil on the cloth?" Some days I shush her, others I let her go on.

Half a day with the laundry, eight sheets got to go through the wringer-washer, then hang on the line. Once they're dry, Bibi insists the tops of them get ironed. Days when I not got much left in me, I only iron hers and Uncle Ray's. Hawk doesn't care and I'm happy to sleep on wrinkled sheets, long as I can sleep, which I never get enough of.

Hawk gets home from school about when I'm done with the house, and we go to the grocery store. I wish I had a day off besides Mondays, when the stores are low on stock after the weekend. But no helping that. Every once in a while I get a Saturday, which always tickles Bibi. No matter how often I tell her, she can't seem to get it that the S&W needs us there on weekends for the crowds. And she tags along with me to the grocery store, bothers me with picking up first one thing and then the other, worse than Hawk. She sees baked beans on sale, starts going on about buying ten cans to save fifty cents, no matter that we eat beans too much and we've got no room left in the hall closet that she calls the pantry. "We can set them on top the fridge, is what," she say, putting two more cans in the cart. "Ray likes them with molasses and bacon. Could eat a whole can by himself."

Hawk takes a jar of cherries off the shelf. "Can we get these, Mama? They're pretty."

Bibi grabs another can of beans.

"No, Bibi." My voice is sharp, making her jump. "The canned tomatoes on sale last week, we stacked them on top the fridge, remember?"

She looks ashamed, like she always does when I remind her of something she forgot, then I feel bad, too. I leave the beans in the cart. We'll put them on the board over the washer. Little enough I can do to please her, and canned beans on sale don't amount to much.

Hawk whines when I put the cherries back, but for the same forty-nine cents I can get a pound of ground beef.

So that's the way it is the day we bump into Mr. Griffin. I'm pushing a cart along the aisle of the A&P with Hawk tagging behind and Bibi beside me, her taking things off the shelf, me putting them back. We come to the end of the cereal aisle, he comes from bread, and we almost run our carts head-on into one another. Smiling. Embarrassed. I catch myself and say, "Bibi, this my boss man, Mr. Griffin."

At the same time he say, "Hello, Loraylee."

"My, my," say Bibi. "A pleasure, a pleasure."

"This my grandmother, Bibi—" I stammer. "I mean Livinia. Mrs. Livinia Hawkins. You've heard me mention her."

"I have. Nice to meet you, Mrs. Hawkins." He looks at

Hawk, who is by my side, close to me. "And you must be Hawk." Mr. Griffin puts out his hand like he was meeting another man, but Hawk steps back, stares at the floor, his arms behind his back.

"You good to my Raylee," say Bibi. I'm thinking she doesn't know how good. My eyes meet his for a second, the same thing on his mind.

"I'm lucky to have Loraylee at the S&W, don't know what we'd do without her." He smiles at Bibi while he say this. "Last week one of my customers told me how much he enjoys talking with her on the line, and—"

Hawk pushes our cart against his, shouts, "Go on!"

"Hawk!" I say, my voice sharp. "Hush."

Mr. Griffin steps back, bumps into a shelf, face red. "I startled him, that's all, stopping y'all in the middle of your shopping."

Hawk mumbles something and turns away.

Mr. Griffin tells Bibi goodbye and goes on down the aisle. I'm thinking Hawk has a first-rate man for his daddy, even if they never gon know each other.

"Mm-mmm," say Bibi. She tips Hawk's chin, making him look at her. "Why you sass that nice man?"

Hawk turns away from his great-grandmother. She looks at me like she suspects something but can't think what. Time was she would know for sure and would say it right out. I take a package of pork chops from the meat case, telling Bibi, "Uncle Ray does favor pork chops and baked beans." I push the cart toward the milk cooler.

The next day Mr. Griffin calls me to his office, saying out loud for the others to hear, "We need to go over your schedule." He closes the door behind us. I sit in the chair across from his desk. He sighs, standing by the side window, staring out at the parking lot, a vast array of cars. Drums his fingers on the windowsill before coming around to me. Kneels beside my chair, puts his head in my lap. I want to cry, but what I do is pat his head, like I would if Hawk came to me this way.

"What're we going to do?" Mr. Griffin ask me. "What're we going to do?"

CHAPTER 8

Before Nettie got sick and died, those awful months in 1958, Eben's favorite part of the day was early morning. He'd sit at the kitchen table and watch her reach for a pot, fill it with water, set it to boil, adjust the gas flame. The morning sun, streaming through the soaring windows of their kitchen, silhouetted her graceful form, her feet never moving as she made breakfast. This appealing economy of motion was typical of her, something he hadn't noticed in his first flush of feelings.

Benjamin Stone, one of his best friends, told him about Nonette Hasty. "My cousin Nettie, nineteen. She's going to teach in the Vacation Bible School at St. Tim's."

Fresh out of divinity school, Eben returned to Brooklyn that summer of 1938, hoping to be pastor of St. Tim's someday. Reverend Younger Tilley, long ensconced in the pulpit, assured him, "Don't worry, many a church looking for a preacher, especially one dat's got hisself educated. Meantime, we need us a youth minister. Kids too much on de streets nowadays. What you say?"

He took the job to keep his ties with St. Tim's, stay close to what remained of his family. The problem was a salary that wouldn't feed a church mouse, forcing him to work several jobs, his favorite at the colored library on Brevard Street, where he'd spent many hours as a child.

The first time he saw Nettie he could not look away from her warm brown eyes, her pretty face, her mellow voice that made him want to hear her sing. He wasn't used to looking eye to eye with girls, and her confident height made him nervous, gave her the upper hand from the start.

Benjy saw how it was. "You're a dead duck, my friend."

He was determined to pursue Nettie and to marry her. His thoughts centered on this idea whenever he saw the tawny girl who carried her leggy self with such assurance, giving him a stirring unlike anything he'd felt in his thirty-one years. He manipulated the Bible school schedule so the two of them could teach the senior high students together in a study of the New Testament—two hours of class that breezed by like two minutes.

He spoke to her about a possible future together, but Nettie made herself clear. "I'm going to finish college. Get a degree. Teach. Nothing's going to stop me. Not a husband. Not children."

He saw in her direct gaze that it was so. She left in August for her sophomore year at Spelman and he began his letter-writing campaign. He sent her two- and three-page missives twice a week, writing on Sunday afternoons as he relaxed after a lunch hosted by a church family, and again on Wednesday evenings after choir practice. He wrote about St. Timothy's and the people she'd come to know over the summer. Never again mentioned marriage, but stated plainly that he was available for Thanksgiving. Every other week he got a brief response, acknowledging his letters, thanking him for news of their mutual friends, but with no hint of anything he could take as personal. In a postcard in mid-November she said she was leaving to do "mission work" on St. Helena Island on the South Carolina coast. One sentence gave him hope: "I'm sorry I won't see you during the holidays, but I'll write again upon my return to school."

He remained steadfast in his pursuit through her graduation from Spelman and the teaching job she took on the island in the fall of 1941, seeing her as much as he could on her visits home, and encouraged by an increasingly responsive correspondence from her end. "I want to work for at least a year before I settle down. Then we'll see," she wrote. She never said no.

After services on the first Sunday in December 1941, Eben visited with two of his favorite members of the congregation, Livinia Hawkins and her brother Ray Glover. Ray, a fit man in his fifties, was talking about a tree he'd planted in their small yard on Brown Street. "Magnolia. It's coming along real nice. May get too large for where I set it, but I'm willing to take a chance. Only a few magnolias in Blue Heaven. I asked—"

"Listen!" Loraylee, Livinia's five-year-old granddaughter, came running into the kitchen. "Listen to the bells ringing."

The air filled with the sound, all over downtown. The deep iron bells from First Presbyterian, the clanging brass bells at the House of Prayer, the bell at St. Timothy's, which to him stood out among the others.

Dooby Franklin burst through the front door, holding his great belly, gasping. "The Japs has attacked us."

Loraylee climbed onto her grandmother's lap. "What're Japs, Bibi?"

Livinia, her face troubled, held the girl, rocking, saying, "Oh, Lordy. Oh, Lordy."

Ray Glover asked, "Where'd it happen, Dooby?"

Dooby took a cup off a shelf above the sink and poured coffee into it, squeezing his bulk into a chair. "Radio say Pearl Harbor, in Hawaii, island in the Pacific."

"That's not us," Livinia said.

Ray said, "Yeah, it is, Livvie. We own it, something like that."

"I'd better get to the church," Eben said. "Folks are going to want to see me and Reverend Tilley."

He heard Livinia's plea as he left. "Pray for us all."

The second week of January 1942, Eben went to the local recruiting station, the lone colored man in the crowd milling outside the storefront army office on West Boulevard. The only man in a suit and tie, and at thirty-five, one of the oldest. He kept his eyes down, stood off to the side, and touched his breast pocket for the reassuring crinkle of paper, the letter of endorsement from the dean of the theology school at Shaw. Most of the men wore shirts and trousers beneath heavy coats against the winter chill, brogans or boots, hats and scarves. Had he made a mistake wearing his Sunday best? Maybe, but he lived by what his mother had taught him: "You wanna be as good as the white man, you gotta be better."

The door to the recruiting station opened. A young corporal called out, "Next!" Five men went inside.

He asked a man standing nearby, "Sir? How do we know when to go in?"

The man flicked a cigarette into the street. "Five men go in together. How long you been here?"

"Since eight-thirty."

"You're next. Go stand by the door."

"I don't want to break in line."

The man finally looked at him. "You want to join up?"

"Yes, sir."

"Stand on the steps."

When the door opened again, he entered with four others. The room smelled of cigarettes and a tangy odor he couldn't identify, maybe furniture polish. There was a compulsive neatness to the room, a bustling air of efficiency. Three desks, the corporal at one of them and sergeants at the other two. He was glad now that he'd studied army insignia, could identify soldiers by rank.

One of the sergeants motioned to him. A heavy man with slick black hair parted near the middle, icy blue eyes, an Errol Flynn mustache. "You're next, boy. C'mere." The tag on his chest said Lindsay. He pushed papers across the desk. "Fill these out."

"Yes, Sergeant Lindsay. I believe I already have, if these are the same forms." He put the completed papers on the desk, used the tips of his fingers to move them toward the sergeant. "Picked them up yesterday."

With a flicker of surprise, Lindsay rotated the forms, studied them, grunted, "Chaplain?"

"Yes, Sergeant." He pulled the letter from the pocket of his coat and held it out. Lindsay thumped the desk.

He dropped the letter, watched the sergeant pull it toward him, open it, read it. The man sat back in his chair, touched his mustache. "I might have just the thing for you. There's a colored unit forming at Fort Bragg. Got a bulletin about it yesterday. They gonna need a chaplain, don't you reckon?"

"Yes, Sergeant."

Thus he became an official army chaplain, though not an officer, as he'd hoped. He swallowed the sting of the insult and focused instead on bringing solace to colored soldiers, wherever he was stationed.

On the way home, he thought about all he had to do in

the ten days before he reported for duty, with the first order of business being to write Nettie, now settled in her mission work, but more and more receptive to talk of marriage. He hoped she would be pleased to hear from Sergeant Eben Polk, United States Army Chaplain.

CHAPTER 9

Persy's first pregnancy was over almost before it started. She missed one period, was due for another when she expelled a bloody lump that would have been a baby if she'd been able to keep it. Early in her second pregnancy, she had a series of random aches, low in her back, which Dr. McInulty said were not unusual. He ordered bed rest for two weeks and during that time the woman who cleaned for Mother came over every other day to help out. For a while the rest seemed to have helped, but at three months a backache awakened Persy at midnight; she prodded Blaire out of a sound sleep. "I don't know if we should go to the hospital, but I'm in a lot of pain."

He held her till she fell back asleep near dawn.

The next night when she woke Blaire, he said, "Jesus, Persy, again?"

That time they did go to the hospital. She lost the baby.

In December of 1954, when they'd given up hope, she got pregnant once more, and all went well. In her eighth month neither of them felt there was any harm in Blaire going on his army reserve duty, a weekend of tactical maneuvers "in the boonies" with thirty other men. Such tours occurred twice a year, and she found herself welcoming his brief absences. She wasn't due for another three weeks and her prenatal signs were healthy; they agreed he should go ahead. "After all," he assured her, "I'll only be half an hour away. Call, they'll come get me."

On Friday afternoon they stood in the driveway, waiting for Blaire's ride to the departure point. She was never comfortable with him when he was dressed in his green fatigues, wearing an infantry cap with crossed rifles, the bill shadowing his eyes. His boots and brass belt buckle were polished to a high shine, his lieutenant's bars gleaming on his collar. He smelled of cigarettes and English Leather. He kicked at his khaki duffel bag. "I may have packed too much." A station wagon carrying four other uniformed men turned in the driveway. Blaire pulled her close, kissing her in a way she felt was for show. He hefted the duffel. "See you Sunday night!" Then he was gone.

Her labor started slowly the next morning, mild contractions that moved from her low back to her pelvis every hour or so. She left word with Dr. Mac's answering service and dialed the number Blaire had left but got no answer. She called Mother, waited through a dozen rings before giving up on her.

She was tempted to drive herself to the emergency room for a medical opinion. Three weeks, not terribly early. Lots of babies made it earlier than that. But she got the bag she'd had packed for a month and called a taxi to take her to Memorial Hospital, a mile away, feeling great about how well she was handling things. At admissions, she gave them the contact information for Blaire: "Call him, please, right now, and if you don't get an answer, keep trying." The woman assured her she would. Persy decided not to try to reach Mother again, at least until things had moved further along.

When he arrived, Blaire would be confined to the waiting room, a smoke-filled room where men gathered to console one another on the misery of waiting.

Laboring women nearby moaned and screamed, unnerving her. The unit was so full that several, including her, labored on gurneys in the hallway. She watched a wall clock, timed her pains, and stared at the uneven perforations of the ceiling tiles, wondering if she could count the holes if she concentrated. She tried to read what was posted on a bulletin board on the wall above her head, but could make out little on the papers thumbtacked to the framed cork.

At one point they considered sending her home given how slowly she was progressing, but when the pains got five minutes apart, they let her stay.

A nurse stopped, took Persy's pulse and blood pressure, put a hand on her belly, waiting for another contraction. Her starched bosom hovered above Persy's nose as she leaned over her, reading something on the bulletin board. A name tag identified her as Nurse Maxwell. She straightened, pushed back a lock of gray hair, revealing a half-moon of sweat in her armpit. "Okay, hon, your vitals are great and you're making progress. I suspect we'll be moving you to delivery soon."

"Soon" became an hour, an hour and a half. A man wandered down the hall looking dazed. Rumpled suit, tie loose at his neck, glancing anxiously around. She asked him, "Is your wife in labor?"

He nodded. "They won't let me see her."

"Yes, I know. That's standard."

"It's been almost twenty-four hours."

"Is it your first?"

"Yes."

"That can take a while."

He straightened his tie. "Your first?"

My first full term, my first that has a chance of living? "No."

"Okay. Well . . ."

She asked, "Are you heading for the waiting room?"

"Yes."

"Would you ask if a man named Blaire Marshall is there? My husband. He's on army reserve duty this weekend and I don't know whether anyone has reached him. I keep thinking they would say something if he's here, but in case . . ."

He touched her shoulder. "Blaire Marshall. Of course I will. What should I tell him?"

"That I'm okay." She couldn't think of anything else.

"It's my pleasure, Mrs. Marshall. I wish you the best."

"You too, sir."

He walked away, a lilt in his step.

Before she saw Mother, she heard her strident voice. "I know she's here. I'll find her—never mind, I see her." She strode toward Persy, arm out as if fending off tacklers. When she reached her she said, "Why in the world didn't you let me know?"

Persy burst into tears. Someone who cared for her had come. She'd thought she could do this by herself. She was wrong. Mother put her arms around her. "Dear girl, I'm here now. I'm here." She straightened. "So where are we? How close are the contractions?"

As Mother spoke, she felt that tightening in her back, around her hips to the front, and couldn't speak. Mother held her hand until it passed, timing her on her wristwatch. For as long as Persy could remember, Mother had worn the same delicate gold band attached to a tiny watch that had been Grandmother's, insisting it would run for another hundred years. Mother smelled faintly of L'Air du Temps.

"How long since the last one?"

She looked at the square black-and-white wall clock. "Five or six minutes."

"Any pushing yet?"

"I feel like I should, but—"

"Believe me, you'll know."

A young nurse she hadn't seen before rushed up, spoke to Mother in a stressed shrill voice, "Sorry, but we can't have you here. The waiting room is down the hall." She pointed.

Mother growled, "Not on your life."

To Persy's astonishment, the nurse scurried off without another word.

"I was working in the garden." Mother's silver hair was pulled back roughly into a disheveled bun. She had dirt under her fingernails. No makeup, no earrings, a sleeveless cotton blouse, plaid Bermudas. "I kept going inside to call you." She brushed at a smudge on her shorts. "With Blaire gone, I wanted to be sure you were okay, but when you didn't answer, I drove to your house. Called Memorial from there and found you'd been admitted. So here I am."

Yes, here she was in her gardening shorts with her alligator bag hanging over her shoulder, wearing her L'Air du Temps.

Within a few minutes, she felt a fullness between her legs. A need to push, as if she'd reached the end of prolonged constipation. There was no longer a clock on the wall. No perforated ceiling tiles or muffled screams and groans from the labor suites. Only Mother, feeling her belly.

After a couple of contractions when she began to push, Mother lifted the sheet, dropped it immediately and shrieked, "She's crowning."

Nurse Maxwell appeared as if she'd been ten feet away, looked between her legs, shouted, "Delivery, stat!"

Mother kissed her and spoke to the nurse. "*Now* I'll go to the waiting room."

Nurse Maxwell got behind the gurney, rolled her down the hall away from the bulletin board, the clock, beneath a procession of overhead fluorescents, and into a busy bright room. She was transferred from the gurney when the nurse barked, "On three. One, two, three!" They lifted her by the sheet she'd been on for hours, deposited her onto a table. Rolled her to remove the sheet, soiled with amniotic fluid and shit. Lifted her legs, put her feet in the stirrups. A pain hit her. She groaned. Nurse Maxwell called out, "I'll deliver this baby if I have to, but where the hell is McInulty?"

"I'm here." Dr. Mac's voice from the hallway.

"Just in time to catch it," said Nurse Maxwell.

Another pain. She grunted, pushed, and felt the baby leaving her. Immediately she heard a high-pitched bawl.

"Good job, Mother," said Nurse Maxwell.

Mother. She was a mother. She'd made it.

"It's a boy," another voice said.

"Let me have him," said Nurse Maxwell. "I'll pink him up."

Someone else called out, "Four-eighteen p.m., six pounds, two ounces."

In the bustle and clatter she said, "I want to see him." Her voice came from a great distance, from some other woman who'd become a mother.

Dr. Mac said, "In a bit, Persy. You're not done here. Got to get the afterbirth." He patted her cheek with a hand that smelled of soap.

Later, much later, she was alone in a room when Dr. Mac walked in carrying her baby in his large square hands.

She held out her arms. "Give him to me."

"There's a problem, Persy."

"Give him to me."

He handed her the wrapped bundle. She smoothed the blanket away from her son's face. Saw brown hair like Blaire's, a blue tinge to his skin. Nurse Maxwell hadn't pinked him up at all. She looked at Dr. Mac. "He needs another blanket. He's cold."

"There's nothing we can do, Persephone. It's a congenital heart defect, a valve problem. He won't make it."

"Yes, he will," she said, touching his cheek. "Hello, Whitney."

He breathed in gasps, struggling for life. She wanted to cover his mouth with hers, breathe into him.

She looked up at Dr. Mac. "Please help him."

"I can't."

He always knew what to do and now he didn't.

"Help my baby!" she screamed.

Dr. Mac shook his head, tears in his eyes. "I'm so sorry, Persy. Be with him now. It won't be long." He turned off the overhead light as he left the room, leaving them in the glow of the bedside lamp.

"No," she said to the baby. "No, no."

The door opened. A uniformed man came in, hurried toward her. She clutched the baby close.

"No," she said again. "You can't have him."

"Persy?" The man touched the baby's head. Blaire, the bill of his folded cap sticking out of his pants pocket. He kissed her forehead, stretched out on the single bed with her, his booted feet nudging her bare toes through the sheet. She leaned into him, inhaled his dependable scent. He laid his head on her pillow, one hand holding hers, the other caressing their son. And it wasn't long. Not long enough.

CHAPTER 10

A blustery day, after a week of rain, been cooped up by the weather too long. "C'mon," I say to Hawk. "Let's get Desmond and go to the playground at school. How about it?"

"Oh, boy! What you think about that, Bibi?"

Bibi is shelling peas at the kitchen table. "A fine idea."

"Wait till Uncle Ray gets home before you start cooking, okay?"

"Okay."

I hope she remembers. Last week she burned the bottom out of a pot when she turned on the stove and forgot it.

We stop for Desmond and head for the tunnel the city built when they cut big Independence Boulevard through our neighborhood. The underground crossing worked well when it was first carved out, giving folks a way to navigate six lanes of traffic. Stoplights weren't enough, and after two fourth-grade boys were killed on the way to school, the city finally paid attention to the awful intersection at McDowell and Independence.

"C'mon," Desmond shouts. He and Hawk race down the steps ahead of me.

"Y'all wait," I holler, my voice echoing. Before I'm down the concrete stairs, a stench rises up to meet me. The boys stop at the entrance.

I take them by the hand. "Hold on till we get across." The city put four lights in the tunnel, but it's still too dark. I look into the gloom, try to see if anyone's sleeping there. In bad weather bums use it for a shelter, for a bathroom, too. Now the city's talking about putting up gates at both ends, with school principals having keys to lock and unlock them.

"Yeah," Uncle Ray say when I tell him about that plan. "It'll hold them off about a week till somebody picks the locks."

We near the middle when a man's voice say, "Hey, honey. You got some cute boys there."

I whirl around, see him sitting against the wall, a wine bottle in his lap. He holds it out. "Want a sip, young lady?" He's filthy, with a gray beard down his chest.

Hawk shouts, "You leave my mama alone, mister!" He sounds much older than he is.

The man lowers the bottle. "No offense, young fella. Just being friendly."

I pull the boys along to the other end, where we race up the steps.

At the playground I sink onto one of the metal benches, cold on this early June day. "Okay, y'all go have some fun."

Hawk say, "If my daddy was here, he would take care of us."

I'm too surprised to say a word.

Desmond say, "You got a daddy?"

"He doesn't live with us," Hawk say. "But someday he will. Right, Mama?"

"We'll talk when we get home, okay?" I need to think. The boys climb the monkey bars, leaving me wondering how in the world I'll explain Mr. Griffin to Hawk. I could start by telling him how I got my name, how he got his. Go from there.

Loraylee Alexander Hawkins, Lo-Ray-Lee, named for Auntie Lorena, for Uncle Ray, and for my cousin Lee who lived three hard years before I was even born. Granddaddy Vester believed that naming me for Lorena would fix Bibi's hurt—got my daddy to write it on my birth certificate and in the family Bible.

Vester has been gone nineteen years. But when Bibi carries on about Uncle Rupert, her first sweetheart, it's as if her forty-year marriage to Vester never happened. What she doesn't want to think about is that Uncle Rupert chose Auntie Lorena.

I like Auntie Lorena and Uncle Rupert, but Bibi throws a fit at the mention of them. They live out near Johnson C. Smith, where he teaches history, another thing that bothers Bibi. She say they think they're too good for us. But I take Hawk to see them, want him to know that enough schooling can get you a fine brick house.

Then there's Hawk. Alexander Clarence Hawkins, who got to be "Hawk" shortly after he was born, a sweet baby with reddish fuzz that grew into curls. Uncle Ray said his gray eyes and silky auburn hair reminded him of a hawk. That stuck. If anybody calls him Alexander, like on the first day of school, he'll say, "You call me Hawk." I've heard him do it, proud of his name. He has never asked about "Clarence," but he will.

Mr. Griffin is Archibald Clarence Griffin. I put Clarence as Hawk's middle name on the birth certificate, telling Bibi and Uncle Ray, "It's a name I like." Clarence means bright, shining, clear. Like both Mr. Griffin and Hawk. Alexander, our family name, goes back as far as we know to when Bibi's grandfather was emancipated on the Alexander plantation that's long gone now. As far as we know.

On the way home from the playground, after we say goodbye to Desmond, I cross our yard with Hawk, sit on the back steps. "How come you said what you did about your daddy, that if he was here, he'd take care of us. Don't I do that?"

"Yeah."

"And I'm going to keep on taking care of us. You know that?"

"Yeah." He looks at the ground.

I put my arm around his shoulder, pull him to me, resting my chin on his head. "Hawk, baby, I know it's hard on you not having a daddy. I don't have either my mama or my daddy. But you and me got each other, got Bibi and Uncle Ray. More family than many folks have."

"Yeah."

I can feel the sad in his voice.

The kids are a block away when I hear them coming home from school, singing loud enough to wake the dead. Nobody in the neighborhood home this afternoon except Dooby Franklin trying to sweep his front yard, Mr. Stone on his way back to the store. The kids peel off as they go into their houses till it's only Hawk and Desmond. The silly song they're singing echoes off the sidewalks. I look out the front door, see him doing what he call skipping: hop on one foot, leap with the other, while carrying on with the song. Sounds to me like he's saying, "Hair he go," and something about Lulu, like the girl in the comics. He gets closer and I start understanding the strange words:

Here we go loopty loo,
Here we go loopty light,
Here we go loopty loo,
All on a Saturday night.
You put your right hand in . . .

He winds up his right arm and throws his hand out in front of him.

You take your right hand out . . .

He throws his hand up in the air.

You give your hand a shake, shake, shake . . .

Which is what he does.

And turn yourself about . . .

He whirls in a circle.

"Hawk!" I call from the front door. He stops and whoops out laughing when he sees me.

"Hey, Mama, I'm loopty-looing."

"I can see that."

He say "Bye!" to Desmond, who waves to him and heads for his house. "This my right hand," he runs up the front walk, wiggling his hand out to his side. I've been trying to teach him left from right. Now here he comes home singing a song, knowing which is which.

"How'd you learn that?"

"Miss Madison. I got a pocket here"—he touches his shirt—"and my heart is under it, going thumpety-thump. See? My right is the side with no pocket or heart."

Simple thing. Why I'm not a teacher.

He comes bouncing up the steps. "You got me a sandwich?"

"I do if you got me a kiss." He jumps up, brushes his mouth on my cheek, runs into the house. I like working first shift so I can be here when he gets home from school.

He sits at the kitchen table, slurping milk while I spread

peanut butter on one piece of bread, grape jelly on another. "Mary Anne, at school . . ."

"Yeah, I know, you're always talking about Mary Anne."

"Her mama cuts the crust off her sandwiches."

"Okay, I can do that." I reach behind me for the bread knife. "'Course if I do, it'll be less for you to eat."

He thinks on that. "Leave 'em on. No-crust sandwiches are for girls." I put his plate on the table and he takes a bite. "Mary Anne's mama fixes her hot chocolate when she gets home." His red-brown curls make his head look big.

"Good for her mama."

"I want hot chocolate."

"And I want a convertible."

"I want one, too, like Mr. Franklin got."

"Then you gotta get you a job."

He laugh. "I'm six. What can I do?" His gray eyes—his daddy's eyes—are hard to look away from.

"Your friend Mary Anne's mama, does she work?"

He takes another bite. "How'm I gon know that?"

"Don't talk with your mouth full."

"Then stop axing me stuff."

"Asking. You say asking, not axing." I sit down beside him, pat him on his shoulder. He shrugs me off. Lately he doesn't like being touched much. Use to crawl up on me and go to sleep, his head on my chest.

He pulls some papers from his book bag, pushes them across the table to me. "You have to read this."

Another notice about the PTA, Parent-Teacher Association, asking me to sign up for hall monitor or safety mother, to come to meetings, to "get involved in your child's education." First few he brings home I throw away. No way I can do more than I do, and I don't like them keeping after me. But here I am, feeling bad for not joining the PTA. I crumple it.

"No! Miss Madison say for you to read it."

Uncle Ray comes through the back door. "Read what?"

I smooth out the paper. "Notice about a parent and teacher thing, meeting at the school. They want me to work there."

"For pay?"

"You're dreaming. They wanting me to help out, make things better for the students."

"You gon do it?"

"Between the S&W and mopping the floor and mending your britches is when I'm gon work for nothing."

"I might could do it." Uncle Ray spreads peanut butter on a cracker, his fingers twisted around the knife, his knuckles lumpy. "You haven't got the time and Livvie hasn't got the mind."

"Uncle Ray, you're not serious."

"I'm not Roebuck."

Hawk giggles. Sears Roebuck is his favorite place to go. "Uncle Ray, he's not Roebuck." Hawk laughs and laughs.

Maybe it's not such a bad idea, Uncle Ray and the PTA. He is the closest thing Hawk's got to a daddy, always showing him how stuff works, telling him why things happen the way they do. Once I heard Hawk ask Uncle Ray about Adam and Eve and the Garden of Eden. "Adam and Eve, were they white or colored?"

Uncle Ray was quiet for a minute. "The way I look at it, one had to be white and the other colored, else how did we all get here?"

I think about me and Mr. Griffin, and I like that answer.

Raining off and on since early morning, bus running late. I'm glad all over again Uncle Ray's there for Hawk and Bibi. What would I do without him? I come huffing home, toting the cardboard containers of beans and potato salad left over from yesterday at the S&W, one more thing Mr. Griffin does for my family. He leaves stuff for me in a paper bag under the counter, nodding to it when nobody's looking.

"Hey!" I hear the radio Bibi leaves going, even after her stories are finished in the afternoon. "Anybody gon say hey?"

"Hey, Mama." Hawk comes sliding down the hall in his socks on the waxed floor, explodes into me in the living room. I grab him, laughing into his neck. "What you learn in school today?"

"Everything."

"You already know everything? Then you don't need to go back."

"Mama, you silly." He pushes away, runs back down the hall to our room.

Uncle Ray's in the kitchen. "Chicken is baking. What you got in the bag?"

At least once a week, he bakes chicken with lemon juice, garlic, and butter. He only has a few recipes, but he does well with them.

"Beans and potato salad, plenty of both."

Uncle Ray stares out the window at the rain coming down. "If I do that PTA thing, Loraylee, maybe I can make the school better, get us a bus. Something."

CHAPTER 11

Eben was fixing lunch when the phone rang.

"I'm calling from Mayor Jones' office," a woman said, "to extend an invitation—"

"Yes?"

"—for you to attend the meeting of the Redevelopment Commission." Her voice was deep, a smoker's voice. "The meeting is scheduled for seven p.m. next Tuesday. That's April 24, 1962."

Does she think I don't know what year it is? "Yes, I believe I'm free then."

"It's in the second floor conference room of the City Hall on East Trade."

"I know the building."

She cleared her throat. "The mayor wants you to consider joining the commission. It's a real honor, you know. Bye-bye." A click and a dial tone.

Tuesday evening Eben stood in the doorway to his closet, wishing he could ask Nettie's advice. She always knew how to dress for these occasions, which of his two business suits looked best with this shirt or that tie. After considering the few possibilities, he chose his black suit and clerical collar. He'd been invited for two reasons: first as a Negro, and secondly as a preacher. A proper representative of Brooklyn, a man who had to have at least some education. As he left the manse, he took a last glance in the oval mirror of the hat rack, assuring himself that he looked every inch a minister, and that he was getting old. *Ah, well,* he thought.

He parked on Trade Street in front of City Hall in the eerie after-dark quiet, no traffic, no pedestrians. He climbed the stone steps to the lobby, feeling lost under the towering ceiling as he waited for the pain in his knee to ease before taking the elevator. In the wide hall of the second floor, he heard a rumble of voices muted by closed doors.

He entered the meeting room and talk subsided. *I'm the only one here who could stop them in their tracks.* At the first encounter he extended his hand. "Reverend Ebenezer Polk. Is this the meeting of the Brooklyn redevelopment project?"

"This is it." The man mumbled a name he didn't quite catch, dropped his hand immediately, looked around. "Reverend, you say?"

"Yes. St. Timothy's Second Presbyterian."

The man walked away, left Eben standing alone as the room filled again with talk.

Windows on the west wall looked out at downtown. The Liberty Life building was lit up. Eli Patterson, a member of St. Tim's who worked as a janitor there, had come to see Eben when his job title changed to sanitation supervisor, with no raise in pay. "They seem to think," Eli had said, "that a fancy title puts food on the table." All Eben could offer was sympathy.

He saw Mayor Hiram Jones among a group of men by the head table, talking animatedly, patting one man on the shoulder. He knew enough about Jones to have a grudging respect for the man, the never-met-a-stranger sort, but with an impressive sincerity. In his mid-fifties, the mayor maintained the athletic build that had made him first-string basketball at Davidson, where he'd displayed amazing agility and speed to compensate for his height disadvantage at six feet even. Jones had pulled his own type of sit-in, after the one in Greensboro. When a similar protest happened in Charlotte, the mayor quietly organized an "eat-in," pairing white and black leaders to dine together in prominent restaurants. Though he was sure that the mayor's motive was to prevent drawing national attention to an imbroglio in Charlotte, at least the man had taken a stand. He liked thinking about the delightful fiasco Jones created by making a lunch reservation for two at the City Club, then arriving with a black man as his guest. Where was that man now? Had he been invited to this meeting?

The mayor saw him, called out across the room, "Welcome, Reverend Polk," and turned back to the man beside him.

Ashtrays littered long rectangular tables set in a square such that all attendees could be seen from any seat in the room. A slide projector on the table at the bottom of the square faced a screen on the opposite wall. Cigarette smoke wafted toward the ceiling. He looked around to see where he might sit to best advantage, then noticed the triangular nameplates, printed front and back to be read from anywhere in the room. A seat near the projector identified him as PASTOR EBENEZER POLK. Across the room a short white man in clerical collar stood by a seat labeled THE REVEREND TERRENCE TIMMONS. The minister crossed the room. "Reverend Polk? Terry Timmons. Glad you're here." He shook Eben's hand vigorously.

"Good to see you, Reverend. I believe we met at the Ministerial Association last year, over at Covenant."

"Oh, yes, knew I'd seen you before." Timmons touched the lapel of his black suit with pudgy fingers. "Forgive my poor memory, but where are you?"

"St. Timothy's Second Presbyterian, McDowell Street."

Understanding lit the man's face. "So that's why you're here. Brooklyn."

Eben decided to test the waters. "Yes, and as a token."

This brought a twinkle to Reverend Timmons' eyes. "Of course you are." He touched his thinning gray hair.

He began to feel more at ease. "You're Providence Methodist, right?"

"I am. Was associate at Myers Park Methodist for several years, then Providence called me." Both men chuckled at the unintended pun. Timmons took out a pack of Tareytons, offering one to Eben.

"No, thanks, I quit when I got a bad cough I couldn't shake." True, if not the entire truth.

Timmons lit the cigarette. "Someday I'll quit, but not today. Are we going to shake them up, Ebenezer?"

"I believe I've already done that by walking in the door."

Timmons' laugh was interrupted by a loud tapping.

A woman stood in front of the head table, holding a gavel. "Gentlemen? We need to get started." Eben recognized the scratchy voice of the woman who'd called him. A nameplate on a stenographer's stand identified her: RHONDA OLSEN, SECRETARY TO THE MAYOR.

She glanced his way, stared from black cat's-eye glasses, looking not at him but through him as she opened the meeting. This was clearly an important moment for her. "All those convened before the Honorable Hiram B. Jones, Mayor, and the City of Charlotte Redevelopment Commission, gather to speak now before this august body."

Mayor Jones motioned for her to proceed. She introduced the Reverend Timmons, who bowed his head and gave a pro forma invocation, not so much a prayer as an acknowledgment of God's blessing for any action taken by the august body.

Once the minutes of the previous meeting were approved, Mayor Jones introduced the first speaker. "Mr. Blaire Marshall, real estate attorney, will address the commission on an ongoing matter: the proposed disposition of properties in the Second Ward area of Brooklyn, also known as Blue Heaven." At these last words someone laughed, stopped abruptly. The mayor and several other men who'd been seated at the head table moved their chairs to the side, with a great clatter. Once they were seated again, Blaire Marshall walked to the slide projector. Tall and tanned, he spoke in a confident courtroom voice. "Good evening, gentlemen and Mrs. Olsen."

So it is Mrs. Eben wanted to remember that if he spoke to the woman again.

Marshall touched a button on the projector, and a slide lit up the screen on the wall over the head table:

REDEVELOPMENT SECTION NO. 1

Project no. N.C. R-14. BROOKLYN URBAN RENEWAL AREA.

This 36-Acre Redevelopment Project is the First of Five Projects
Scheduled to clear the 238-Acre Brooklyn Area.

Renewal of this Area is funded with Financial Aid from

URBAN RENEWAL ADMINISTRATION,
UNITED STATES HOUSING & HOME FINANCE AGENCY,
and THE REDEVELOPMENT COMMISSION OF
THE CITY OF CHARLOTTE.

Marshall said, "This next slide—"

The door opened and a man came in. A stocky Negro. He raised his arm, addressed the crowd. "Sorry, gentlemen, we experienced an undue delay."

Mrs. Olsen spoke louder than was necessary. "Your name?"

The man lowered his glasses. "Gideon Rhyne, ma'am. If you're the mayor's secretary, we spoke yesterday."

Mrs. Olsen sounded confused. "I, yes, Mister—I mean, a man by that name called our office." She turned in her seat and spoke to the mayor. "I gave you a note about him."

"Mr. Rhyne, your attendance caught us unprepared." Mayor Jones stood. "We don't have a nameplate for you, but there are plenty of extra chairs."

"Thank you, Mayor. Apologies for the interruption."

The mayor spoke again. "What brings you to the commission, Mr. Rhyne?"

"As explained to Mrs. Olsen yesterday, we have only just arrived in Charlotte, which we hope to make our home. We'll be living in Brooklyn for the present, and after hearing what is planned for that neighborhood, we found ourselves quite interested. This is an open meeting, is that right? Open to the public, that is."

"That's correct." The mayor turned back to Marshall. "Blaire, please continue."

Marshall waited until Rhyne sat. "I've been given the pleasurable task of showing you the model drawings prepared by the architect, Lloyd Lewiston, for the areas contiguous to downtown Charlotte, how they will look after the proposed redevelopment." A click. A smoke-filled beam projected a section of Trade Street between Caldwell and McDowell, featuring the proposed new County Courthouse, followed by murmurs of approval. "The roughly rectangular hash-marked section surrounding the courthouse represents the two hundred and thirty-eight acres of blight known as Brooklyn."

Eben felt a wave of nausea. *It is coming. All those families, schools, churches. The graves.* McDowell Street between Fourth and Stonewall, which included St. Timothy's and the graveyard, sat in the middle of the hash-marked area.

He felt someone's gaze, turned to see Gideon Rhyne grinning at him, nodding.

Marshall touched the projector. *Click,* the same slide. *Click, click,* again the awful pronouncement of the purpose of the committee. "Someday we'll have something more reliable than slide projectors," Marshall said. Another click, a new slide. "There we go. This and the following are photos of the slum areas." The first slide depicted the houses on Cedar Alley, which Eben knew to be the worst of Brooklyn. The next photo showed a listing outhouse that you could almost smell. The only such structure he knew of was down on Morrow Street, near the creek, not in use for many years. Slide after slide showed dirt streets, decaying dwellings, garbage piled in front yards, sagging foundations. *What about the lovely old homes on McDowell, the well-kept cottages on First and Myers, the successful business district on Second Street?*

Marshall's presentation went on and on, slanted and deadly. "Instead of blight, there will be upscale restaurants, nightlife."

The commissioners nodded, took notes.

"But it won't come to Charlotte if we don't plan now."

Another slide: "Independence Square at Trade and Tryon, the heart of Charlotte. As you see, there's a drugstore on one corner, a dry cleaner on another, a dime store on the third, and a haberdashery on the fourth. These photos were taken in the heavy pedestrian traffic of late afternoon."

When people, the majority of them Negroes, were getting off work in the inner city, Eben added to himself.

The next slides showed colored people leaving the drugstore. Catching buses. Going into and out of Kress Five and Ten, which for decades had one of the few bathrooms for blacks in the whole of downtown.

The display ended with a photo of a colored man slumped on the sidewalk outside the dry cleaners. Passed out, apparently.

Marshall was winding up for his finish. "In a few years the Square will have a skyscraper, an art plaza, a major hotel." He beamed at his audience. "Questions?"

Eben raised his hand.

"Yes, Reverend?"

He stood, wanting to be sure all the commissioners could see him. "These businesses," he projected his booming pulpit voice to every person in the room. "These businesses that currently fill the four corners of Independence Square, will they be forced to close, and if so, will they be given options for relocation?" He glanced at Reverend Timmons. Their eyes met and Timmons gave a slight nod.

"Those shops are used mainly by residents of the wards."

"Colored people?" This was both a question and a statement.

"Yes, for the most part."

"And again, will the merchants have any choice about closing?" Eben looked over his glasses at Marshall, who returned his steady gaze.

"Sacrifices must be made for progress." Around the room heads bobbed.

"Yes, sacrifices will be made." Eben paused, looked at the mayor as if directing the next question to him. "How many members of the board have help who live in Brooklyn? Maids, yardmen, carpenters, plumbers? Do you frequent the shoemakers, seamstresses, and bakers in . . ." He paused. ". . . Blue Heaven? And how will your employees get to work if they move to Biddleville or Belmont or Fairview Homes?"

Rhyne grinned, mouthed, "Amen."

"I raise these questions to bring up a topic that perhaps has not been addressed. Most of these service people avail themselves of public transportation—buses. How will they commute when they're forced to move?"

He steeled himself for reactions or—worse yet—no reaction at all. The questions had an impact, reflected by downcast eyes.

"Before I conclude, I want to tell you of a conversation I had last week with a neighbor. The man was born in his home in Brooklyn, had planned to live out his life there. He owns the property outright, but struggles to keep it"—Eben paused—"fit. Many repairs are needed."

Around the room men mumbled, "Yes," or "Uh-huh." Someone said, "Exactly."

Eben continued. "So I asked him how he felt about redevelopment, the prospect of leaving his lifelong home in Brooklyn to move into a new house, with a new mortgage. He replied, 'Now, Preacher, that puts me in a trickbag.' " Eben saw puzzled looks.

"A trickbag, gentlemen, is a question with no right answer." Eben spoke to Blaire. "One last thing. Will the suggested sites for relocation of downtown merchants offer the same amount of foot traffic?"

"We'll be making every effort in that regard." Marshall pointed to another raised hand. "Yes?"

Eben ignored him. "What about the people?"

"A renovated downtown, geared toward the growth in the banking industry, will attract thousands of professionals,

I guarantee it. Charlotte is uniquely situated between Washington and Atlanta to appeal to bankers, stockbrokers, lawyers, politicians."

"I meant those living in the wards."

"Of course, an important part of the plan is affordable housing, multistory complexes—"

"High-rise tenements?"

"I'm speaking of apartments with air conditioning and indoor plumbing."

"But not in Brooklyn—or Second Ward, as I'm sure you'll call it—where the land is too valuable."

"Rest assured, we're going to take care of the people who leave the Brooklyn community."

"That's a nice word, 'community.'" Eben sat down.

At the end of the meeting, Rhyne followed him out. In the elevator he clapped Eben on the shoulder. "You made some points in there, Pastor Polk. We got their attention."

"I hope so." Eben pushed the down button. "Where are you staying in Brooklyn?"

"With my sister, Roberta Stokes."

"The seamstress?"

"Yes, she speaks highly of you."

"You said you were going to settle in Brooklyn. A peculiar choice, given its certain fate."

"Certain? We're not convinced of that." The elevator door opened. Rhyne waved good night and took off before Eben could respond.

There was something too slick about Gideon Rhyne, from his highly polished brogans to his pomaded hair, a whiff of bay rum, but he was brother to a decent woman.

Eben felt he'd scooped up water in a great thirst, only to have it slip through his fingers. He longed for the solace he always found in his study. As he approached St. Tim's, he passed a group of men at the corner of First and McDowell, their faces lit by a fire in the barrel they surrounded, mouths open in song. He recognized Eli Patterson. Just this evening he'd been thinking of him. He pulled over to listen: *"When the night has come, and the land is dark, and the moon is the only light we will see, I won't be afraid just as long as you stand, stand by me."*

CHAPTER 12

In June of 1962 Persy felt drawn to go back to Windy Hill, to get away from Blaire's interminable involvement with the planning commission. She often spent evenings alone anyway, when he went back to the office, and she was attracted by the thought of solitude at the beach rather than in Charlotte.

Her second morning at the shanty she woke before daybreak, went to the porch to catch sunrise over the ocean. The water was flat, colorless in the predawn, lazy waves lapping the shore. The sun, when it broke the horizon, was tepid, disappointing. After breakfast she cleaned the small kitchen, thinking it strange that Mother had kept the shanty sparsely furnished, unlike the overcrowded mess she lived in at home.

Persy had seen Mother go on binges of straightening up, getting rid of stuff, swearing, "I'm clearing out my clutter!" It seemed not to bother her that some of the things she tossed weren't hers. Like the baby shoes Persy had planned to have bronzed. "You wouldn't have wanted to preserve them," Mother had said. "The leather was cracked." Or the flowered shawl Persy wore to her senior class dance, hoping someday she'd have a daughter who'd want it. "But it was so dated," Mother said.

That might have been when Mother got rid of the letters Persy's father had written her from California when she was a toddler. Every letter began, "My Sweet Persy," carefully written in block capitals, the only cursive being "Daddy" scrawled at the bottom. He wrote about living near the Pacific Ocean, how it sounded and smelled. When she was in the second grade she found the letters in a shoebox in Mother's closet. She sat on the floor in Mother's bedroom, stared out the window, holding a letter, trying to imagine the waves crashing. Then her hands were empty. Mother towered above her. "What are you doing?" she yelled.

"Reading Daddy's letters."

Mother grabbed up the box. "They're private!"

"He wrote them to me."

"He left you." Mother looked tall and mean. "He's never coming back."

After that, when Mother was out Persy searched through her things, hoping to find the letters. As she got older, she created her absent father from fragments of dreams. If she'd ever talked about it, she would have said he haunted her sleep. She had dreams about a man, though it wasn't always the same man. Just the same sort of fatherly fellow: in the auditorium when she won the spelling bee in fourth grade, and shouting hooray at Municipal Pool when she got a blue ribbon for the hundred-meter backstroke. Persy felt this father's presence at her elbow during her small wedding. She never found a single photo of him, but over the years she formed an image of Robert Rochester Alexander: slender, kind, and funny, she decided. Like James Stewart in *It's a Wonderful Life*.

Mother hired a maid when Persy was ten, the third or fourth since Persy's father left, and finally one who stayed, who brought order to the household, and who seemed to understand Persy's mother, Gracie Nell Alexander.

The big house in Eastover got calmer and more organized under Augusta Baxter's firm hand; Persy soon learned that she could count on that order. Augusta spoke with a directness that was at first abnormal to Persy, who was used to Mother's way of stating what she wished was so rather than what was. When Augusta found Persy going through her mother's things, searching for the shoebox, she said, "Your mama got rid of those letters. Don't ask me how I know, I just do. They're gone and you got to stop looking for them. You got to remember that your mama is the one who stayed, not your daddy."

Sometimes Augusta would tell Persy something about her father, though Persy never knew how Augusta got her knowledge. Augusta didn't respond to direct questions, but at odd moments she'd share a tidbit such as, "You're tall like your daddy, got his eyes, too." If Persy followed up with, "How do you know?" Augusta would change the subject. One day, Augusta said, "Your daddy was wrong to leave the way he did, but he had his reasons." Persy wanted to scream when Augusta would say nothing more, but was grateful for any scrap, waited for the next one.

Augusta knew her place, understood exactly how far she could push Gracie Nell, but she had a way of getting what was due. This wasn't something Persy understood until the matter of social security came up, long after she'd left home. During her second pregnancy, when Persy was told to rest as much as possible, Augusta came over to Persy and Blaire's three days a week to cook and clean, run errands. She must have been in her fifties by then, had been working for Mother for thirty years, but her smooth skin made her age hard to judge. Persy had never considered the issue of social security for a maid, but Augusta must have given it a great deal of thought.

One afternoon when she was clearing the lunch dishes, Augusta said, "You go on and take a nap now, and while you down I'm going to make a phone call to the government. Your mama has to start paying my social security." Augusta turned to the sink, began running water hard, humming as she washed the dishes.

"Good luck getting her to do that." Persy went to her bedroom, imagining Augusta's confrontation with Mother. But if anyone could maneuver Gracie Nell Alexander, it was Augusta.

That evening Persy found a paper by the phone with notes in Augusta's careful hand: "Work at least 2 days a week—50% paid by employer. Retroactive. No exceptions." She smiled to think how this matter would be greeted by Mother, and wished she could be around when Augusta approached Gracie Nell about paying the government two percent of her salary into social security. Augusta deserved it, and Mother deserved whatever grief the payment caused. *Retroactive, my goodness,* Persy thought.

Once when Persy had taken Augusta home in weather too harsh for the usual bus ride, she'd seen an astonishing garden in the tiny front yard, a mass of flowers framed by a neat redwood fence. She knew so little about the woman, her personal life, or what social security would mean to her. It had never occurred to Persy to wonder what would happen to Augusta when she got too old to work. After all, she had a nice little house in Third Ward. A husband and two children—Persy remembered the pregnancies, the inconvenience to Mother of having Augusta out for a month or so each time. During the last ten years that Augusta worked for Mother, Persy had spoken with her a few times, but she never saw Augusta again after she retired in 1961, upon her sixty-fifth birthday. The only thing she ever heard Mother say about the woman was,

"There'll never be another Augusta. She took such good care of things and stayed out of my business."

How could it be, Persy often wondered, *that someone was in our lives for forty years, then gone. Only five miles away, but gone.*

After lunch Persy took a long walk to the pier and back, pushing herself, going in and out of the water to cool off. At the groin she sat to catch her breath, heard laughter coming from Atlantic Beach to the north. A man and woman ran along the edge of the water, tossing a ball back and forth. The man was very dark, his long arms and legs flailing awkwardly. Not an athlete. He threw the ball to the woman. She caught it, threw it back, her movements fluid and natural. She was fair-skinned, her hair a frizzy bouncing mass. The woman must have felt Persy watching. She turned, looked at Persy, raised her arm as if to wave, but didn't.

Late in the afternoon Persy swam out beyond the breakers where she floated on gentle swells. The ocean was running south, and she frog-kicked to stay near the shoreline at the shanty, the most contented she could remember being in a long while. She heard someone call out. The man had drifted well south of the groin. The woman shouted from beyond the segregating rope, "Louie! Louie, come back!"

The man noticed where he was, and began a strong crawl toward the groin. He turned his head to breathe, saw Persy, continued stroke after stroke.

She watched the man swim away feeling a sadness she couldn't explain.

After supper she sat out front, nursing a Scotch, enjoying the wind off the ocean and contemplating something that had occurred to her in the heat of the day. She set down her glass, rose with a purpose, and went to the storeroom for the toolbox. Thirty minutes later she shoved the first-floor A/C unit from where it had been moored in a front window. The unit landed with a satisfying crunch on the sandy lawn, leaving an unobstructed view of the moonlit ocean. The wooden frame around the window had apparently been painted several times since the unit was installed, and no matter how she tried, she could not get the window to close. She was sweating heavily, had scrapes, scratches, and broken nails, but the result was worth the pain and trouble. A beach towel would do to cover the gaping hole until she could hire someone to come to the shanty, remove the two upstairs units, and get all the windows operational again.

Restored by a long hot shower, she took the phone to the porch, stretching the curled cord, which was just long enough, and called Blaire. He was at first incredulous at what she'd done. She listened through his mild rant, then said, "I hate those units. They're ugly, inefficient."

He surprised her by laughing. "Fulfilling neither form nor function."

"Right!"

"And it is your house, after all. I guess if I were there more than once a year I'd have a right to object."

"But you aren't." She smiled to herself.

After they said good night she sat a while longer, finishing her Scotch. Mother had been right in her advice, ". . . put it in your name only." What an amazing gift it had turned out to be. Most of all, regardless of her shortcomings, Mother had been there all Persy's life.

A falling star streaked the eastern sky. Instead of a wish, she vowed: "I release you, Robert Rochester Alexander, my long-departed father, wherever you are."

CHAPTER 13

We having supper when Jonny No Age comes in the back door carrying a bouquet for Bibi like he does from time to time. Flowers he can't sell but are still pretty.

"Hey, Jonny," say Bibi. "You want a glass of tea?"

"No, ma'am. Can't stay." He puts the flowers in the sink, runs water over them. "Stick 'em in a mason jar after supper." And that quick he's gone.

"A nice boy," say Uncle Ray.

"Uh-huh, shame, though. A shame." Bibi shakes her head.

Jonny—he tells folks his name is Jonny, no *h*, but they hear it wrong—is six and a half feet tall, thin as a rail, and pitch-black. If Bibi sees him walking down the street she say, "There go that licorice whip." She's fond of Jonny, even if she doesn't approve of what he is. Several men use to go in and out the back door to his shop, now only the one, a bookkeeper from Raleigh who moved in with him two-three years ago.

Steadman's Flowers is a bright spot in a gray block of run-down stores, so no one makes a move to push Jonny No Age out of Brooklyn. But he's got two strikes against him, being Africa black and a queer.

We still at the table when Mayrese Hemphill calls from the front door, "Loraylee?"

Bibi looks up, her eyes round. "We Grand Central Station this evening."

I push my chair back. "It's Mayrese, Bibi, for me."

"Go on." She stabs up a forkful of green beans, cocks her ear to the radio we listen to while we eat. WGIV Weekend Jive. She starts singing, waving her fork, beans dropping, *"Mama said there'll be days like this."* Hawk tosses a bean back on her plate, laughing.

Mayrese is standing inside the front door in a cloud of perfume. "Hey!" She's in her glad clothes, glad it's Saturday night, glad to have a friend girl. "Y'wanna go hopping?" Got her hair piled up in a wave, glossy with Lustrasilk, a purple flower in it, her red satin blouse tucked into her swirly purple skirt.

She plops into Uncle Ray's chair, crossing her legs, swinging one foot. There's scuff marks on her red ankle straps.

Uncle Ray comes into the living room, stops when he see Mayrese in his chair. "You got on some powerful cologne, Mayrese."

She pays no mind to his frown. "Thank you, Ray."

He shakes his head, goes out to the porch with his pipe.

"Mama!" Hawk calls from the kitchen. "Can I eat your pork chop?"

"No!" I holler. I ask Mayrese, "You want to wait for me?"

"I'll go on over to Tocky's." Mayrese gets up, waves her polished nails as she opens the screen. "See you there in a bit."

Half an hour later I go down our front walk into the warm night, walk up Brown Street. At McDowell I cross Independence, not wanting to use the tunnel on a Saturday evening—no telling how many bums gon be in it.

I stop to speak to Mr. Stone, who is taking in crates of fruits from the sidewalk. He calls to his wife, "Hildie, come say hey to Loraylee."

Mrs. Stone steps through the door. "You looking real fine, Loraylee. Stepping out on a Saturday night, are you?"

"Yes, ma'am, to Tocky's."

She picks up a box of apples, goes back inside.

In the light from the storefront, my shadow moves ahead of me, disappearing when the store goes dark. I hear Mr. Stone closing the grille over his door.

Uncle Ray thinks nobody needs a lit-up sign saying STONE'S GROCERY because anyone shopping there already knows what it is. But Mr. Stone say with Charlotte growing and McDowell being so busy, he wants folks from outside Second Ward to know about his store. "Men going home from work downtown can stop in for beer or if the missus calls them saying to get eggs."

Tocky's is a block up First Street, and I take my time, speaking to folks I pass, my heels making a pleasant sound on the sidewalk. The air smells faintly of sewer, drifting up from Little Sugar. I don't know how folks in Blue Heaven can stand living right on a branch of the creek where the stink can get bad, especially in the heat of summer. Passing the alley between the drugstore and barber shop, I hear the clack of dice, the clink of coins. Craps. Milk money going down. A boy runs past me, skids into the alley, shouting, "Why y'all start without me?"

A light goes out across the street. "Hey, Loraylee!"

"Hey, Jonny, you been open on Saturday evening?"

"No, making a wreath for a funeral tomorrow." Jonny looks up and down First, then crosses over.

"Who died?"

"Dicker Phillips. You remember him and Morella?"

"Sure do. The Parkinson's got him, huh?"

"From what Morella told me, maybe a stroke. He passed out Thursday evening. Dead by the time they got to Samaritan."

Jonny is so tall and skinny it's like talking to a lamppost.

"Things will be easier on her now," he say, "after him being sick such a long time."

"Is Morella okay at the Courts?"

"She says it's noisy, got roaches, people fighting. She's hoping her daughter will take her in." He looks around again.

"You expecting somebody?"

His eyes dart. "Naw."

Something's coming down for sure.

"That's a pretty dress. Where you headed?"

"Gon meet Mayrese Hemphill at Tocky's."

A couple heads toward town on the other side of the street, arm in arm, laughing.

Jonny touches his chin, nervous, jerky. A car drives by, moving slow, tooting the horn to people it passes. He jumps back.

"I gotta go." He walks away fast, his shoes clapping the pavement.

I've been knowing Tocky McGuire since first grade. He has a juke joint in what was once a dry cleaning store. The store closed after a new one opened over on Caldwell. The front counter that had clothes on it, dirty one week, clean the next, is now a bar with stools. Where the swinging half door was is a space wide enough to pass into a big room that use to be filled with hanging racks of Sunday best in paper bags—dresses, suits, pants. Tables fill that space now, some with two chairs, some with four or six, around a dance floor. The jukebox on the back wall shoots rays of color—orange, green, blue—the only light except the glow from brass wall lamps with dark shades. So dim I can't even see what's gritty under my shoes. The place smells of cigarettes and popcorn.

Mayrese is sitting with two men at a table in the corner. What am I doing here? If she wants to set me up with some good-time Charlie, that doesn't interest me, but not to be rude, I go over.

A fat man in a red suit stands, pulls out a chair for me. He's short and wide, like a fire hydrant. "Hello there, sweet thing. Can I get you a beer?"

The other man has on a shirt the same purple as Mayrese's skirt, and I wonder did they plan that. He stares at me. "Hey, girl. You got pretty brown eyes, now don't you?"

I sit, look over at Mayrese, shake my head a bit trying to let her know I don't want to be hooked up with anybody. She grins. Her eyes shine like maybe she's already had a couple of drinks.

Fireplug sets a mug of beer in front of me. "I'm Lester. You live round here?" He settles back in his chair.

"Yes." I take a sip of beer. Icy, bitter, good.

He takes a gulp, spilling drops on his tie. "You work at the S&W, don't you?"

"I do."

"Seen you coming and going." He laughs, like that's funny.

I drink my beer, thinking I'll leave when I finish it.

Mayrese say, "Loraylee been at the S&W since God was a baby." There's a smear of mascara on her left cheek.

"Loraylee," say Lester. "A name like music."

On the jukebox "Shop Around" starts playing, and Purple Shirt sings along with it, dipping his chin and going bass on the line, "You better shop around," winking at me. Somebody kicks my foot under the table. Mayrese frowns at me, smiles at Purple Shirt. I get the message. I turn my head to stare out at the couples fast dancing, coming in close together, then stepping back. Some dance I don't know yet.

"You shy all of a sudden?" ask Purple Shirt. "You friendly enough to get you a kid."

Mayrese say, "Hawk. He what now, six?"

"Eight," I say.

"Yeah," say Purple Shirt. "He mixed. His daddy white?" When I don't answer, he say, "Earlier this evening, didn't I see you talking with that tall piece of work? Nigger what sells flowers."

I can smell how bad this man is.

"Jonny No Age. The fag."

I say to Mayrese, "Believe I'll go on home, now." Purple Shirt stands up fast, his chair hitting the floor with a crack like a pistol. Talk stops. Folks turn, look.

He starts laughing loud, a scary sound. "Didn't mean to startle you, girl. Just axing if you friends with Jonny No Age."

"Like I said, Mayrese, I'm gon—"

Tocky walks up. "Loraylee, you okay?"

"Can you get somebody to walk home with me?"

Lester say, "I can, my pleasure." He starts to stand, but Tocky pushes him back in his chair and takes my elbow.

At the register Tocky say, "How about I call Ray to come get you?"

"Yes, please do that."

He dials, pushes the hang-up button, dials again. "Busy. You got a party line?"

"Doesn't everybody?" Across the big room Mayrese is laughing at something Purple Shirt say.

Tocky speaks into the phone. "Operator? I need you to interrupt a party line. Emergency? It will be if you don't let me call through." In a minute or two he say, "Dooby? This Tocky. Get off the phone so I can call Ray. Loraylee wants him."

I say, "Tell him I'm okay."

"Tell Ray she's okay but she needs him to come get her." He hangs up the phone. "Dooby say he'll come down here hisself, if Ray's not home."

"He's home." I cannot imagine Dooby, who seldom leaves his house, coming to get me.

"Stay with me till he gets here."

I sit on a stool by the bar, thinking how much fun a Saturday night would be if I could go out with Mr. Griffin. The music, the dancing, the beer.

Twenty minutes later Uncle Ray comes through the front door. "You okay, Loraylee?"

Tocky say, "Hey, Ray, how you doing?"

"Oh, hey, Tocky. I'm okay, you?"

"Doing great. How about a beer? On the house."

"No, that's okay. Livvie's alone with the boy. Don't like leaving them too long. What's going on?"

"Some tough guy trying to hit on your pretty girl here."

"Glad you called me." Uncle Ray touches my shoulder. "Let's go."

We walk along, not talking, past Jonny's flower shop, past Stone's. At our front walk, Uncle Ray say, "I don't like that Mayrese."

"I'm done with her."

Sunday morning I wake to Uncle Ray shaking my shoulder.

I sit up. "Time for me to make breakfast?"

He shakes his head, frowning. "Jonny No Age is in the hospital. Couple of policemen want to talk to you."

I rub my eyes. "What'd you say about Jonny?"

"He got beat up. Hildie Stone told them she saw y'all together last night."

"We passed on the street." I look across the room. "Where's Hawk?"

"The kitchen. Bibi's fixing him some oatmeal. You'd best get dressed."

I wash my face, brush my teeth, put on my church clothes

as fast as I can, smooth my hair, and go to the living room. Uncle Ray is in his chair, looking at the floor. Two white men stand by the front door, one tall and skinny, the other shorter, heavy. Both of them in suits, ties, not looking like police. The tall one say, "Loraylee Hawkins?"

I nod.

"Sgt. Mahaley, Charlotte Police Department." He pulls something from his pocket and holds it out to me. A badge. Then he sits on the sofa. He's young, about my age.

The other one say, "Detective Blackmon." He stays by the front door, looking out the screen. Stocky, gray hair, in charge. "You know why we're here?" he ask.

"Jonny Steadman. My uncle say he's in the hospital."

"We'll get to that."

Bibi comes in carrying a tray with cups on it, sets it on the end table, and backs out. I say to her, "Please keep Hawk in the kitchen." I close the kitchen door, sit in the straight chair near Uncle Ray.

"Who's Hawk?" ask the one on the sofa. Was his name Mayley?

"My son. He's eight."

The detective gets a cup, takes a sip. He doesn't like being here—it shows on his face—doesn't like the coffee. Did Bibi offer them milk and sugar?

Mayley say, "Jonathan Steadman, owner of Steadman's Flowers. You know him well?"

"Yes, sir, he—"

"You see him last evening around eight o'clock?"

"Yes, coming out of his shop."

He pulls a notepad from his pants pocket, writes something on it.

The detective say, "Unusual he'd be open on Saturday evening, isn't it?"

"I asked him why was—"

"What did he tell you?" Mayley's voice is sharp, like I've done something wrong.

"Dicker Phillips passed from a stroke and Jonny—"

"Dicker died?" Uncle Ray say.

"Sorry, Uncle Ray, should have told you about Mr. Phillips." I look back at the policeman. "Jonny was making a wreath for the service."

The detective say, "This was around eight?"

"Uh-huh. I left home a little before. It's not but a few blocks from here to Jonny No—to the flower store."

"Jonny No?" ask Mayley.

"We call him Jonny No Age. His first name, Jonny, got no *h* in it, and that's how come—"

"So Jonny No Age is a nickname."

"Yes, sir. Folks joke he doesn't know how old he is."

Mayley scribbles something on his pad and the other one say, "What'd y'all talk about?"

"Not much, like hey, how you doing, then Mr. Phillips."

"He mention anything about a friend he, uh, rooms with?"

I shake my head. "He told me Dicker Phillips passed, and I say how that must be bad for Morella—Dicker's wife. And Jonny say he reckon things would be easier for Morella if she could get outta the Courts."

"Why was Morella in court?" the detective ask.

"Not court like the law. She's at the Courts, what we call Piedmont Courts, over there on Caldwell. Apartments and such."

Mayley say, "You mind if I smoke, Loraylee?"

"No, sir." Bibi doesn't like anybody smoking in the house, but I get our ashtray from the cupboard, sit back down.

Mayley ask, "What did Jonny say after he told you about"—he looks down at his notebook—"Dicker Phillips?"

I stare at our faded rug. "He looked around like he was waiting for somebody."

"Loraylee, you know what a homosexual is?"

"I do."

"Is Jonny a homosexual?"

"Rumor is."

Mayley coughs a bit. Fiddles with a lump of thread on his jacket where a button is gone. "Is it pretty well known that he's queer?"

I straighten my skirt over my knees. "People talk. They can be wrong, and—"

The detective interrupts me. "Jonny say anything else?"

"Say he gotta go, headed up First Street toward where he lives."

The detective say, "Excuse us, be right back." They go out, voices rumbling on the porch for a minute or two. Mayley steps back in. "That's all for now."

"Wait," I say, louder than I mean to.

He looks irritated. "What is it?"

"You never said how Jonny is doing, what happened to him."

Mayley say, "Sorry, I meant to. He got beat up pretty bad."

"Is he at Samaritan?" Uncle Ray ask.

"Yes."

He pushes himself up out of his chair. "Why y'all come here?"

The two men look at each other like they're considering what to tell us. The detective say, "We've made an arrest in another matter—"

"It might be connected to Jonny's beating," Mayley say.

"And I guess you don't want to tell us about that other matter?" Uncle Ray say.

"Not now." The detective takes Mayley's arm, pulls him toward the steps. They go to the car parked out front.

"Huh," say Uncle Ray. "This is a strange thing. Mighty strange. Sure hope Jonny gon be all right."

"I'm on second today, could go see him if we leave church right after Pastor Polk's sermon."

"Let's do that." He opens the kitchen door.

Hawk comes in. "What did the police want, Mama?"

"To talk to Uncle Ray. You save me any oatmeal?"

Bibi sniffs. "What you thinking, Raylee, letting them smoke in my living room?" She picks up the ashtray. "Come get breakfast, then we going to church."

CHAPTER 14

Eben was in the choir loft, pushing a dust mop, when the front door of the sanctuary opened, splitting the aisle with a beam of sunshine.

"Ebenezer Polk?"

He dropped the mop, shaded his eyes. A woman walked toward him, her long shadow shortening as she approached. She was vaguely familiar, but he couldn't recall her name.

"Georgeanne Wilkins. Edward's sister. You were in sixth grade when I started at Myers Street School."

"Georgie Bee?"

She smiled. "Georgie Bee. Yes, that was me back when you were Neezer. I'm Georgeanne now."

A few years younger than he. "What brings you to St. Tim's this morning? Would you join me in a cup of coffee?" *The cleaning will wait.*

"I'd love that." She looked at the pews, the mop. "I've interrupted you."

"Thank goodness."

"You're pastor here?"

"Pastor, janitor, yardman, depends on when you catch me." He motioned for her to follow him toward the rear of the church. "Let's go up to my study." He climbed the stairs in his usual halting manner.

Halfway up she asked, "How old is your church?"

"Began in 1842, in what I gather was a room in someone's home." They reached the top of the stairs and he stopped at the newel post to ease his right knee. She waited by his side. He caught a whiff of something tangy, like lemon, and the dusky smell of cigarettes. "My study is down the hall." He pointed to the door and followed her.

She couldn't be more than five feet tall, though that was difficult to judge given her high heels. A seersucker suit, pill-box hat, jewelry. She'd come a long way from Myers Street School. As had he.

He switched on the overhead and she sat in the easy chair. "I was sorry to hear about Nonette's passing. It's what, three years ago?"

"December of fifty-eight. Four."

"I met her my freshman year at Spelman. A lovely girl."

Girl. All those years ago. He went to the percolator. "Cream, sugar?"

"Black." She took off her gloves, smoothed them on her knee, and folded them into her pocketbook.

He gave her a cup, added milk to his. "What did you major in?"

"I doubled in history and political science. Then law school at Howard."

"You're an attorney?"

"I am." She settled into the armchair. "I came to see you about the urban renewal."

He sat behind his desk. "Are you for it or against it?"

That smile again. "Eddy says nothing can stop it."

He judged his coffee, found it better than usual and was

glad for that. "Folks don't know what to do. All of a sudden they're ordered to move from where they've spent their whole lives and I can't offer much solace."

She opened her purse, took out a pack of Salems.

He held up his hand. "I'd rather you not, please. I'm an ex-smoker, constantly tempted."

"Oh. Of course." She closed her bag. "Maybe I'll try to quit. Again. What do friends call you now? Ebenezer?"

He chuckled. "Eben, mostly."

"Okay, Eben. Eddy tells me the cemetery is threatened."

"That's right. As of now, the city wants to move the graveyard. It's only a fourth of an acre. Sixty-three graves, but there may be over eighty souls buried there."

"Properly identified graves can't be moved without appraisal by a qualified archeologist."

He swiveled his chair, stared out the window at the sliver of the cemetery he could see behind St. Tim's. "What's proper identification?"

"I can show you statutes."

"Some graves are only a depression. Others have rocks. Family plots may have more than one body." He turned back to her. "Do you remember Reverend Tilley?"

"Younger Tilley put the fear of God into me when I was a child."

"He told me about a register. From what he said I gather it had information about the burial sites, but I haven't been able to find it."

"Something identifying the unmarked graves? That would be verification."

"Yes, but it's most likely lost." He could still hear Reverend Tilley's words, "De register's got everything . . . In de cellar, back of de coal bin."

"Why would it have been hidden?"

"Habit. Before emancipation slaves weren't supposed to

read and write. Literacy was forbidden and punishable. I've speculated that the register might have linked black families to whites, here in Mecklenburg County. Such things wouldn't be well received, as I'm sure you can understand."

A siren sounded, got louder, horn blasting at an intersection near the church.

"Someone's got trouble," she said.

"Sirens always make me think that."

She waited until it faded. "The gravestones are a treasure. It's a shame there aren't more." She shifted in the chair. "I've walked the cemetery."

When had she done that? "During my first year after taking over St. Tim's I came upon a lot of papers, did my best to deal with them." He pointed to a door. "What used to be a nursery is now a library." He stood. "Come, I'll show you."

He took a key ring from the top drawer of his desk and unlocked the door. They entered a cramped room filled floor to ceiling with books. "There," he said, pointing to three boxes on one of the bottom shelves.

Georgeanne knelt gracefully, touched a box made of wooden slats. She was lithe; he envied that. The overhead light showed strands of silver in her hair.

She stood, brushed her skirt where it had touched the floor. "Would you let me go through some of these papers?"

"Be happy for another pair of eyes."

"May I take the box labeled 1880 to 1910?"

"Help yourself."

She bent, pulled the small crate from the shelf, looked at a faded sticker. "Oranges?"

"The original cardboard boxes were falling apart, so I transferred things to sturdier containers. Fruit crates I get from Stone's—do you remember Ben and Hildie?"

"Of course. Stone's Grocery, an institution." She balanced the box on her hip. "You sorted everything?"

"Yes, went through the records, sorted them by dates."

"Thank you for trusting me with this." She carried the crate back to his office, opened her pocketbook, closed it. "Sorry, I was about to light up. I am hooked on nicotine. Never mind. What I'd love to do is go with you to the cemetery. See what we can find out. Could we go now?"

"Yes." He liked the sound of "we."

They went down to the kitchen at the back of the sanctuary. She put the box of papers on a counter and stopped outside the back door, looked up at the trees, walked a few feet away from him. "Downwind of you," she said as she lit a cigarette, clicking her lighter shut and dropping it into her purse. "My apologies." She waved away the smoke, pointed at the manse. "You live there?"

"Yes, with Noah, my nephew. Do you remember my brother, Oscar?"

She shook her head. "I remember you had a brother, but he was out of school by the time I got there."

"Out after tenth grade, truth be known; never was much for books and lessons, has been on the street most of his life. He got married when he was forty-three and I hoped that would settle him, but his wife died having Noah. Oscar's in prison now, out in six months if he behaves himself."

"How long has Noah been with you?"

"Just since April this time. He's thirteen, a good boy, easy to live with. And he's family. Didn't know how much I missed that until he moved in."

At the cemetery gate she stopped, nudged the end of the cigarette until the glowing ember fell to the grass. She stamped it out and flicked the remainder of the butt with a finger. Slivers of tobacco drifted down. She twisted the empty paper of the depleted butt and dropped it into her half-full pack of Salems.

"Field stripping," he said.

"Yes, my husband learned it in the war."

Married. Why no ring?

She preceded him through the gate. He noticed again how slight she was, but she felt solid beside him in her determination to help.

He saw the cemetery as she must have seen it. Run-down, most of the graves ill-kept, weeds choking those near the back where the crumbling brick wall had been replaced by a fence. The graveyard appeared to suffer from a general lack of care, which couldn't be further from the truth. The more recent plots, those with headstones, had flowers, were well maintained.

"I can see that families take care of the sites of their relatives. Of course, the unmarked graves aren't tended to."

He felt defensive. "Once or twice a year the congregation does a general tidying up, but it doesn't take long for weeds to take over."

"Yes," she touched his arm, "I didn't mean to criticize." She walked toward the back, stopped at one depression marked by rocks at head and foot. "Given the number of stones, I'd guess there's more than one body buried here."

"I believe so." He stood beside her, next to the fence. "Are you in practice or do you teach?"

"Both. I teach a course in the School of Law at North Carolina College of Durham, and I'm also with a firm."

"What brought you back home?"

"Eddy wrote me about the urban renewal, asked if I'd look into the legal aspects." She walked to another grave, bent to examine the faint inscription on a tilting marker. "As you may know, our father died last month. I'm helping Eddy with his estate."

"How long will you be here?"

"I've got four weeks' leave." She looked up at him. "I'm startled to have such strong feelings about Brooklyn. It's like this cemetery, half well maintained, half not."

He let out an exasperated sigh. "According to the planning commission, it's over seventy percent blight."

She stood. "Someone knows how to fudge numbers."

CHAPTER 15

Retta Lawrence got to be six foot tall, with hands and feet bigger than most men. Everything about her is so fair she must burn easy. Her hair's the color of oatmeal, more wrinkly than curly and thick as a mop; gets out of the nets the S&W makes us wear.

When the dishwasher breaks down, which isn't often, thank the Lord, and we have to do them by hand, the two of us stand together at the metal sinks, her washing, me rinsing and drying. Her hands get bright pink in the hot water, and I ask, "Why don't you wear gloves? They're specially for washing dishes."

"They keep me from feeling if the dishes are clean." She washes another plate.

"You gon be chapped."

"That's nothing new."

Retta's friendlier to me than any other white person at the S&W besides Mr. Griffin, any other white person in the world, for that matter. We don't generally visit much, but one afternoon she follows me outside on a break, settling on a wood crate. She gets a cigarette lit, puffs a bit. "I'm going out to Lake Wylie next week."

I take a sip of my Coke, wondering why she's telling me this.

"How old's Hawk?" The question comes out of nowhere.

"Was eight in October."

She takes a deep drag, lets it out slow. "Becky turns nine in January. Can Hawk read?"

"Some."

"Becky's always bringing books home. She reads to me now. Used to be the other way around."

We quiet for a bit, her smoking, me thinking. She say, "You and Hawk want to go out to the lake with us?"

I don't answer her right away.

"Loraylee?"

"What're you talking about?"

"My cousin has a place on Lake Wylie. He told me I could go out there and bring friends. We could swim, fish."

"I can't swim."

A crash in the kitchen echoes up the dumbwaiter shaft.

"Uh-oh. I'm glad we're not down there," Retta say. "You ever gone fishing?"

"Once with Uncle Ray."

"We could go on our day off. There's a little cabin. My cousin Bobby and his brother hauled in sand, made a beach, put in a dock."

"You saying it'd be okay for me and Hawk, being there with you and Becky?"

She stares at me with her blue eyes behind her thick glasses. "Yeah, that's what I'm saying."

I watch a garbage truck backing up in the alley. How can anybody drive backward in something that big? "You're from up north. You don't know how it is here."

"The cabin's private property, two or three acres. Nobody'd

see us." She drops her cigarette, smashes it under her shoe, then picks up the butt and tosses it in a trashcan. "We can take a picnic, beer and Cokes, have fun."

Retta and I make our plans to go out to the lake on our next Monday off, and I wait till Sunday night to tell Bibi and Uncle Ray. Bibi won't remember much of anything I tell her late in the day, and I don't want to give Uncle Ray time to object. After I clean up from supper, I go to the living room where Bibi is settled in her chair, knitting needles clicking. For a long time she's been making a sweater for Hawk, and if it started out as a sweater for a four-year-old, she'll need to find another boy. Uncle Ray's on the floor, fiddling with the TV again.

I sit on the sofa. "I'm taking Hawk on a picnic tomorrow with Retta, my friend girl from work."

"What's that?" Bibi looks up.

"We going on a picnic tomorrow."

"Retta you say?" Uncle Ray ask. He's behind the TV, the top of his head visible, curly white hair fading in the middle where he's going bald. When's he going to give up on that TV?

"Yeah, Retta Lawrence. You've heard me talk about her. Started at the S&W a year after I did."

Bibi pulls out a few stitches, then gets to knitting again, lifting the yarn over the top of the needles, rocking a bit as she works. "How you getting there?"

"Retta's got a car."

Uncle Ray stands up. "And where y'all going?"

"You heard of Lake Wylie?"

"Been fishing out there." He sits in his chair. "Where-abouts? It's a big lake."

"Retta's cousin has a cabin. She's got a daughter, Becky, about Hawk's age, who's going with us."

Bibi rocks and knits. Uncle Ray stares out the screen door.

"We going"—I stand up—"tomorrow."

"Huh," say Bibi.

Monday morning, nine o'clock, Retta pulls up in front of the house in her Ford. The rust bucket, she calls it, always adding that it runs good. Uncle Ray hollers back to my bedroom, "She's here. Your friend girl."

"Tell her to come on in."

Then I'm wondering if Bibi put her knitting away and did Uncle Ray leave his tools lying on the floor by the TV? Is the morning paper spread out on the sofa? Where's Hawk?

Bibi stops at my door. "Somebody out front, Raylee."

"It's Retta, from work. Go meet her. I'll be there in a couple minutes."

"She white?"

"Uh-huh. Is that a problem?"

"Not for me. Might be for you." She goes.

"Mama?" Hawk whines from the bathroom, "No more toothpaste."

"In the medicine cabinet. Hurry, now."

He's been excited since he woke, talking about going on a picnic, and asking can he take his bike Uncle Ray got him. "No place to ride it," I tell him. "Take your ball. You and Becky can play with it."

"Girls can't play ball."

"Girls can do anything boys can. Or more."

"Huh." He sounds like Bibi.

When he comes out of the bathroom, I give him a long look.

"My shirt the right way?" He twists to look over his shoulder.

"Yep, label in the back." He's got on shorts and a T-shirt, socks and sandals, buckled up and all. His hair slicked back, wet. When it dries it'll be in a tangle of curls, auburn, like his daddy's. "Get a paper bag from the pantry, and stick your blue jean shorts in it, for if we want to go in the lake. I'll bring towels."

"Is the lake like Little Sugar?"

"Bigger."

"Bigger and bigger?"

"Yep. Go on, now, Retta's here."

He takes off running. When I get to the living room, Retta's sitting on the sofa talking with Bibi. "Yes, I work at the S&W with Loraylee."

Bibi looks at me. "Where you say y'all going?"

"Out to Lake Wylie. On a picnic. I told you last night."

I walk over to her chair, kiss her cheek. "We going now, Bibi. Back later on."

"About eight this evening, is that okay?" Retta ask.

Hawk comes running in, carrying a grocery bag. "Got my jean shorts!"

"Good. Where's Becky?" I say to Retta.

"Outside with your uncle Ray. He's showing her the henhouse."

Through the screen door I see Uncle Ray and a little girl coming around the house from the backyard, holding hands. She's not much taller than Hawk, skinny like her mother, but with straight black hair and brown eyes. Makes me wonder about her daddy. First thing she say to me, "I like your chickens." Her voice is quiet, shy.

"Do you like eggs?" I ask.

"Yes, scrambled. And sandwiches."

Uncle Ray ask Retta, "Where y'all going on the lake, exactly?"

Why's he being so nosy?

"My cousin's place is over the state line, near the marina."

Uncle Ray seems to think on this. "Y'all be careful."

Then I know what he's thinking about, and I reckon Retta does, too. Yeah, be careful.

We get everything loaded in the car, the children in the back, Retta apologizing, "It's a junk heap, like I said, no A/C and a bad muffler, but it runs great."

"Never been in a car with A/C anyway."

As we pull away, I wonder is Dooby Franklin watching out his window, and does he think I'm getting uppity, going off with a white girl?

Retta gets us over to Tryon and heads south. "There's fishing poles my cousin says we can use, but we have to stop for bait. I need gas anyway."

"Bait?"

"Yeah, Bobby says get worms. If we were going out in the boat, we'd get minnows, but we'll fish from the dock."

"Worms?" Hawk laughs. "We getting worms."

Becky say, "So we can fish."

Hawk bounces on the back seat, excited, talking nonstop with Becky, who answers him in her quiet way.

When we get to Highway 49, Retta pulls into an Esso station with a sign by the pumps, WORMS. MINNERS. LURES. LUNCH. Ask In Doors. A man comes up to her window. "Gas 'er up? Check your oil?"

"Just gas, please, and we'll come in for some worms."

"Yes, ma'am." He looks at me, glances in the back at Hawk and Becky, doesn't say anything.

While the man's filling the tank, Hawk say, "I need to pee, Mama."

"Me too," say Becky.

Retta ask, "Will you take them?" She points to a sign to the restrooms. "Soon as I pay, I'll drive around there."

A sign on the door to one bathroom say White Men but the "White" has a slash of orange paint across it and beneath that, BROKE printed large. The other door has WHITE WOMEN on it. The whole thing is slashed out with orange paint, and beside it is written ANY BODY.

When we get back in the car, Hawk say to Becky, "Your hair's shiny."

She laughs. "Yours is curly."

We bump down a dirt road off the highway, the car rattling, making me wonder what's keeping it together. Retta turns onto another rutted road and there it is, the cabin, the sandy beach, sun bouncing on the water. Hawk yells, "The lake!" He and Becky scramble out of the car as soon as it stops. The cabin is a shabby-looking thing between the driveway and the water. When we go into it to change into our swimsuits, I see it's one big room with a curtained-off section that passes as a bathroom. That does come in handy, though.

The rest of that June day stays in my mind. Warm breezes, the kids running along the shore, tossing rocks into the water. Me wearing a bathing suit borrowed from Retta, tight on me. Hawk shy seeing me in it. Him and me going into the water a bit—neither of us can swim, so the lake is both fun and scary. Retta and me fishing, not catching anything worth keeping, but having fun trying. After a while we lie on the dock, her cigarette smoke drifting in the breeze, the sound of motorboats out on the lake, Becky and Hawk singing the "Itsy-Bitsy Spider" song when they come on a web.

"You been to the ocean?" I ask Retta.

"Sure, grew up near it in New Jersey."

"I'm thinking I'm gon go see it."

Two weeks later I call Auntie Violet. She lives in Atlantic Beach, in South Carolina, and is happy for me and Hawk to come stay in her place. All we have to do is get there. Our very first trip together, far from home.

Mr. Griffin puts my dates on the vacation calendar in his office. "Sure wish we could go off together, you and me and Hawk."

"Yeah, me too. Maybe someday. Someday when things change."

Last thing Uncle Ray say to me when we get into a taxi at home: "Call me when you get there. You don't call, we're going to worry."

At eight-thirty in the morning on a bright June Sunday, Hawk and me get out of the taxi at the Trailways station, where we board a bus that'll take us to the beach. It's got more colored on it than white, so I feel easy about the trip. We settle into our seats, him by the window, up on his knees, looking out. "The ocean is bigger than the lake," he say. "Miss Madison told me. It's the biggest water there is."

"Yeah, that's right. In pictures of it, you can't see across to the other side."

The bus finally rolls out of the station, onto West Trade. Hawk grabs the bottom rail of the window. "We going!" he shouts.

He didn't sleep much last night. I'm thinking he'll nap on the bus, but he stays up on his knees, telling me what he's seeing. "Look, Mama, cows!"

We not even to Monroe and already it's farms, tobacco, cotton, beans, and corn, the land rolling on and on.

I open my purse, take out the map Uncle Ray got me. "See." I point to the state line, show Hawk. "That's where we are, and that's where we going, Atlantic Beach."

In a couple of hours we get to Cheraw, where we have to wait forty-five minutes for the next bus. I get Hawk some Lance crackers and a Coke, so he's happy, runs all around the waiting room talking to folks. Then we board the bus to Conway, driver telling me it'll be about three hours, with two stops, and we'll transfer again to a local.

While we rolling along I'm thinking that South Carolina doesn't look like North Carolina. All flat and washed-out, tan dirt instead of red clay, miles and miles of pine trees. About twenty minutes before we due to stop, Hawk finally falls asleep, and I let him be until most folks are off the bus and the driver yells at me, "Hey, girl, you going to transfer or not?" He's gray-haired, got knuckles swoll from arthritis, like Bibi, but he can't be as old as she is and still be driving.

"Yes, sir, let me get my boy here." I wake him up and he starts fussing right away, not a thing I can do. I'm feeling fussy, too. We get inside with our suitcase and me mostly carrying Hawk till we can sit down on a bench, where he goes right back to sleep and I'm wondering if I should leave him be, knowing if he naps too much, he won't go to bed when it's time. It's more than an hour till the bus to Windy Hill, where Auntie Violet gon meet us, and I sit with Hawk's head in my lap, wondering how he can sleep with all the noise in the waiting room. My eyes get heavy, too, and I'm about to drop off myself when I hear them announcing our bus.

The driver say it's three stops before we get to Windy Hill. He talks with Hawk, who is wide awake again.

"Mama, do I know Auntie Violet?"

"She saw you when you were a baby, is all." Auntie Violet is Uncle Ray's sister, my great-aunt. I remember her as friendly, a talker, at least around Bibi and Uncle Ray. Unless she has reduced, she's fat.

"She lives at the ocean, right?"

"Yes, she does, has a house on the beach, but it'll be just you and me. She's going to be gone for a few days on business, letting us stay in her place."

When we climb off the bus in Windy Hill I'm looking around for Auntie Violet when I hear my name, "Loraylee, Hawk, here I am."

She walks toward us and she hasn't reduced at all, is maybe

even fatter. I'm so glad to see her I almost cry. Hawk runs ahead of me and puts his arms around her. She bends down, kisses his cheek, smothering him in her bosoms, then holds out an arm for me. "You must be tired, Loraylee. That's a long trip, and I am so glad you're here."

After we get settled in her car, she say, "I'm leaving this evening for Columbia, sorry about that, but y'all will be okay. There's groceries in the kitchen. I've got electricity, of course, not always dependable, so I've put out candles in case you need them. My house is a duplex, but nobody's in the other side right now. Renters are coming in next Sunday." She talks almost all the way to her place.

As soon as we pull up, Hawk jumps out of the car. "I can see the ocean. Look!" His small voice is lost in the roar of the waves. The ocean goes on forever. Hard to believe there's something like Africa on the other side that we can't see. Hawk runs up and down the sand yelling, "Hey, ocean!"

When we get inside Auntie Violet lets me call Uncle Ray. "A collect call, station to station," I tell the operator, wanting Auntie Violet to know we won't be adding to her phone bill. She ask to speak to Uncle Ray when I'm through.

"Hey, Ray. Yeah, they're tired but they got here." A pause. "No, it's an NAACP training session. I promised to attend, can't miss it. I'll be gone all week, but they've got everything they need, don't you worry. I love having Hawk here, what a boy. Say hey to Livvie for me."

She leaves right after supper. I'm so tired I want to crawl in bed even if it is still light outside. I put the candles and matches on the nightstand in case we need them, get out our pajamas, but Hawk won't let up about the ocean. Got to see it again. "Okay," I say, "one more time. We not staying long this evening."

"And we going to the ocean in the morning, too." He pulls me toward the door.

"Hold on . . . we need something to sit on." I get the beach towel Auntie Violet gave me. "Okay, boy, let's go say good night to the ocean."

Soon as we get over the dunes, Hawk squats and picks up something from the sand. "Look, Mama!"

It's smooth and pink, like a piece of a china plate. "Part of a seashell," I tell him. "They get broke crashing on the beach, I reckon." He picks up more and more, some curved, some flat. Pretty. "My, my, aren't they something." I spread the towel on the sand, sit and watch him.

The next morning I wake in Auntie Violet's house, unsure where I am. Hawk's not in a bed across the room, the sun's coming in through a window that's in the wrong place. Then I remember. We are on vacation, what a wonderful thing that is. I laugh out loud.

"That you, Mama? You awake?" Hawk runs in, jumps up on the bed. "Let's go to the ocean!"

CHAPTER 16

Eben walked over to the church, a staccato of raindrops on his umbrella, going through a mental list for the Fourth of July celebration. Firecrackers. Ben would get them on his trip to Gaffney where he went to buy the first peaches of the season. In early July Ben set crates of ripe freestones on the sidewalk in front of Stone's Grocery, and even whites showed up to buy them.

At St. Tim's, he had to force the door, which always stuck in humid weather. He climbed the stairs to his office slowly. He'd never paid much mind to the old saw about wet weather aggravating achy joints, but these days he knew it to be true.

The phone rang as he propped his dripping umbrella outside his office. Gideon Rhyne, now Brother Rhyne, calling. Eben hadn't seen him since the first commission meeting, but gossip had it that Rhyne had become a member of the House of Prayer. The man's voice boomed through the phone, telling Eben about plans for an Independence Day parade. "Sweet Daddy McCollough will be in town, an enormous tribute to us, and the Brooklyn churches will join in honoring him.

We're calling to tell you where your church is in the lineup, and your people—"

He interrupted. "Brother Rhyne, we're planning a parade of our own that day."

Rhyne said, "The bishop won't be happy about this."

"Ours is a bit more of a neighborhood thing. Perhaps we could stagger the times."

"We'll consult with Bishop McCollough and call you." The phone went dead.

Eben let go of a long breath he didn't know he'd been holding. He'd do everything he could to avoid a disagreement among the Brooklyn churches, but he didn't want to kowtow to the House of Prayer, as he so often felt he had to do.

He stood slowly, feeling a need for fresh air, and pulled down the top half of the window behind his desk. As cool damp air blew in, he remembered a visit last week from Loraylee Hawkins and her son, when they'd come to see him about the parade. He'd watched them from this same window as they skipped toward the church, Hawk shouting "Whiz! Bang!" and whistling a long note that started high and ended low, "Weeeeeeeeeeeeeee! Boom!"

A few minutes later they had burst through his office door. "Pastor," Loraylee said, "we here to help with the Fourth of July."

He motioned to the chairs across from his desk. "Please, please, have a seat."

Hawk jumped into the straight chair and sat, his legs swinging, fingers snapping.

Eben looked at Hawk. *A happy, healthy boy.* Reddish curly hair on a round skull, startling gray eyes. "Ben Stone's going to get firecrackers for us in South Carolina, when he goes to buy peaches."

"Yippee!" the boy said. "See, Mama, I told you!"

Loraylee laughed. "Hawk's been a firecracker himself for

days." Loraylee's brown eyes were almond shaped. Her high cheekbones, her dusky skin—*Maybe a streak of Cherokee in her blood.* She asked, "How can we help with the parade?"

"You could distribute fliers around the neighborhood."

"That'll be easy," Loraylee said. "Hawk wants to carry the American flag when we march, and Uncle Ray's gon be Frederick Douglass if he can find him a wig. He'll help me be Sojourney Truth."

"Sojourner," Eben said.

"Oh, is that right?" Loraylee stood to leave. "Just wanted to let you know because we leaving tomorrow to visit my auntie Violet for a week at the beach."

"Gon see the ocean," Hawk said, jumping from his chair.

"We'll get in touch again when we get home," Loraylee said. "G'bye!"

She'd whisked Hawk out the door and the air in his office had seemed to settle as in the wake of a whirlwind.

After the upsetting call from Brother Rhyne, he spent an hour on the phone, lining up a meeting with other churches to discuss the holiday. His objection to the House of Prayer once again trying to take the focus off smaller congregations went deeper than he could have explained. Thus far, ministers and minions alike agreed to meet.

The rain had stopped when he left the church, greeted by a glorious June afternoon. He headed for Stone's, counting on Ben to understand that the festivities must not be centered around Bishop McCollough. He entered the grocery to the ringing of the bell on the door, the pleasant creak of the floorboards beneath his feet. The store always smelled the same, sweetness from the produce; a rusty scent from the meat case, where a cured ham hung above pale plucked chickens nestled side by side. "Ben?" he called out. His friend came through a door in the back, wiping his hands on the bib of his long white apron. In his middle years Ben had gotten a potbelly Eben hadn't noticed before but was otherwise as fit as ever.

"Hey, Eben. You want a Coke?"

"Don't mind if I do." He sat down on a crate beside the drink cooler.

Ben pried open two bottles and settled on the floor, knees bent, his back against a box of canned beans. "How're the festivities shaping up?"

"Fine, until early this afternoon. That's why I'm here."

Ben drank, swallowed, and belched.

Eben shook his head. "We can dress you up but we can't take you out."

Ben tipped his bottle in a mock toast. "So what's going on?"

"Gideon Rhyne, who fancies himself an emissary of the esteemed Bishop McCollough, has importuned me to join our Fourth of July parade with theirs."

"Importuned by an emissary? My, my."

Eben laughed so hard he had to hold his nose to keep from spraying Ben with Coke. He touched his handkerchief to his eyes. "They've got the AMEs, McDowell Baptist, the Church of God, a couple of others. We were low on their list, right above Mount Sinai Holy."

"Could have been at the bottom."

Eben said, "What gets me is someone like Bishop McCollough, with no connection to Brooklyn, sweeps in here a couple of times a year and takes over. Makes things all about him. Riles me, Benjy. He doesn't understand we're fighting for our lives here, those with tarpaper on the roof and those with asphalt shingles."

"United we fall?"

"You got it." He held the cold bottle against his arthritic

knee. "The House of Prayer here in Charlotte, they're with us, but when the mighty Sweet Daddy comes to town, they forget their local pride. They truly worship the man."

"And not his God?"

"Sometimes I wonder."

Ben said, "Follow me, brethren. I'mon teach y'all to fish."

"Yowsa, yowsa, I'm wit you, Daddy."

The front door opened, the bell tinkling. Ben looked at his watch and spoke to the rectangle of afternoon sun. "That you, Bertha?"

A young voice called back, "Hey, Mr. Stone, yes, it's me."

"Get set up. The cash drawer's ready. I'll be with you in a few minutes."

"Yes, sir."

Ben said, "My new girl. I think this one's going to do well, though I never have these kids for more than a year. They get a better job and move on."

"But you get them started."

"I do, yes, I do."

"Can you meet with us on Thursday evening?"

"I'll be there, but I want you to be thinking about something."

The tone in Ben's voice told Eben he'd better pay attention. "What's that?"

Ben held up his Coke, looked at the bottom of the bottle like there was a message on it. "When I said 'united we fall' I was joking, right?"

"Right."

"Not a joke. Brooklyn's on the way out, Eben. We both know it. And I'm going to say something to you that I won't be saying Thursday night. We've got a mess here and there's only one way to clean it up, which is to wipe it out."

"Brooklyn, wipe out Brooklyn?" Eben straightened, studied his old friend's face.

"Yes." Ben tightened his lips, ran a forefinger down the wet Coke bottle. "Of course what I wish the city would do is rebuild, but that's never going to happen. The land's too valuable, close as we are to the Square."

"You're right about that. Georgeanne Wilkins has been doing research about this urban renewal thing, the redevelopment, and she came on a story that was in the *Observer* in 1912." He pulled a piece of paper from his shirt pocket and put on his reading glasses. "Almost forgot to show it to you. Remember, this is fifty years ago, and when they say 'this section,' they mean Brooklyn." He read aloud, "'. . . farsighted men believe that eventually this section, because of its proximity to the center of the city, must sooner or later be utilized by the white population.'"

"Good Lord," said Ben. "Only surprise there is that they'd say it in the paper. Couldn't get by with talk like that today."

"But wipe us out, you're in favor of that?"

"I'm in favor of cleaning up the god-awful chaos we've got here. Too many people are living on the edge, in shacks, in filth, and something's got to be done about that. But when we go down—and go down we will—I want them to see us shoulder to shoulder, not fighting amongst ourselves. The strongest thing we have is unity or, as Reverend King said, when he spoke in Raleigh, '. . . the creation of the beloved community.' Remember that?"

"Yeah, I do."

Ben rubbed his chin, looked toward the front of the store. "You and I see through the Sweet Daddy pomp and circumstance, but one thing he does well is get the beloved community together behind him. Doesn't matter who's out in front. What matters is the enormous crowd we'll show the city."

"Hmph," Eben chuckled. "So what you're saying is we should join the other churches, parade with the House of Prayer."

"Yep."

They finished their Cokes in silence.

Eben returned to St. Tim's to find the *Charlotte News* on his desk with an article circled, and a note paper-clipped to it, "See, Preacher, this queer got his due." The hatred stunned him. ANOTHER MURDER CORNER DEATH:

> Jonathan Steadman, 39, died at Good Samaritan Hospital early Tuesday, from a brutal assault at the intersection of East First Street and South McDowell in the Brooklyn Neighborhood. Steadman, a.k.a. Jonny No Age, owned Steadman's Flowers. No immediate family has been identified.

The term "a.k.a." made Jonny sound like a criminal instead of what he was, a gentle man who'd been donating flowers for St. Tim's Sunday services as long as Eben could remember. Nothing elaborate, vases of jonquils or daisies nestled in ferns, but always there by late Saturday afternoon. A brutal assault. He shuddered at the idea of anyone beating Jonny, a decent man whose only crime was loving another man. Jonny had lived openly with his friend Joseph—Eben couldn't remember the man's last name—for several years, and many in the community could not abide that. But to beat a man to death?

The police had come by St. Tim's to question Eben about Jonny, but apparently were never able to connect him with anything illegal. There'd been rumors of Jonny's store being a front for the sale of marijuana, even that he'd grown it in the garden behind the shop. No plants were found, no evidence Jonny had ever been other than exactly what he was, a florist.

He swiveled in his chair to look at the wall calendar, setting aside the following Sunday for Jonny's service. He picked up the phone. Joseph answered on the first ring.

"Why, Preacher? Who hated us so much?"

Us. Had Joseph been threatened, too? "There's no understanding such people, Joseph. All we can do is remember Jonny with love."

The man on the other end of the phone sobbed. "The police aren't even trying to find out who did it, a few questions, then they dropped it. One more dead queer, that's Jonny's epitaph."

After Jonny's funeral, Eben sat at his desk, pondering something that was bothering him. He'd gotten some solace from the service. Among the dozen or so people in the pews of St. Tim's were the Hawkins family. Livinia Hawkins made no attempt to hide her disdain for Jonny's lifestyle, but she was also outspoken in her fondness. What was it she'd said? "Jonny No Age, good in his heart. Odd one, though. Odd." With Livvie's increasing senility had come a directness Eben admired.

He struggled to accept what he knew for a certainty: His congregation believed homosexuality to be a sin—right up there with murder, infidelity. And doubt. He could preach love from the pulpit but he couldn't change the age-old prejudice. If he tried, it was a battle he'd lose. His people, so long targets themselves, needed someone to shun.

CHAPTER 17

Wind scalloped the beach under a cloudless sky that promised a fair day. Gulls congregated at the end of the groin, making Persy want to startle them into the sky. Beyond it a woman and boy walked in the sand at the ocean's edge. The boy jumped over ripples of incoming waves, shouting, laughing. The woman, much darker than the boy, had black hair; his gleamed like copper wire in the sun. He ran back and forth, squatted, picked up something, threw it into the water; the woman spread a towel in the sand, sat and stretched her legs toward the ocean. *She must be the boy's mother.* The woman propped herself on her elbows while the boy circled her, never still.

Whitney would have been full of energy and curiosity, like that boy.

Persy left her Keds at the bottom of the dunes, headed for the rocky groin, seeking purchase with her knee on one stone, her hand on another. The rough flatness on top invited her to walk, her arms out for balance on the slippery, guano-splattered rocks. At the end, the gulls departed in a flurry. She felt triumphant, embraced by the wind. *Briny fishy me.*

The woman on the beach yelled, "Hawk! No!"

Persy turned, saw the boy as he climbed onto the rocky wall, stood. Fast, sure-footed, he headed her way. "Hey, lady." He neared her, swaying, his arms splayed, imitating her stance to balance himself. His mother ran along the base of the groin, shedding her sandals and stepping into the water. "Hawk, get back here!"

The boy came on unsteadily, reached for Persy and slipped, his fingers brushing hers. His head bounced off a rock as he tumbled into the billowing waves. The woman shrieked. Persy saw bubbles where the boy disappeared and jumped into the churning eddy, cutting off the woman's scream. She went down, down, blinded in the turmoil, groping. Exploded back to the surface for a gasping lungful of air and under again, arms spread, seeking. She brushed a piece of shirt, an arm, pulled him to her. Surfaced, spitting salt water. With both feet she pushed away from the groin, her arm around the limp boy, holding him close.

"I've got you," she told him, "I've got you now." He lay against her, arms hanging.

She kicked, kicked. Her free arm propelled them toward shore. Her left foot brushed the bottom before a wave lifted them. They rose and dipped. The wake of a breaker sucked them back out. She thrust her feet down, felt the bottom again. Dug her toes into firm sand, took a step, two, carried him into the shallows, fell to her knees, coughing. Feeble swells brushed her thighs. The woman reached them, pulled the boy from Persy, gulped with sobs that distorted her face. "Hawk, you okay? Hawk?"

He gagged, vomited water, groaned.

The woman thumped the boy's back with the heel of her hand. "Hawk, speak to me," she screamed. "Hawk!"

He spit another mouthful of water, opened his eyes. "Hurts, Mama."

Mama.

The woman sat on the wet sand, held her son close, rocked back and forth. His tight curls leaked rivulets of ruddy water.

"Look." Persy pointed at his head.

The woman's hand found the gash. "You cut yourself," she told him.

The boy cried out.

"He needs a doctor." *The woman must know this.*

Blood seeped through her fingers, down his neck. "I got no car."

"Is that your place?" Persy pointed to a duplex.

"Yes, where we staying." The boy buried his face in her chest, his shoulders shaking.

"Carry him to the road. I'll drive around." She stumbled toward the house, pulled on her shoes, snatched towels from the clothesline, keys and pocketbook from inside the front door. In the car, her hand shook so badly she could not get the key in the ignition. She could still feel his small limp body against hers. Nausea overcame her. She opened the car door and threw up. Ocean water drained salty and clear from her stomach, her sinuses. Trembling, she eased the car onto the empty road.

Persy pulled into the driveway as the woman crossed the patchy lawn, holding her son, calling out, "He needs to lie down." Persy helped her into the back seat, handed her a towel. "Press this on his cut."

She got back in, started the car. "We'll go to the clinic in Myrtle Beach. I'm Persy Marshall. Our house is on the other side of the groin, where your son fell."

The boy moaned.

"He's bleeding bad."

"Press on the cut. We'll be there in ten minutes." She smiled at the anguished face in the rearview mirror. "Last year my husband got stitches in his foot. I know right where to go."

"Is my boy gon need stitches?"

"Maybe. Probably."

The woman talked to her son in a murmur as they headed south on Highway 17, the car quiet except for the low voice from the back seat.

A woman in a white uniform and nurse's hat was unlocking the front door of the clinic when they pulled into the parking lot. She looked at Hawk in his mother's arms, at the bloody towel, at Persy. "The doctor will be here soon, but he doesn't usually—oh, well, come on in. I'll look at the wound and we'll see." She took them inside, flipped on lights, showed them to an examining room.

"I'm Mrs. Marshall. We have a place at Windy Hill, and this is—" Persy stopped, looking at the boy's mother.

"Loraylee Hawkins. My boy is Hawk." The woman's shorts and sleeveless blouse were blood-splattered, but she had a calm dignity. Persy felt disheveled in her wet clothes, her squishy Keds.

"Put him there," the nurse pointed to a table. "I'm Nurse Hastings."

Hawk kept his hand on his mother's arm after she put him down. He cried out when she removed the bloody towel from his wound. "You gon be okay, baby. It's not too bad." She touched his fingers to her mouth while the nurse inspected his head.

"No, it isn't bad," the nurse said. "Dr. Rivers may want to take a few stitches. His decision, of course, but in my experience . . ." With metal pincers she took cotton balls from a glass container. "Hawk, I'm going to clean where you got hurt, might sting a bit, all right?"

He looked at her, his eyes large. "Okay." She moistened

the cotton with clear fluid from a brown bottle, dabbed it on the wound, talking to the boy all the while. She covered the wound with a gauze pad. "You'll be fine, Hawk." She looked at Persy. "What happened?"

"He fell off the groin, hit his head."

The nurse turned to his mother. "When was Hawk's last tetanus shot?"

"Got all his shots when he was born. He's eight now." She smiled at her son, then spoke to the nurse again. "I got insurance."

"That's good. Eight years? He'll need a booster."

A door opened and closed in the outer office. A man called, "Nancy, I'm here."

"Hey, Doc. We're in Room One."

A short, fat man came in, wearing a business suit, starched blue shirt, tie. Persy caught a whiff of aftershave. He took off his straw fedora, ran a hand over his bald head, peered through round glasses. "What have we got here?"

"Dr. Rivers, this is Mrs. Marshall from Windy Hill. She brought this boy in. A scalp laceration."

The doctor frowned at Loraylee and Hawk.

"They have insurance," the nurse said, "so I could send them over to the hospital. Stallings would be happy to—"

He cut her off. "When's my first appointment?"

"Nine-thirty, the Ramsey woman, eight-month checkup."

"Hmmm." The doctor rubbed his chin. "Tell you what, let's not involve Stallings in this. If it's only a couple of sutures . . . I'll be right back." He left the room.

Nurse Hastings said, "He's going to change his coat."

He returned in a white coat with HEWITT RIVERS, MD, stitched in green script on the breast pocket. "Your name?" he said to Hawk's mother.

"I'm Loraylee Hawkins and this my boy, Hawk. He's eight."

Dr. Rivers touched Hawk's shoulder. "You're eight, are you?"

"Be nine in October."

"Would you let me see where you hurt your head?"

Hawk looked at his mother. "Okay."

The doctor gently lifted the bloody gauze. The nurse cut open another bandage, held it out at the ready. After inspecting the wound, the doctor put the clean gauze over it. "Loraylee, I think four stitches will do." He asked Hawk, "Do you know your numbers?"

"I'm almost in third grade." He sounded indignant.

Dr. Rivers held up his hand, thumb and pinkie folded. "How many fingers?"

"Three."

"I'm going to look in your eyes, okay?" Dr. Rivers held out his hand and the nurse put a penlight in it. He examined Hawk's eyes. "Loraylee, has he been asleep since he fell?"

"No, sir."

"There's no sign of a concussion, which would be like a bruise on your son's brain. Let's get him stitched up and I'll tell you what to watch for, but I believe he's going to be all right."

"We supposed to go home on the bus Sunday, six or seven hours' trip. That okay?"

"If he has no problems before you leave, it's all right for him to travel. Your own doctor can remove the stitches in a week or so." He said to Hawk, "Nurse Hastings will shave your head a bit, give you a bald spot."

"Okay."

"I'll do something so you won't feel it when I sew up the cut."

Loraylee whispered to Persy, "I left my purse at the house, with my insurance card."

"When we're finished here, I'll take you back to get it."

For the first time, she smiled at Persy. "I thank you."

Persy stood off to the side in a corner of the room, shivering in her damp clothes in the air-conditioning. She wanted to be out of the way, but hoped they wouldn't ask her to leave.

Dr. Rivers explained everything to Hawk as he proceeded, letting Loraylee stay close to her son, perhaps persuaded by her effect on the boy. Even with a local anesthetic, Hawk must have felt the pull of the needle passing in and out of his scalp. With each suture he squealed and began to wiggle. His mother spoke quietly to him. "I know, I know. It's scary, but we almost done." A few minutes later Dr. Rivers tied off the last of four neat black sutures and dropped his instruments on a tray littered with bloody gauze. He taped a bandage over the wound.

Nurse Hastings gave him a syringe. "The tetanus."

Dr. Rivers took Hawk's arm and swabbed it with wet cotton. "Take a deep breath, Hawk. Hold it."

At the moment of the injection, Hawk squealed, "Ow!" but it was over.

"We're all done." Dr. Rivers patted Hawk's shoulder. "You're a brave young man."

Persy touched the boy's foot. "You did great."

"Keep him awake until his regular bedtime," the doctor said to Loraylee. "If he seems unusually sleepy, call Nurse Hastings." He left abruptly.

In the front room, a receptionist was at the desk, a small girl with platinum hair and bright lipstick. "Mrs. Marshall, we understand that you'll return later with their insurance card."

Loraylee said, "We will, and I'm grateful to Mrs. Marshall."

Again the girl spoke to Persy. "Nurse Hastings said to give him an aspirin if his head starts hurting."

As Loraylee turned for the door, she said over her shoulder, "I will do that."

When they left, Hawk had two lollipops, one in his hand and one in his pocket. They all sat in the front, the boy between his mother and Persy. Hawk was warm against Persy's side and smelled like alcohol and grape sucker. He put a finger to the edge of the bald patch that showed under the stark white bandage. "How long it gon take to get my hair back?"

"The way it grows, won't take long," Loraylee said.

"Good. I don't particularly like being bald."

"Not particularly, huh?"

"I guess it's okay. Uncle Ray got a bald spot, too."

Persy turned off Highway 17 onto the road to Windy Hill.

Hawk sat up straight, peered over the dashboard, shouted, "There it is, the 'Lantic Ocean!"

She felt his excitement.

"Soon as we get back home I'm telling Desmond I got stitches after falling into the ocean."

Persy pulled into the gravel drive behind the duplex. "Who is Desmond?"

"My friend. We in school together."

She stopped the car. "I'm going to get cleaned up. I'll come back for y'all in an hour or so."

"Honk when you get here."

Persy went back to the shanty, where she stayed in the shower until the hot water turned tepid, thinking about how wonderful it felt to be around a child.

The evening gaped before her, hours until bedtime, but even so too brief for her to think about all that had happened. Moving quickly around the kitchen, she fixed a poached egg, slice of boiled ham, cantaloupe, toast, forcing herself to wash up after she ate, to leave a peaceful kitchen that wouldn't nag her later.

At dusk she sat in one of the rockers with a beer. The sun setting behind the house was reflected on the breakers, a golden pink no one would believe if it were in a painting. She looked north to the duplex where lights were on in second-floor windows. Imagined Loraylee putting Hawk to bed in short pajamas, smelling of soap and toothpaste, fussy because his head hurt. Did she remember to give him aspirin? Did she read him to sleep? *I would.*

We could have drowned.

The beer was sharp in her throat. Clearly, Negro patients weren't welcome at that clinic, evidenced by a familiar unacknowledged byplay. But on the whole, the doctor treated Hawk and Loraylee well.

During the drive back to the clinic with the insurance card, Loraylee had told Persy they lived in Brooklyn. The neighborhood that Blaire was working to destroy, and where Persy visited Roberta Stokes to get a christening gown for Whitney, all those years ago. Persy hadn't told Loraylee that she was from Charlotte, too, hadn't offered her a ride home on Sunday, though she could get them home in half the time it would take on the bus.

Sitting there, rocking, she made up her mind: This wasn't going to be another missed opportunity. Inside the house the phone rang. *Blaire.* They hadn't spoken since yesterday. She let it ring.

CHAPTER 18

Mr. Griffin's got something special planned for our Monday off, and I've gone to Lamarr Beauty Shop, got my hair heat treated and styled, got a manicure and pedicure. I'm feeling shiny.

"You're gorgeous," he say, when I get in the car.

"Been to the beauty parlor." I touch his leg.

He drives out of town, the sun setting behind us.

At a sign saying Matthews five miles, he turns onto a dirt road. We stop at a lake, silver in the dim evening. Mr. Griffin say, "You stay here while I set things up."

I roll down the window, listening as he opens the trunk, walks back and forth down to the water, carrying stuff. The air is full of sounds I don't recognize. I've heard night noises all my life, living near Little Sugar, but out here in the country a band of critters is playing strange music. No traffic, no radio playing next door, nobody out on the street talking. Frogs, crickets, a hooty owl and other birds settle down for the night.

Mr. Griffin call me, "Okay."

I get out and walk to where he got a blanket spread on the ground. "Wine," he say, "cheese, boiled shrimp, fruit . . . a sunset picnic."

I can't tell him how happy this makes me. I sit down on the blanket. It's almost dark, but the sky glows with a moon rising. "You plan for the moon, too?"

"Of course." He hands me a glass of wine, clinks against mine. "To us." He takes a sip. "How's Hawk doing? When are the stitches coming out?"

"He's grumpy, can't wait to be done with it. We see Dr. Wilkins Tuesday afternoon."

"Have you heard anything else from the lady who brought y'all back to Charlotte?"

"Mrs. Marshall? No. We talked a lot in the car coming home, but that trip was a one-time thing and we both knew it." The wine is cool and sweet. "She took us all the way home, I tell you that? I mean, she could have let us off anywhere in town we could catch a city bus, but she wouldn't have it. When we pulled up in front of the house, she tell me something like, 'You have a lovely home.' "

"Did she come in?"

"Oh, no. I grabbed our bag, got Hawk. I thanked her for saving us such a long trip. That was that."

We sit in the dusk, in all those sounds coming through the trees, touching each other, drinking wine.

He say, "I wish we never had to sleep."

"You being silly. We got to sleep or we couldn't work. Be too tired to do anything."

"But what if we didn't need to sleep and never got tired? We could work eight or ten hours, and have all the rest of the day to read or play or make love." He kisses me good. "Think about that."

I can't think about anything but kissing, anything but his

hand slipping down from my shoulder till I'm shivering. "Listen! I never knew critters made such commotion." We're in a bowl of night noises.

Mr. Griffin puts his mouth close to my ear. "Hear that bullfrog? Know what he's saying?"

"What?"

He makes his voice real deep, his mouth against my ear. "Want some. Want some. Want some."

I laugh out loud. Some of the night noises stop, then pick right back up.

"Listen to that lady tree frog. You know what she's saying?" This time his voice is high. "Huh-uh, huh-uh, huh-uh."

"She should say 'Uh-huh, uh-huh, uh-huh.' "

He nuzzles my neck. "I grew up out here listening to all the critters talking among themselves."

"You never told me that."

"My parents still live in the house my great-granddaddy built when he settled here after the Civil War."

His parents. Hawk's grandparents. "They don't know they got a grandbaby."

He's quiet for long time. "No, they don't," he say, finally. He picks up a stick, tosses it toward the lake. "Mom wants me to be happy." But he doesn't sound happy.

"And your father wouldn't want a colored grandson, is that it?"

"No, he would not."

"I don't understand how come you are the way you are."

"I met you, Loraylee. I can't say more than that. Just everything is different from what it used to be, since the day you walked into the S&W looking for a job."

He takes my hand. I can barely see him in the rising moon, but I can feel how serious he is.

"Another thing they don't know is that you got a colored

girlfriend." Even if me being black doesn't matter to him, it would to his parents. That could change him. Suddenly I feel like I don't know him at all.

We sit there in the night sounds, the moon above the trees now. "You think I'll ever meet them?"

"If I have my way, you'll never set eyes on my father."

We next to each other, but apart. The air smells of grass, flowers, the lake.

He breaks off a piece of cheese. "My parents own all the land between here and the highway. A dairy farmer rents most of it, Mom and Dad live on the rest."

"So all this will be yours someday."

"I guess, but I don't want to live out here, never again. I'm a city boy now, and they've got a vegetable garden, a milk cow, a bunch of dogs. Oh, and a henhouse."

"Uncle Ray has chickens."

Mr. Griffin pulls me to him. "I wish we could get married."

"Mr. Griffin, we need to talk about something else."

"Can't you at least call me Archie when we're alone?"

"Not gon happen, any more than we gon get married."

We sit in the moonlight, eat our supper, drink our wine, then lay back on the blanket, the noises we make blending in with the sounds of the night.

I get home about midnight, come across the porch as quiet as I can, open the door, and there is Bibi, sitting on the sofa in the dark. "Bibi?" She doesn't answer. I say her name again, louder, turning on the lamp on the end table.

She's in her nightgown. "Hey, Raylee." She doesn't seem startled. "You been out?"

"Yes, ma'am, to dinner and a movie with a friend." The lie comes easy.

"What you see?"

"*Splendor in the Grass.*" I saw the name of that movie when we passed the Manor Theatre coming back to town. I almost choke to keep from laughing.

She say, "I'd love to go to the movies."

"I'll take you soon. Why you sitting here with the lights off?"

"Trying to think of something that woke me up. When I opened my eyes, I couldn't remember what it was. I came in here to see if I could."

"You had a dream, most likely."

"Most likely." She shake her head. "Didn't seem like a dream."

"Let's get you back in bed. You need to pee first?"

"No, just did." She stops. "I think I just did."

I'm hoping she's right. Don't want to deal with wet sheets in the morning.

As I turn off the lamp by her bed, she say, "Glad you got to go out with your friend. Y'all need to do that more."

At first I think she doesn't know it's somebody special as Mr. Griffin, but then I think she does.

After I get her settled, I try to sleep, but I'm wide awake, wondering what kind of father Mr. Griffin would be.

We spent the night together, once, back before Hawk, when Mr. Griffin first moved into his apartment on Seventh Street. His roommate was out of town and Mr. Griffin say we'd have the whole night, him and me alone. First thing when we got there I looked around to see what he put in the apartment to make it home. Books everywhere. How'd he have time to read them? Pictures on the walls, some of them magazine pages he taped up, others in a frame. The only picture in our living room is Jesus standing in a field, feeding a sheep. Bibi loves that picture, but it has always bothered me that Jesus is white. She say it doesn't matter. It matters to me, and someday I'm gon ask Pastor Polk about that.

Mr. Griffin's apartment only had one bedroom. "Where's your roommate sleep?"

He pointed to the sofa. "It opens out into a bed."

"No!"

He lifted up the cushions. Sheets, a mattress folded up on itself. "But this isn't for us."

He led me down a short hall, past the bathroom and into his bedroom. Had me sit on the edge of the bed while he lit two candles, his hand shaking, nervous as I was about getting into bed together. But then he started unbuttoning my dress. So slow I almost couldn't stand it. I took his shirt off him the same way, one button, then the next. Even if I'd been with him in the back seat of his car, I'd never seen him totally naked, and before we lay down I ran my hands through the curls on his chest. Thick hair, even redder than on his head. The most handsome man I ever saw.

That night he tells me he loves me. We in his bed wrapped around each other. He squeezes me. "I love you." That simple. I've been knowing for a long time that I love him, but I haven't said it out loud. I don't have to, because he say, "And you love me, too."

"Okay," I say. And that's that.

CHAPTER 19

Eben woke at three a.m. to a pounding on his front door. "Fire!" Oscar yelling. "Fire!" He stood, groggy, peered through the blinds at St. Tim's. The frame church—built in 1880, a potential tinderbox—was dark. He pulled on his bathrobe and slippers, padded to the front door to find his brother silhouetted by an unnatural dawn on the horizon.

"Fire," Oscar gasped, "least two dozen houses."

"Was anybody—"

"Don't know, don't know." Oscar bent double, breathing hard, holding his stomach.

Eben stared at the strange glow in the sky. Caught a whiff of smoke.

Sleet peppered the front windows.

Oscar shook his head. "Morrow Street is bad. Real bad, what I heard." A biting wind whipped through the open door.

Dread swept over him. Much of Brooklyn was built of dried-out timbers, the roofs no more than tar paper. Row after row of dilapidated shacks standing like daddy longlegs on brick pilings where wind whipped through.

He threw on slacks and a shirt, his clerical vest and coat, heavy shoes. In the living room he shoved his arms through the sleeves of his winter overcoat, snugged a hat down over his ears, yanked on fur-lined gloves.

Oscar had on his ancient leather windbreaker over a T-shirt, not warm enough for such a night. Eben gave his brother a flannel shirt, knit cap, gloves, and scarf, and handed him the car keys. "Turn on the engine, the defrost. There's an ice scraper under the seat. I'm going to unlock the church, turn up the heat."

The frigid air was heavy with the smell of smoke. He headed across the grass toward the church. His foot slipped on the icy steps and he landed on his bad knee, the pain stunning him. He pulled himself up onto the porch, dry under the overhanging roof.

"You all right?" Oscar called from where he stood, scraping the windshield.

"Yeah, okay," he lied, flexing his leg. He opened the church, turned up the heat, flipped on the outside light. A yellow cone lit the porch, the steps. The front walk glistened; he chose the frosted grass instead, limping with care to the car.

The engine ran sluggishly, the wipers scratching back and forth on the frozen glass, but Oscar had scraped enough for Eben to see directly ahead. "Horrible to be homeless on such a night."

Oscar looked past him at the church. "You gon leave it unlocked, the light on? Anybody can go right in."

"St. Tim's is open to those who need shelter."

The car slid as he turned onto Third. He slowed to a crawl. People stood in scattered clumps watching as flames rose above the rooftops a block away. He pulled up at a rope across the street, a policeman standing guard. The inferno raged, contained, he hoped, by the creek. Water from fire hoses sent silver arcs through the flames. Sirens filled the night air. "More help is coming, thank God," he said.

"Took 'em long enough. Fifteen minutes 'fore the first one showed up." Oscar opened the passenger door and got out.

Hoses saturated the roofs of nearby houses. "Hope that works," Eben said.

"Not gon keep the fire from jumping alleys."

Firemen crisscrossed the street, their bulky figures black against the blaze. One man holding a hose shouted to another, "Pressure's bad. Not enough hydrants." The second man shrugged.

A car horn began to honk in a pattern he recognized instantly, though he hadn't heard it since the war. *Beep-beep-beep BEEP-BEEP-BEEP beep-beep-beep.* The sound came from somewhere not far away.

"Whus zat?"

"SOS."

"I'll go see can I find it." Oscar ran into an alley toward Fourth Street.

At a touch on his arm Eben turned to see Ben Stone. "Benjy, you heard? Not enough water pressure."

"They've got a lot of hoses going. Maybe that's the problem." Ben's breath came out in cloudy puffs.

"The water department is the problem," he said. "Injuries, deaths, anyone—" he couldn't voice the question.

"Don't know. People are missing, some houses on Morrow. Nobody's allowed down there till the fire's under control."

"How many houses?"

Ben's face showed the fear Eben felt. "Fifteen, twenty maybe. Probably started with a coal stove. Night like this, getting warm is all folks can think about. Those old burners, if they get too hot . . ."

The honking continued without pause. "SOS. Oscar's gone to see if he can help," Eben said. His eyes began to smart, and smoke filled his nostrils. He pulled out his handkerchief, dampened it in runoff at the curb, put it over his mouth.

"I'll fetch Hildie, we'll open the store. Folks can get what they need, pay us later," Ben said. He headed up Third toward his grocery.

People huddled together, their faces lit by the fire. "Preacher?" A woman stepped away from the crowd, walked toward him. She had on mismatched shoes, a man's plaid shirt over a pink nightgown. Elmira Swinson from St. Tim's, the choir, the women's circle. Her face was anguished. "My sons live next door to each other down on Morrow."

He put his arms around her, felt her body trembling, touched her wet cheek. "The street's closed off. Soon as we can get through, I'll take you myself."

As if she hadn't heard him, she said, "Both my sons. One of them married, two kids."

A man took her hand, "C'mon, Elmira, your sister's looking for you." They walked away.

An approaching siren grew louder, wound down, ground to a halt. The SOS honking stopped abruptly.

He walked toward the crowd milling in the street. Several people surrounded a woman who sobbed, "My husband, my babies." He recognized her as he got closer. She worked in the Laundromat, married to a man who'd been arrested for breaking and entering. *In prison, isn't he?* "Mrs. Mason?"

She turned to him, tears tracking her ash-grayed face. "Oh, Pastor, they all gone, my man, my two young'uns."

"Your husband, isn't he in—"

"Paroled last week, started work yesterday." She leaned into him. "Dear Jesus, we only had a couple days, the kids so glad to see they daddy."

How could he console such a loss? "There's room at the

parsonage. People will help. We'll take care of you." As she collapsed into his arms he realized how little she was wearing. A bathrobe, nightgown, slippers. He took off his overcoat and put it around her, gave her his gloves and hat.

People in nightclothes stood in the street. *Are they all burned out of their homes?* The icy air bit into him. His knee throbbed.

Oscar walked up. "That car horn. Man broke his leg jumping from a upstairs window, his wife in his arms. Dragged hisself to his car." He coughed. "She not gon make it. Pregnant and burnt to a crisp. Ambulance took 'em away." He looked at the crowd across the street. "You tell 'em the church open?"

He felt a sudden fierce love for his brother. "Yes, of course, I must do that." He wiped his face with the damp handkerchief.

"Please, gather around, folks. St. Timothy's is open, warm. There's hot water, a shower in the upstairs bathroom. Food in the kitchen. More will come when word gets out."

"How we gon get to the church, Pastor?"

"Is there a place my kids can sleep?"

"Clothes? We freezing. Got nothing left."

"How many of us can you take in?"

He called out above the voices. "Who has a car, a truck?"

A man shouted, "I got a pickup, if it ain't burnt."

Ben appeared at his side. "My van's around the corner. Holds at least ten, maybe more. I'll make as many trips as necessary." He handed Eben a paper bag, whispering, "A sandwich, an apple, a Coke, set it aside for later. You gotta eat."

With a gigantic huff another house fell in on itself, sending out a great shower of sparks and a wave of hot air.

A man grasped his hand, doubled over coughing, trying to talk. "Pastor, that's our place just went."

He touched the man's shoulder. "What's your name?"

"Willie Simpson. My wife, my son, my mother-in-law, we lost everything. I ain't got a shirt to wear to work." He stood barefoot in soot-streaked long drawers, a do-rag around his hair. As if realizing how little he had on, the man began to shake.

Eben said, "Get your family and go to St. Tim's. The church and manse are both unlocked. My bedroom's in the manse, clothes, shoes, whatever you can find. Where do you work?"

A woman behind him said, "He on a tree crew, Jones Construction."

"Are you his wife?"

"Yes, sir, Preacher. Orabelle Simpson."

"Y'all go in Ben's van over to St. Tim's. He'll be back for another load soon."

Adrenaline had fueled him, but now the biting wind slashed through his jacket as if he were naked underneath, penetrated his slacks. Even with his brogans on, he'd lost touch with his feet. Not yet five a.m. The sun wouldn't warm the air for at least two more hours. The night felt endless.

Oscar stood off by himself, looking bewildered. Not much he could do, on the edge of living in the street, only out of jail a month this time. Eben went to him. "Noah okay?"

"Yeah, I hope he still sleeping."

When Ben came back, he returned Eben's coat, hat, and gloves. "Mrs. Mason sent these, said someone else would need them."

Three more times during the next several hours, Eben gave his garments away and three more times they came back to him.

By early afternoon the fire was reduced to a smoldering pile of ashes. The smell of burning wood was replaced by a harsh acrid odor that filled Eben's mouth with a foul taste. Firemen walked through the wet black mess, yellow helmets bright amid the ruined remains. Downed electric lines left half of Brooklyn powerless and freezing.

Six city blocks remained roped off. He asked several people about the Swinsons, their houses, but no one knew anything.

Members of St. Tim's came to the church to offer temporary shelter, clothing, food. A woman from the Red Cross stopped Eben in the street. "We'll coordinate with the Salvation Army, see about funds. Tell me what you need. I'll see what we can do." People showed up from St. Paul's Baptist, the AMEs, the House of Prayer, eager to help.

At eight in the evening he got back to the parsonage where he settled a family in the spare bedroom, several more in the living room. He'd left dozens on cots and pallets in St. Tim's. He was weary to the bone, but more than that, angry. Low water pressure. Not enough hydrants. Firefighters slow to respond. He shook his head to prevent himself from screaming in rage.

In the bathroom he shed his clerical vest and tossed it toward the hamper, where it landed on the rim, half in, half out. The collar, blackened by soot, was almost indistinguishable from the vest.

He pushed everything into the hamper. Sat on the side of the tub, his head in his hands. Fourteen dead, a dozen missing. Almost four blocks of Brooklyn in ashes, many more houses beyond repair.

Nettie's throaty voice came to him clearly. "We have to rise when we're least able, and know the Lord is with us."

CHAPTER 20

The news on the radio caught Persy's attention as she sat at her desk in the kitchen, going over a shopping list: "Several blocks of Second Ward were engulfed in flames around one o'clock this morning. Firefighters have contained the fire to Third and Morrow Streets, along Sugar Creek. There are fourteen confirmed deaths, many yet unaccounted for. Property damage is extensive."

She called Blaire at his office.

He answered, sounding breathless and impatient, as he often did when she reached him at work. "Yes, Persy, what is it?"

"There's been an awful fire, I heard on—"

"What? What did you hear?"

"On WBT, the morning news. A fire in Brooklyn, where—"

"Yes, it's horrible, and not unexpected."

"You expected a fire?"

"No, no. I meant it was bound to happen with all those shacks, this freezing weather, decrepit coal stoves." He paused, cleared his throat. "Of course, in a way the fire clarifies things—" She heard a woman say, "Mr. Marshall, a call on line three." Blaire said, "Okay, in a minute. Sorry, Perse, I'm really busy. Anything else?"

"I wanted to be sure you'd heard."

"Thanks. See you tonight." *Click*. Dial tone.

She stood there holding the phone. *Clarifies what?*

Loraylee Hawkins lived near the creek. In the car coming home from the beach, she'd told Persy that in Brooklyn they call it Little Sugar. Persy remembered feeling there was a world she'd never known that existed less than two miles up the creek from her home in Myers Park.

In the confines of the car during the drive from Windy Hill last summer, Persy and Loraylee in front, the little boy, Hawk, in the back, their conversation had at first been restrained. What Persy always thought of as who-are-you stories. After only a short time they became two women whose lives had been incredibly different, even living so near to each other, and they talked a lot about Charlotte. One memory jumped out. When Persy said that Freedom Park was behind her house, Loraylee told her about taking Hawk there on the bus, last year. They would have been right across the creek from Persy and Blaire's backyard. But Loraylee said they only stayed in the park for an hour. "Not a single other colored person there. No signs saying we couldn't be in the park but I felt it." Hawk, oblivious to what this implied, said, "I liked the teeter-totter in that Freedom place."

Persy hadn't known how to respond. *Freedom Park doesn't mean freedom for all.* They'd been silent for several minutes until Hawk spoke up again. "We go to the playground at my school. It's got a teeter-totter *and* a sliding board. Desmond likes the monkey bars."

Persy said, "Oh, yes, your friend. You want to show him your bald spot."

"Yep, that's Desmond."

Loraylee must have sensed the awkwardness. She immediately asked Persy how long she'd lived in Charlotte, and where she'd gone to school. She spoke with pride of her job at the S&W, how happy she was to be working on the serving line. Another connection. Persy had eaten at that cafeteria many times, had no doubt been served by Loraylee.

"They've got great banana pudding," Persy said.

Hawk said, "The chocolate pie is the best."

Persy had wanted to know about Hawk's father, but there was no way of asking that wouldn't have sounded nosy or rude.

The radio continued with updates. The fire was out, with the damage limited to one block of East Third and three blocks of Morrow Street. She got out a map of Charlotte and saw that the fire had not been near Loraylee's house on Brown Street. But she wanted to talk to her, let her know she'd thought of her when she heard about the fire. She finally got an answer a little after three in the afternoon, a man who asked her to hold on. Loraylee came on the line.

"Hey, Loraylee. This is Persy Marshall, we met at the beach last summer when Hawk hurt himself."

"Sure, Mrs. Marshall, how you doing?"

"I'm well, hope you are."

"We all right. I guess you heard about the fire last night."

"That's why I called. I wanted to be sure you were okay."

"We got smoke, but the fire didn't cross the boulevard, and lucky we got power. Lines down everywhere from the ice and the fire. It's bad. School's closed, and Hawk likes that."

"Of course he does. So I guess Mrs. Stokes is okay, too." Persy had told Loraylee about meeting Roberta Stokes, but hadn't mentioned the christening gown.

"Miss Roberta? Yeah, she should be. Might be without power, but the fire didn't get to Myers Street."

* * *

Blaire almost never brought his work to the dinner table, but that evening he had a file open beside his plate, hardly looking up from it as he ate, too involved in it to talk. The page he was studying had a graph with horizontal lines intersecting verticals, dots where the lines crossed, headings at the top, numbers down the side and across the bottom. She finger-walked across the table and tapped a nail on the label of the open file folder, "Renewal Dates." She asked, "What is that?"

He closed the file. "Sorry, I shouldn't be looking at it during dinner. There aren't enough hours in the day right now for me to do all that's needed."

She put down her fork with a thump, louder than she'd intended. "I wish you'd talk to me about what's going on."

He looked at her with a flash of irritation he tried to hide.

"What did you mean when you said on the phone that the fire clarifies things?"

"Oh, that. Well, it clarifies our point that Brooklyn is long overdue for a clean sweep. It's an indication"—he cleared his throat—"an indication of how bad things have gotten there." He pushed his chair back, picked up the folder, thumped the tabletop with it, straightening the papers inside. "Sorry, Perse, I've got so much to do."

"Wait a minute, Blaire. A story in the *News* quoted people in Brooklyn saying there aren't enough fire hydrants, that water pressure was low, that the fire department was slow responding."

Blaire's eyes narrowed, his face flushed. "Multiple alarms went out. Seven trucks responded. Almost fifty firemen, Persy. Fifty. Some had to be treated for smoke inhalation."

"What about the hydrants, the water pressure?"

"You shouldn't trust the *Charlotte News.* They always want to stir things up, you know that." He stood. "Those people in

Brooklyn don't have the means to take care of themselves. We have to see that they have decent housing and schools. We've got to step up and imagine a better way for them."

"They don't all need our assistance."

"You're talking about that seamstress, aren't you, and that girl you brought home from the beach? I understand that some of them are doing okay. But if you'd seen what I have, you'd be the first to want more for them . . ." He went toward the living room. ". . . more than what they have now." He closed the sliding doors behind him.

CHAPTER 21

My back bothering me again, has been since I was carrying Hawk, like being pregnant threw me out of whack. But what's on my hips is probably the blame. Last week I saw myself in the window at Woolworth's and wondered who is that big girl, about to tell her she could look better, but it's me, dressed the best I can in Auntie Roselle's hand-me-downs.

Uncle Ray sees me in something that was Auntie Roselle's, gets quiet, and I know it's a dress he remembers, or a blouse she wore when they went out for the evening, or a scarf he bought for her. He never talks about her, just gets quiet and I know she's in his mind. I was a baby when she died, so I never knew her, though I felt like I did when I came on the trunk with her stuff in it. Some of it real old-fashioned, all of it exactly my right size. But I'd still like to have a dress bought new for me and picked out only because it's pretty.

At supper last night he say, "You reckon rosebushes can be moved?"

He means the ones he planted for Auntie Roselle. "Why you asking?"

"Just got to thinking, the fire has made it easier for the city to run us out."

"What?" Bibi looks like she's about to cry. "Who gon run us out?"

I say, "We staying right where we are, for now, Bibi."

Uncle Ray gets up, puts two slices in the toaster.

Last week I walked down Morrow far as I could, until I got to the barriers put up since the fire. Stood by Little Sugar looking at the burnt-out places people use to live, black sticks jutting up now. All the footbridges folks built across the gullies are gone, too; you couldn't get to a house even if it was still there.

Most places when the city tears down a house or a church, they take every living thing, anything green—trees and grass and bushes and flowers—nothing left but a dirt field, and come the first rain, mud runs off into the sidewalk and streets, coating them with slippery red clay. But that didn't happen where Dicker Phillips and his Morella use to be. For some reason when their house got torn down, the city people left a big oak that's bent in the middle with a flat place you can sit on. Something must of got in its way when it was sprouting, and the tree grew up around whatever that was. Got to have been there a hundred years or more, and I like to think someone with the city had respect for it and let it be.

There aren't yards, no trees or grass over in Fairview Homes or the Courts, where they send families whose houses are already gone, just buildings with folks living on top of each other, packed in like peaches in a can. Maybe you'll see a dried-up bush or two and not a single real house, only what they call apartments but are really cells.

Bibi told me about where she was born, a mill house on Stonewall, lived with her mother, father, her brother, two sisters, and later on with Uncle Vester and their son. Hard to imagine all of them in one small house close to the curb on the boulevard, no yard to speak of, cars whizzing by day and night. And here we are only a couple blocks away, the four of us, a yard out front with a magnolia, and a backyard with a couple of trees, three rosebushes, and the falling-down henhouse by the stoop.

So many things will be lost when we have to move, nothing to do with the reasons the city wants to redevelop—what they're calling it. Get rid of Negroes in downtown Charlotte—what it is. No way we all gon wind up in the same neighborhood. People I've known all my life won't be nearby anymore. Won't be able to walk to the doctor, the dentist, to church, to school. To work. What will happen to the Savoy Theater, St. Tim's, the Queen City Classic, Tocky's, the library, Stone's Grocery? Steadman's Flowers will be closing soon; with Jonny No Age gone, his friend Joseph has tried to sell the shop, but nobody's buying in Second Ward these days—the city will get it eventually—so Joseph's gon move back to Raleigh quick as he can.

Lately, and maybe because of all the talk about how we'll have to move soon, I can't stop thinking about my mama and daddy, wondering what the truth is. Wondering, I guess, what the truth is about me, about where I come from. Mostly wanting to know so I can tell Hawk someday.

Daddy died at a place called Guadalcanal. I imagined it was like the Panama Canal, which I learned about in fourth grade. The teacher pointed to a map and said how important it was for boats to be able to go from the Atlantic to the Pacific without going around South America. I imagined my daddy on an important piece of water that was a cut-through to some other important piece of water. Uncle Ray, who told me about Guadalcanal, say he reckon that might be true but he didn't really know. When I looked it up, I found out it was an island, not a canal at all, and that my daddy was in a terrible place early in World War II. Knowing that made him more real to me than he'd ever been, even in the few memories I have of him: a handsome man who tickled me, making me laugh, same way I do with Hawk.

I want to know about Shushu, once and for all, and that means I have to ask Grand and Pap. Again.

On my next Monday off, I decide to try one more time. It takes me almost an hour to get there, transferring at Johnson C. Smith, then walking another couple of blocks.

Grand answers the door wearing an apron, a delicious smell drifting out around her, making me hungry even before I know I am. "Come on in, girl. Long walk from the bus stop." She puts her short fat arms as far around me as they'll go, say in my ear, "Wish you'd brought Hawk with you."

"He's in school."

"Course he is." She taps her forehead. "My memory isn't what it once was."

"Your memory is great, at least compared to Bibi's." We walk into the living room. "What're you cooking?"

"A roast for this evening. I get one from the A&P on Sundays because they reduce the price. Then we have two-three meals off it." She starts to sit. "Where are my manners? Can I get you a cup of coffee? I've got a pot on the stove."

"I'd like that, thank you."

"Cream and sugar?"

"No, ma'am." She always ask, and I always say the same thing.

She comes back with a tray, and lets out a sigh as she sinks into an easy chair, rubbing her shoulder. "Bursitis. Hurts something awful. And taking aspirin for the pain gives me heartburn." She stretches her arm, moves it around. "All those years writing on the blackboard is what caused it, I reckon."

"Where's Pap?" I ask.

"Gone to his meeting at Tabernacle, a bunch of men who

get together once a week. He says they're doing church business, but mostly they share stories about how things used to be."

I compliment her on the doilies she's crocheted for the chair I'm sitting in, then it comes out: "Grand, I reckon you'd tell me if you'd heard anything from Shushu, but I have to ask."

"I have heard nothing." She gets that set look that say not to go into this again, so I don't. We sit and sip and I like being here, being taken care of by my grandmother, even if she won't tell me about Shushu, or can't, maybe is ashamed she doesn't know anything. When light hits her face in a certain way, or Pap lifts an eyebrow in an expression I know, I see Hawk in them. I'm not going to get what I want from them, so I reckon it's best if I be grateful for what I got.

On my way home I stop by Clancy Tyler's shoe repair, a small, bright shop that smells like leather and polish. I tell Mr. Tyler I need new half soles. He say it'll be a dollar each and I get him down to a dollar fifty for both. New shoes be at least five dollars and that dollar fifty buys me maybe another year on these that are already broken in, important for somebody on her feet all day. New shoes could give me a month of blisters. While we talking a white lady comes in and Mr. Tyler motions to me to stand aside. He knows where his bread's buttered. She say, "Mr. Tyler's work is so good. I used to go to the shoe shop out Providence Road, but I'm glad I found Mr. Tyler. He's better."

I say, "Yes, ma'am," but I'm thinking she comes here because yes, he's good, but mostly because he's cheaper than any Eastover shoe repair.

After she goes, he gets back to me. "She's been coming here for years." He picks up my shoes in his gnarly hands, scarred and twisted from arthritis, but strong. There's a streak of black shoe polish smeared on the kinky white hair above his left ear. He's got to be seventy, I reckon, but sharp. Wish Bibi was.

He looks out the front window. "Got my notice yesterday."

"Mm-mmm." My stomach hurts. "They say when?"

"Give me six months to relocate. Got my eye on a place over in Third Ward."

"Don't you reckon sooner or later they'll get Third, too?"

"They're not saying."

"They're not saying lots of things."

"I'm thinking on it." He picks up his hammer and taps the sole of my shoe. "Might close the shop. Don't know if my white customers will follow me to Third."

"You got lots of whites?"

"Enough. About like Roberta Stokes. She's moving to Third and her ladies gon go with her. That's what they're telling her."

After I leave the shoe shop I walk past Myers Street School. Something going on there this afternoon, maybe that PTA thing Uncle Ray's been doing. He say he's enjoying it. "I am the only man in that group, and the only one over fifty. Those young ladies were astonished when I first joined them, but now I'm one of them. I make them laugh, and we're getting things accomplished. Gon get a new sliding board for the playground, and we're talking about how we might persuade the school board to get us a bus." I'm pleased that Hawk has family in the PTA.

A woman comes toward me on the boulevard, carrying a shoebox. Medium like me. Medium height, medium hips, medium brown, her heels clacking on the pavement. Could be my mother passing me by, same way she left me all those years ago. I want to ask, "Aren't you ashamed you left your baby?"

I wonder have I passed my mother a dozen times, don't have to go to Chicago to find her. Maybe she's right here in Charlotte, just not eager to see me. Or maybe it's not me she left, but my daddy. Everyone's always saying what a good man Ronald Hawkins was. Could be he hurt her bad, she had to run, but that doesn't explain how she could leave her baby girl and never look back.

"Shushu," I wish I could ask her, "didn't you like me? Was I ugly?" I'd touch her face, so like mine, put my nose in her hair, pull her smell into me. She didn't just rob me of a mother when she took off and left her squalling baby girl. No, not just that. She took with her the chance I would ever have a brother or, more what I would want, a sister. I do think on what my sister would be.

If I could talk to Shushu, I'd tell her about our house, about the backyard and how Hawk has made it his own private jungle, about his swing from the maple tree, the rosebushes Uncle Ray planted for his Roselle, the henhouse. Ask her did she know my great-auntie? Uncle Ray got one picture of Roselle. Fair-skinned and pretty in an old-fashioned way, in a black dress, shoulder pads, a white flower in her hair, like Billie Holiday. The way I'd want my sister to look, if I had one.

CHAPTER 22

Eben sat on the bench in the tiny Myers Street park, tuning out the faint rumble of traffic on Independence Boulevard. He sought a rare moment to enjoy the fall colors across the street: the maple he thought of as a flaming tree, if not a burning bush. And the brilliant yellow of the ginkgo—the only one in Second Ward as far as he knew. He hoped he'd be here the day it dropped all its leaves in a golden flurry so unlike the measured shedding of nearby trees. Did whoever planted it live long enough to see it become such a star?

Every so often he caught a whiff of the fire. The smell of burned wood, wet ashes. Even after eight months, he would wake in the night in a terror, thinking he heard Oscar's voice calling out to him. The charred rubble had been cleared, leaving three blocks of blackened flatness along Little Sugar, a block of East Third in ruins. He'd walked down those streets last month, saw the dead ground. But at the creek he was relieved to see the banks covered with grass, cattails, flowers, several hopeful saplings. There'd been an official sign admonishing anyone from trespassing the vacant land. What municipal moron had come up with that idea?

He sat in the sun, twisting his wedding band, a habit since Nettie first put it on his finger. He could see himself walking down the aisle, newly wed, twisting the ring. She'd teased him about this unconscious manipulation, had asked whether he really wanted to wear it, or if perhaps he felt it restricted him in some way. He laughed at her nonsense while he nudged the plain gold band round and round. Almost five years now since her death, he wore it steadfastly, and never once considered removing what was as much a part of his identity as his clerical collar.

From his seat by the sidewalk in the minuscule park—ten by twelve feet of grass, one bench, an azalea, a plaque dedicating the space to Rufus Talford, who voluntarily swept the streets of Second Ward for forty years—he gazed at Myers Street School, thought of all the hundreds of small feet that had traipsed those halls, his own included. A rich history there, with its Jacob's Ladder fire escape where his sixth grade posed proudly for a class picture, the only photo he had of his elementary years. He was struggling to accept the inevitability of bulldozers tearing up Brooklyn, the looming probability of the cemetery being violated; he knew what the community meant to the people he'd vowed to comfort, and ached at the thought of it disappearing forever.

He heard shuffling, hesitant steps and turned to see an old woman with a cane headed his way, eyes down. She stopped, lowered herself heavily onto the other end of the bench with a groan and a sigh. "Oh, my. Oh, my." She rubbed her hip through a voluminous skirt. "Sure am glad to sit for a spell."

"Yes, ma'am. I'm grateful for this bench, too."

"The sun feels so good. Makes me want to lie down in it like I did when I was a girl."

He tilted his head. Sidelong he saw age spots on twisted

hands, ridges of purple veins in the pale skin that conferred such privilege on her. Did she ever think about that? Of course not.

"That collar. You a preacher or something?"

"Yes, ma'am. Reverend Polk of St. Timothy's Second Presbyterian."

"Reverend, huh? Do y'all take confession? No, I guess that's a Catholic thing."

He stopped himself from saying "yes, ma'am" again. "I can offer reconciliation, for those who want it. Not many do."

"Reconciliation? A mighty fancy word for admitting our sins, wouldn't you say?" She rubbed her hip again.

"Arthritis?"

She looked toward the skyline of Charlotte. That she hadn't answered him made him uneasy, but he waited.

The quiet filled with birdsong, a faint diminishing siren—trouble somewhere.

"Okay, yes," the woman said.

"Yes, arthritis?"

"I do have arthritis, but I sat down here because of your collar." She stopped, dropped her head, fiddled with the cloth of her skirt. "Reconciliation? Is that what I get if I confess?"

"That's possible. There's no guarantee, of course."

"Catholics promise absolution. Not sure about Presbyterians. I reckon you'll give me a penance, too." The skin of her face sagged as if gravity affected her more than most. A pinkish flaky residue filled the lines to either side of her nose. Her eyes, a watery hazel, had bruise-like depressions under them that she'd apparently tried to hide with powder. She yawned, exposing teeth too perfect to be real, evoking in him an unfathomable pity.

"Our church suggests penance, but I don't try to tell anyone what they must do to absolve themselves of guilt."

"Who said anything about guilt?" She shifted away. An odor came from her, fetid, as if part of her was dying.

"Sorry." He stood. "I must get back to work. I'm in my office at St. Tim's, over on McDowell, if you—"

Her laugh was loud, more of a bray. "Can't take the heat, huh?"

"I beg your pardon?" He felt a need to escape. "Good day, ma'am."

She pushed herself up off the bench with one hand on the painted planks, the other on her cane, banging it on the paving. The rubber tip made dull thumps as she pumped it up and down.

"All right." He sat back down. "I suppose I can take confession on a park bench."

The woman walked a few paces, pounding her cane on the unforgiving sidewalk. She looked over her shoulder. "You'll do." She sat down as far away from him as she could get on the narrow bench. Surely half her hip must be off the end of the plank seat. "Cancer. It's my fault and I cannot sleep for thinking about that. If I hadn't smoked all those years, and if I'd eaten right, exercised properly. The doctor tells me I might have got it anyway, but I don't believe him."

"Why would you believe me?"

"Because you're a man of God."

If only she knew his doubts. If she knew that he stayed away from those parts of the Bible he didn't like. That his followers would desert him if they learned of his misgivings. "Having cancer isn't something to confess."

"Hating my husband is."

Her abrupt shift rattled him. "What does your husband have to do with your cancer?"

"I wouldn't have smoked if it hadn't been for him. And now that my lungs are rotting, he keeps on smoking, blowing it in my face. I hate him for giving me my first cigarette and for smoking when I can't."

He put his finger inside his collar, pulled it away from his neck. "Maybe I can help you with the hate you're feeling."

"Don't need help with hating. That's easy. But I sure don't like it that I have to live with someone I hate. Don't like that one bit." She tapped her cane on the sidewalk again, as if the motion gave her solace.

"Why do you stay with him?"

"He pays the bills, plain and simple. Nowhere else for me to go. Kids won't have me, family won't have me."

That no one would want her, this was something he could understand. Her problems went too deep for any ministration he might offer, but it would be wrong to walk away without giving her consolation. That was his job. Even if she wasn't in his church, she was in the congregation of humanity. "Where are your children, your family, here in Charlotte?"

Again that derisive, dismissive laugh. "They got out as soon as they could. Daughter in California, son in Hawaii, a beach bum I'm sure."

"Any other family?"

She shook her head. "Maybe my sister is still alive, in Virginia, but I haven't heard of her in many years."

Her misery touched a chord in him, resonated with his own sense of aloneness. "So I gather that your husband is the only family you have now."

"Such as he is."

"You must have loved him to have married him."

"Sure, before he changed."

A fleeting notion crossed his mind. His only stumbling block was his lack of belief that he could help her. That he could help her, help Brooklyn, that he could relieve the members of St. Tim's of the pain of relocation. Could keep the graveyard intact—was it really so simple that all he had to do was believe?

"And you," she asked. "What of your family, where are they?"

Her question startled him. Oscar's future unknown. And Noah, who was back with his father, though that could change any day. "My family are mostly—"

She got to her feet. "What am I to do?"

He understood: He could help her but he couldn't change her fate. Couldn't change his own fate, couldn't have saved Nettie even if he'd known about the cancer when it was just one twisted cell in her womb. Couldn't keep the bulldozers away from St. Tim's. Could only do what he'd been doing all his life, offer comfort. He took the old woman's hand. "Pray for forgiveness in your heart. That'll bring you peace."

She looked hopeful. "Pray to forgive or to be forgiven?"

"Both." He stood, touched her shoulder. Enough, this was enough.

"All right." In a three-pointed gait she headed toward Independence, cane, left foot, right foot.

He walked back to the manse with a buoyancy he hadn't felt in months. He took a shortcut through Bell Court, passing the house where the Swinson family had settled after the fire. Elmira had planted a determined garden behind the shotgun houses that fronted First Street. Over the summer, with little evidence of a design, she'd created an explosion of blossoms, many still blooming on this fall day. The colorful clusters put him in mind of the ladies' hats he saw from his pulpit every Sunday.

CHAPTER 23

"You'll meet Noah today." Blaire started the car. "The kid at the parking lot."

"The car wash boy you've talked about?" Persy asked, settling into the passenger seat. "How old is he?"

"Not easy to tell with blacks, you know?"

She wasn't sure about that. "A guess?"

"Maybe thirteen when I met him last year. Some holiday. Washington's birthday? Anyway, out of school. Came running up, toting pail, brushes, sponges." Blaire's voice goes high, mocking the words, "Wash yo car, mister? I'm de bess in Charlotte, anybody tell you, Noah Polk's a first-class car wash boy."

His mimicry made her uncomfortable.

"Mitchell says Noah's okay." Blaire had worked with Mitchell Spalding, the city attorney, since leaving private practice.

When they pulled into the College Street lot, a raw-boned black boy ran up, his eyes large. He waved, saying something they couldn't hear, sealed in the warm car, the heater going full blast, morning news on the radio. She nudged Blaire. He leaned forward to pull his wallet from his back pocket, extracted two dollars. "Half goes to Danny," he told her.

"Who's Danny?"

"Guy who runs the lot."

She wondered what a dollar meant to the boy.

On that bright February afternoon, Noah didn't seem to have the slightest awareness of the frosty air. There was only the dirty car in need of cleaning, and his head in need of a hat. She and Blaire had other concerns beyond crumbs on the passenger-side floor mat, an overflowing ashtray, and bird droppings on the hood from the tree beside their driveway.

Blaire gave the keys to Noah. "Soon as you're done, you give these to Danny, okay?"

"Yes, sir. Yes, sir. Yo car safe with me, Mista Marshall."

"I'm sure it is." Blaire paid ten dollars a month for parking in the lot, and often said it was highway robbery. In fact, the rate was much less than what he would pay for parking in the town lot behind his offices, and included unlimited ins and outs, an assigned parking space, and the dependable boy who sang while he worked.

They started for the County Courthouse on East Trade, walking swiftly to stay warm, with Blaire shifting his twenty-pound briefcase from hand to hand. For seventeen minutes morning and evening, he could not do a blessed thing but walk. He'd told Persy how much he hated wasting time, but having no choice, he put one well-shod foot in front of the other. Black wingtips on a court day like this, and brown oxfords otherwise. The smooth leather reflected his sensibility, his choice of what looked right as opposed to what pleased him. If he lived in a world where there were no penalties for nonconformance, he'd be wearing suede derbies, slender across the toe. Persy wondered if Blaire guessed that she knew these intimate things about him.

She looked at trains on spurs as they crossed Brevard. The windows of four sleek passenger cars showed the indistinct faces of travelers heading out of Charlotte. What would happen if, one morning, she and Blaire got on the nearest one? A witness had done that a month ago, skipping out of a deposition at the last minute, leaving four attorneys cooling their heels. Blaire said he'd known most of what the absent witness would have added to the facts of that case, but had been looking forward to going fishing to see what might pop up.

In law school, one of his professors had preached a common dictum: "In court, never ask a witness any question to which you don't already know the answer." Blaire said he'd secretly believed the professor a fatuous fool, but nonetheless took the advice to heart until he accepted the truth of legal Q&A. There were questions he had to ask to which he could not possibly know the answer. His hope was that opposing counsel believed the dictum.

He broke the silence. "Today's hearing is to get a temporary restraining order. I hope you're not bored."

"Why would I be? What's the case?"

"The city wants a certain property. The title appeared to be free and clear until a lien holder showed up. If the claim is valid, the debt has to be satisfied before any sale."

"How was it discovered?"

"We got a copy of the lien from the fellow's lawyer. It's Jerry Parker, by the way."

"Wow, old home week. Wasn't there a title search?"

Blaire looked at her. "You've picked up some things along the way."

"I remember the search when we bought on Sterling."

"The lien holder may be trying to pull something, but he has what appears to be a legitimate document from over twenty years ago. It didn't show up until he did."

"Where's the property?" They were approaching the courthouse.

"All will be revealed in the fullness of time. Maybe you won't be bored, after all."

A clerk in the courthouse told Blaire, "Sorry, Mr. Marshall, but the only space available this morning is Courtroom Seven, and there's a jury trial due to start there at ten. Y'all be done by then?"

"I guess we'll have to be. Are the parties here?"

"Everyone's in Seven, getting ready."

Persy would have preferred anonymity, but being the only observer in the courtroom made her presence obvious. The defense attorney, Jerry Parker, a partner in Blaire's former firm, greeted her. "Hey, Persy, what brings you here?"

"Good to see you, Jerry. I enjoy sitting in on Blaire's trial work whenever I can."

Blaire said, "I told her today's hearing will be a big bore."

Jerry raised his eyebrows. "You may be wrong about that, Blaire."

Persy sat toward the back to be inconspicuous, but could hear what was going on as clearly as if she were seated beside Blaire. He and Jerry, now adversaries, were still friends outside the courtroom, often played golf together. She'd almost become used to this paradox among lawyers.

The judge convened the hearing. "Consideration of a temporary restraining order."

The lien holder was sworn in, stating his name, "Laird Carson." Persy felt an instant dislike of the small man, his oiled hair, his eyes flitting back and forth.

Parker established Carson's name and residence, and that he held a lien of forty thousand dollars pursuant to a loan he made to a property owner in 1941. A document detailing the debt was marked as evidence of the transaction.

"Mr. Carson, for the record, what is the address of the

property on Exhibit One that's now up for sale to the city?" Parker asked his client.

Blaire held up his hand. "Objection. Based on a fact that hasn't been established."

Before the judge could rule, Parker turned to Blaire, "Oh, c'mon, Blaire. We all know the city wants it. That's why we're here."

"Establish it for the record and I'll withdraw my objection."

The judge said, "Fair enough."

Parker consulted a paper, then asked the witness, "Where is the subject property?"

"Five-seventeen East Third Street."

Persy thought the address was in Second Ward, might be in Brooklyn.

"And what is on the property at that address?"

"Wholesale Auto Body Parts, or it used to be. Closed now."

"Is the property for sale?"

"Yeah, the owner put out a sign last month."

"Is there a prospective buyer?" Parker sounded smug.

"I heard the city wants it."

Parker nodded at Blaire. "With regard to Exhibit One, your interest is an outstanding lien for forty thousand dollars, is that correct?"

"It is."

After a few more questions about the history of the property, Jerry spoke to the judge. "That's all I have at this point."

Blaire began his examination of Mr. Carson slowly. Persy smiled to herself. Blaire could put someone at ease, then attack before the witness knew what hit him.

"Mr. Carson, Exhibit One represents a lien you took on the property in, let me see, I believe it was January of 1941, so twenty-three years ago, is that correct?"

"That's right."

"In the amount of some forty thousand dollars?"

"Yes, sir."

"A sizeable sum of money in 1941, wouldn't you say?"

"Objection, calls for a conclusion," said Jerry Parker.

"Sustained," said the judge. "Can you restate the question?"

"Never mind." Blaire consulted his notes, appeared to be in deep thought, then said, "I want to clarify. Were you present when the lien was executed, or was the loan carried out by an intermediary?"

Carson cleared his throat. "An intermediary, I guess you could call him. My attorney."

"And is your then counsel now deceased?"

"Yes."

"The property owner who borrowed forty thousand dollars from you, he's dead as well, is that correct?"

"That's right, and that's why . . ." At a look from Parker, Carson stopped.

"That's why, what?"

"Nothing. I got the lien papers after he died, that's all."

"Are you saying you forgot about the debt until the papers showed up?"

"No, no, didn't forget, but . . ." His voice dropped off.

"Because it would be hard to forget such a sum, right? Are you a wealthy man, Mr. Carson?"

Parker stared out the window, his voice flat. "Immaterial."

"Noted," the judge said.

"Let me ask it another way. When you received the papers upon your former counselor's death, did you then remember the transaction?"

"Asked and answered." Parker sounded bored.

"Asked and evaded, is more like it," Blaire mumbled.

"Sir?" the court reporter asked.

"Counsel's opinion is irrelevant and insulting." Parker yawned.

The reporter's fingers moved on her keyboard.

Exhibit One appeared to be a legal document. The judge issued a temporary restraining order, pending an additional title search; if the lien was upheld, the sale of the property to the City of Charlotte could not proceed until the debt was satisfied. As Persy and Blaire left the courthouse, Blaire said, "I don't think another search will clear things up."

"Then what? Right back where you started?"

"Not exactly. I believe we need to look more closely at Mr. Carson."

As they headed back to the parking lot, Persy asked, "The disputed property is in Second Ward, right?"

"It is."

"Brooklyn?"

Blaire started to cross Brevard, stepped back on the curb when the signal turned red. "On the periphery, but yes."

"So that's why the city is buying the property, urban renewal."

"Sure. We're getting as much as we can while it's affordable."

"Does Carson know about the redevelopment?"

"It's no secret."

They both knew that wasn't an answer, but Persy let it drop. They walked toward the parking lot in silence until Blaire stopped in the middle of the sidewalk on College Street. "He's double dealing!"

"Who? How?"

"Carson. Something's fishy. He didn't seek payment of a sizable lien for twenty-three years. Why? And how come the first title search showed no debt?"

"Would that depend on who did the search?"

Blaire looked at her with new respect. "It was a guy in Parker's office."

"Does Parker have anything to benefit from this?"

"His fee, obviously. No, no, Jerry Parker's as honest as they come, wouldn't hide a lien if he knew it existed. But someone . . ." He paused, twisted his mouth. "Okay, here's the deal. I think Carson collected the debt years ago. The original seller's dead, the attorney's dead. If the lien was satisfied by cash or check, and if there's no record of the transaction, well . . ."

"My word, he's trying to collect again."

"That's my suspicion. If I can prove it, the city can buy up the tract at a bargain."

"And Mr. Carson?"

"Goes straight to jail, does not pass Go, does not collect two hundred dollars."

"Or another forty thousand."

"You got it." He stopped at the car. "I'll go get the keys, be right back."

Persy waved to the boy Noah as they pulled out of the lot. He waved back, a wistful look on his face.

Blaire turned onto College, headed toward Trade. Persy asked, "I'd like to ride by the property, it's on our way."

"Why?"

"I'm curious, having heard so much about it."

"Not much to see."

Blaire was right. Two ramshackle buildings on East Third with faded words, WHOLESALE AUTO BODY PARTS.

They sat out front for a minute.

Persy said, "Indulge me. Go down Third to Myers. I want to show you something." But as soon as they turned onto Myers, Persy regretted it. They passed houses that looked unlivable, crumbling chimneys, dirt yards, broken windows.

She would have assumed the dwellings were abandoned if she hadn't seen a woman hanging clothes on a line and children in a front door watching them ride by.

Blaire said, "Persy, we have to help these people."

They passed a storefront advertising coal and fuel, a poolroom, shoe repair, grocery, a café. "But look at all these businesses," Persy said. "And there, drive down the next block." They came to where there should have been a row of pastel cottages, but the only one that remained appeared to be in a state of flux. The picket fence was in sections, the windows of the cottage blank, the bushes uprooted and lying in the front yard. "Oh, no, Roberta's house is gone."

"Yes, renewal began here months ago. It has to happen, Perse. Brooklyn is over seventy percent blight. That's a fact."

Persy was quiet the rest of the way home.

CHAPTER 24

Dooby Franklin is in his porch rocker, staring off like he's sleeping with his eyes open. Not rocking, his stick legs bent at the knee, his belly bulging under the arms of the chair. I holler "hey" to him but he doesn't even turn his head, just looks at a piece of paper he's holding. "Dooby?" I call out again. He crumples the paper into a ball, tosses it in the dirt.

I walk down our front steps, cross the yard, pick up the paper. Dooby pushes himself up. "Got my letter. They give me three months." He opens his door and goes inside.

The letter is dated June 12, 1964, from the Redevelopment Commission of Charlotte, telling him he's got to find a place to live and move out, that his house gon be torn down in three months.

I put the wrinkled paper on his rocker and go home. Uncle Ray is in the kitchen, trying to fix the toaster that burned out yesterday, got it torn apart with stuff all over the table. Bibi's sitting there watching him, frowning. "No more toast coming from that piece of junk," she say.

I suspect she right. "Dooby got his letter this morning."

"His letter?" Bibi ask.

Uncle Ray pats her shoulder. "Where'd you put my pliers you were using yesterday?"

"Oh. Maybe I left them in the bathroom."

She gets up and walks down the hall. I can't think what she'd be doing with pliers in the bathroom.

"How's he doing?" Uncle Ray asks, looking out the window toward Dooby's house.

I shake my head.

"I'll give him some time before I visit."

The next morning after breakfast Uncle Ray goes over to see Dooby. After a short while he comes back. One look tells me something is awful. His skin's gray, his hands shaking. He passes me without a word and picks up the phone in the hall. I hear him dial, say, "Operator? Get me the police. No, an ambulance. No, the police." A pause, then, "Yes, ma'am, emergency. I got to report a death."

When he gets himself calmed down, Uncle Ray tells me he got to Dooby's house, got no answer at the door and went on in. "I called out to him, had to push junk aside and climb over it so I could get down the hall to his bedroom. Found him on the floor on his belly. Dead. Still holding a needle."

"A needle? What you mean?"

"Like for shooting up, but I can't figure Dooby doing that." Uncle Ray shakes his head. "Doesn't seem right, but maybe."

I fix him some ice tea.

He holds the glass with both hands. "Dooby hasn't thrown away a paper in fifty years. Stuff stacked everywhere, magazines, cans, dirty clothes, shoes. I stepped on a dead mouse. Those cats of his running free. Gotta be a dozen." Uncle Ray pulls his handkerchief from his pocket, wipes his eyes, blows his nose. "Had him a path to the kitchen, the bathroom. Stinks bad in there, almost couldn't breathe." He slumps into his chair. "No wonder he never let anybody in his house. No wonder. How can a person live like that?"

Pretty soon we hear sirens. First the police, then an ambulance, then more police. We watch from the porch as they take Dooby out, a huge lump on a stretcher, four men carrying it to the ambulance.

Cats scatter in the neighborhood, yowling, hungry. Neighbors set out food for them, but a man from the pound shows up, starts tossing them in his truck.

City people come and go, men with clipboards, standing in the yard, talking. One man shouts, "I say bulldoze the whole thing, junk and all."

Another say, "I'm not going back inside. Rats everywhere."

Dooby has been dead two days when a woman knocks at our door saying she's his sister. Thin, so different from her brother I would never guess they were related. A fine maroon coat with velvet collar and cuffs, black hat, leather gloves, but she doesn't have airs when she introduces herself as Irene Scoville Franklin, from Alexandria, Virginia.

I invite her in. "Would you like a glass of tea?"

She takes Uncle Ray's chair by the front door. "No, thank you. But of course I do have some questions, if you have the time?"

"Sure." I sit on the sofa.

She takes off her gloves, puts them in her pocket. "I understand you were the last person to talk with James."

"James?"

"Dooby. My brother."

All those years we never knew his real name. "Yes, the day before . . ."

"The coroner says he died of a heart attack, and I don't question that, given his weight, his diabetes."

"Diabetes? Was he taking shots for it?"

"Yes, apparently every day."

"My uncle Ray, the one who found Dooby, will be glad to know that's what the needle was all about."

"Found him?"

"Yes, ma'am, after he passed. Holding a needle."

She's quiet, her face so sad.

"He was upset about the letter."

"What letter?"

I'm wondering how in the world she doesn't know about that. "From the city, telling him he had to move in ninety days. He got it the day before he died."

She stands. "That explains a lot. He may have taken twice the amount of insulin that morning." She puts her hand on the doorknob. "I've given the city permission to do whatever is necessary with the house. They're going to bring in an exterminator, haul away the trash, then tear it down. I'm making arrangements for a service. James didn't have a church, not that I can determine, but the minister at Friendship Baptist—"

"Reverend Coates."

"Yes. He's agreed to officiate and our family has two plots left at Pinewood. James gets one of them."

She picks up her purse, fixing to leave, looking tired, edgy. I reach out, touch her arm. "Would be no trouble for me to fix you a glass of tea. Why don't you sit back down for a bit?"

She looks around like she forgot where she is, and I wish I could make it easier for her. She has lost her brother, maybe her only family. She falls back into Uncle Ray's chair, touches a hankie to the tears on her cheeks. "We hadn't been close, not since our parents died, all those years ago. I wish I'd known about his—" She hesitates like she's not sure how much I know. "About the way he was living."

"That's not your fault."

"No." Her voice catches in her throat and she sits quiet for a minute. "But it's awful, beyond anything I could have imagined." She blows her nose. "Yes, a glass of tea, if it's not too much trouble."

"No, ma'am, not one bit. Come on in the kitchen."

She laughs. "Ma'am? I grew up in Blue Heaven. Went to Second Ward High. But it is strange being back here." She follows me, takes a seat at the table. I get the tea jug from the refrigerator.

She looks out the window. "Your house, is it . . . are you . . ."

"Haven't got a letter. But it's only a matter of time."

"Where will you go?"

"We thinking on it, thinking on it." I get glasses from the cabinet. "What do you do in—where was it you say you live?"

"Alexandria, Virginia, but I work in DC, in the Government Accounting Office. What about you?"

"I'm at the S&W Cafeteria on the Square, ten years now. I'm on the serving line."

She picks up a toy truck Hawk left on the table. "You have children?"

"One boy, Hawk. He's nine, fourth grade at Myers Street School. You know it?"

"Went there myself."

"Do you have children?"

She shakes her head. "I chose a career, never married." Dooby's sister finishes her tea, says goodbye.

As she goes down the front walk, stepping around the magnolia limbs, getting in her shiny blue car, I wonder what it's like living in Virginia, working for the government. I watch as she drives away.

CHAPTER 25

An odor assaulted Eben inside the front door of the manse. Mildew, which he'd smelled for weeks, but stronger than it had been. Where was it coming from? Perhaps a plumbing leak in the basement. Before he reached the bottom of the wooden stairs, he saw standing water, glittering in the gaunt light from narrow windows near the ceiling. He sat on the steps, removed his leather shoes and socks, stepped barefoot into frigid water, an inch, maybe more. What had been on the floor that would now be ruined? Had water gotten into the coal bin? If so, the furnace wouldn't run and he'd soon be needing it. The coal delivery chute ran through an opening in the top of the bin, which was otherwise covered tight, secured by a latch attached to a cross beam. Using all the strength he could muster, he shoved the bin an inch or two away from the wall. The rusty latch gave way. He lifted the lid. There wasn't much coal—he'd planned to get a delivery next week—but what was there was soaked, mildew climbing the walls of the bin.

"Well," he said aloud, "that's that." As he turned away,

something caught his eye, a flash of faint color behind the bin. With his face against the wall, he reached as far as he could, but couldn't dislodge whatever was there. He sloshed over to the tool bench, turned on a work lamp hanging from a hook, took it to the bin. The wavering beam illuminated a book.

With a pipe wrench as a lever, he shoved the coal box a bit more from the wall, reached in and retrieved the book. REGISTER in murky letters across stained leather. His legs trembled. He sank down on the bottom of the basement steps.

Upstairs the phone rang and rang. Eben sat for a long while, the ancient book on his knees, caressing the damp leather. He started to open it, but the cover bent, began to tear from the spine. "No!" he shouted. With the book in his right hand, he pulled himself up by the railing, climbed slowly to the first floor of the manse, getting there as the phone stopped ringing. He spread a thick towel on the kitchen table and put the book on it, pressing to release moisture. Who would value the treasure he'd uncovered, would honor it?

Georgie Bee. She'd know what to do with this precious relic. He dialed the number for her brother's house. When he reached her, she laughed, "I just tried to call you."

"Oh, that's crazy. I was in the basement, heard the phone but couldn't get to it."

"You sound excited."

He sat down, calming himself. "Could you possibly come over here? I've got something to show you, don't know what to do with it, but I'm sure it's important."

"I'll be there in ten minutes."

He was still sitting at the kitchen table when the doorbell rang. He walked into the living room, saw Georgeanne through the screen door. "C'mon in." He felt awkward greeting her in his bare feet.

She touched his arm. "Eben, what in the world? You look like you've seen a ghost."

"I might have. The ghost of Reverend Tilley."

She followed him through the dining room. "Where are your shoes?"

Of course she would notice. "On the basement stairs. Got a problem with water down there."

At the kitchen door she saw the book, reached for it.

"Don't! It's wet, fragile. We've got to figure out how to dry it before we open it."

"What is it?"

They sat at the table. "The register Reverend Tilley told me about, the night he died. Said it was in the basement, behind the coal bin. I thought he meant St. Tim's. Never occurred to me he was talking about the manse, until today, when a problem in the basement forced me—" He shook his head.

"Oh, my. Did he say what was in it?"

"He—I mean, I didn't put a lot of faith in what he said at the end. He was rambling, something about slaves running off, empty graves. Oh, and that what was once vital wouldn't matter after a while."

Georgeanne touched the damp towel. "I wonder how we should go about drying it."

"After I called you I remembered someone who might know what we should do, an anthropologist interested in the graveyard. He'd know about preserving things."

"Let's call him."

Marion Lipscomb was, if anything, more excited than Eben or Georgeanne by the discovery of the register. He inspected it cautiously, his eyes large beneath bushy colorless eyebrows. "I'm in a field where time takes on a new meaning. The time that things have been latent, for example, can be anywhere from days to millennia. Then there's the time that must be respected in the process of extraction. I've seen delicate fragments ruined by hasty hands. When something like this is discovered"—he gestured to the damp book on Eben's kitchen table—"rushing risks destruction." He raised his arms, twirled with glee in the small kitchen, shouted, "Oh! This is a great day. Give me an hour, and I'll bring you what you need to dry this precious book. I promise you we will uncover its mysteries." He ran through the house, slamming the front door behind him.

"Wow," said Georgeanne, "the man's a whirlwind."

"He is that, and his enthusiasm's contagious."

"Is he albino? I've never seen such white hair."

"Don't albinos have pink eyes? Anyway, I'm glad we called him."

Less than an hour later Marion returned with an impressive array of tools: an oscillating table fan, two rolls of paper towels, a variety of tweezers from the most delicate—what might be used to extract an errant eyebrow—to needle-nose pliers. He laid out an assortment of wooden blades so thin they were almost transparent, magnifying glasses, and a canvas cylinder he unrolled to reveal a dozen brushes of various sizes.

"Now we go to work," he said, setting the fan on the kitchen table. "We'll run it day and night on the lowest setting, rotating back and forth to create a gentle breeze. When the cover is dry enough to lift, we'll use these"—he held up a wooden blade, the smallest tweezers—"to insert a paper towel between the cover and the first page. As the drying proceeds—and it will, be assured—we go to the second page, etc."

A week later, under Marion's expert guidance, at the cost of two rolls of paper towels and arduous patience, the register was dry, though permanently bloated. As if returning from the dead, its color was restored: the word REGISTER in rusty red on brown leather, the spine of black cloth, the pages edged in tarnished gold. It sat there on the kitchen table, framed on three sides by paper towels.

They all wore thin cotton gloves Marion had provided.

"Ready?" Marion asked.

"Ready!" Eben and Georgeanne spoke simultaneously.

Marion lifted the cover, removed the first paper towel to reveal a bold flourish across the title page: "Second Presbyterian Church Colored, Charlotte, North Carolina." And below that, "Register of Members Beginning in the Year of our Lord 1842."

Eben said, "According to the church Bible, St. Timothy's was added to the name after the Civil War. Until then, it was simply Second Presbyterian. This confirms that."

"My goodness," said Georgeanne, "I had no idea the church was well over a century old."

"As an institution it's a hundred and twenty-one. In the early years members met in homes in what was then called Logtown, renamed as Brooklyn at some point after the Civil War. By 1880, they had enough money to buy a new two-story house as a permanent location for what is today St. Timothy's Second Presbyterian. The history's in the King James Bible we keep at the pulpit."

Marion inserted the wooden blade, lifted the title page with the tweezers, removed the next paper towel. The second page was a crude map of the cemetery with plots sketched in and numbered, but the last two inches, where it had been soaked, was illegible.

"What a shame," Georgeanne said. "But at least we'll be able to label many of the graves, assuming there's a link to the numbered plots."

The third page was columned and covered in a feathery script, the top clearly legible, the bottom a smear of ink.

Georgeanne touched the soiled lines with a gloved finger, and asked Marion, "Is there any way to decipher this mess, to look under or through where the ink has run?"

He shook his head. "Nothing I know of, and that's a shame."

"It is indeed," Eben said, "but let's see what we can read and go from there."

The seven columns were headed in neat capital letters, repeated on every page: NOMINE, LOCUS, RITES, BIRTH, DEATH, BURIAL, DATUM.

"It's fascinating to me, the mix of Latin," Marion said. "Wonder what that's about?"

"Scholarship," said Eben. "Whoever started the ledger was learned, and wanted that known."

Under "Locus" some entries gave nothing more than "Charlotte, North Carolina," or "Spratt Plantation, Mecklenburg County," but there were some exact street addresses such as 719 East Second Street, LT.

Eben said, " 'LT' must have stood for Logtown."

"Rites" included baptism and communion. Under "Death" was a date and numbers that corresponded to the map of the cemetery. The column headed "Datum" had three mixed alphanumerics.

"A code," said Marion.

"Obviously important to whoever began the register," said Georgeanne, "but signifying what? Children? Siblings? Marriages?"

Marion disagreed. "It's got to be more than that."

"Look at the fourth and fifth entries, right before the illegible lines." Eben pointed to the first page. "Dated 1842. 'Manning Tilley,' born that same year, date of death blank. That could be Reverend Tilley's father or grandfather. And below that, 'Elisa Tilley nee Younger, born 1847, died 1873.' Locus for both, 'Tilley Plantation, Charleston, South Carolina.'" He stretched his stiff leg under the table, accidentally kicking Georgeanne. She reached over to pat his thigh, a gesture he found thoroughly pleasant. He smiled at her. "Younger Tilley grew up on the South Carolina coast," he continued, "so these must be his parents, but why in the world are slaves on a plantation in Charleston listed in a register in Charlotte?"

Georgeanne said, "I've been going through that box I got from you, dated 1880 to 1910. Found some papers with information on the Tilley family." She put her briefcase on an empty chair, opened it, and pulled out several file folders. "Manning apparently became a thorn in the side of his master when he fell in love with Elisa Younger, a slave girl fancied by their owner—one Eliott Tilley. Manning was sold 'up south,' to a plantation near Waxhaw, where he was freed. Nothing more is known of him."

"So he's not Reverend Tilley's father?" Marion asked.

"Apparently not. Their only connection is the name they share from the plantation. Elisa had a child, our Reverend Younger Tilley, in 1863, fathered by her master, as was too often the case."

Marion looked at the register. "When she was only sixteen."

"Yes, probably taken against her will."

"And someone," Eben added, "wanted to be sure the Tilley line was recorded in the register. Strange."

"Not really," said Georgeanne. "Manning was here—I mean at least he was in Waxhaw. Had become a free man. Could have settled in Charlotte. And he loved Elisa. Perhaps he got his birth date recorded in the register and added Elisa's, given that he thought of her as his wife—certainly his beloved—whether or not they were ever married."

They sat in silence until Eben stood. "I need to stretch a bit. One thing is clear: We now know why Reverend Tilley was so light skinned. He's one of those colored men who could have passed and chose not to. Makes me admire him even more than I already did." He laughed. "And that name, Younger. Sounded odd to me when I first heard it. Got used to it, though." He went to the kitchen sink, ran water into a percolator.

"No coffee for me, thanks. Too late in the day, and I've got to go. Tomorrow?" Marion yawned, got up, rubbed his astonishing platinum hair.

"Sunday, it will have to be after three in the afternoon for me." Eben turned on the stove.

"Fine with me, see you then."

After Marion left, Georgeanne said, "I've been reading the statutes, Eben, and they're not in your favor where the cemetery is concerned. The city will have domain over St. Tim's and the cemetery, though they will have to pay for everything, removal of the bodies, re-interment, etc. Of course, they'll find a legal way to do the minimum necessary."

He put the pot on the stove. "Yes, that's inevitable. What bothers me most is those who don't have my options."

"Options?" She got cups from the cabinet, put milk on the table for Eben.

"I've found a potential new home for St. Tim's, a small church that's in trouble financially. We've been talking." He watched the percolator, changing the subject abruptly. "Have you seen anything in those papers about a John Thomas Quarry?"

"Doesn't ring a bell." She sat back down. "You mean that stone at the back of the graveyard, JTQ?"

"That's the one. Reverend Tilley told me there's no one

buried there, that the stone with 'JTQ' etched in it was a ruse, that Quarry supposedly died but instead left town."

"I'm only about halfway through the papers," Georgeanne said. "I'll let you know if I come upon anything about him. Quarry? Like a rock quarry?"

"To the best of my memory." He poured the coffee, added milk to his, sat down across from her. "How much longer will you be here?"

"Fall break ends Wednesday, but I'm looking into moving back to Charlotte. There's a position open at Johnson C. Smith." She touched the register. "It's quite attractive to me. I'd be working with poli-sci students, teaching American constitutional law."

"With what emphasis?"

"How government works within constitutional limits. Contemporary problems. Civil rights in particular, my special interest."

"Soon?"

"I have a lot to wrap up in Durham, but yes, classes start right after New Year's."

He decided not to question what she had to wrap up. There was time for that.

Eben was unbearably bored with the task of writing this week's sermon on the importance of godly work. He'd chosen the readings, music for the offertory, and the hymns. "Jacob's Ladder" seemed especially appropriate, given the recent seventy-fifth anniversary of Myers Street School. But the message needed refinement, focus, a parable with which to bring it to a close. From his office above the choir loft, he heard the voices of children in the sanctuary. Happy at the interruption, he descended the stairs.

The Hucks twins, Mary and Martha, were pushing

brooms around the foyer. A pleasant tang filled the air as Mrs. Hucks cleaned windowpanes with vinegar-soaked newspaper. At his step she turned. "Good afternoon, Preacher. Hope we not disturbing you. I got the girls doing work for the Lord today."

Godly work. "They seem to be enjoying themselves."

"Hey, Pastor Polk." Mary stood with her broom at attention as her sister continued sweeping, head down.

How could identical twins differ so in personality? "Hello, Mary. How're you doing, Martha?" The shy twin swept dust from a corner.

Mrs. Hucks moved to the next window. "That one may not have much to say, but she's deep. Sunday school put them up to this, you know?"

"I'm grateful. I could never keep this place clean without help."

She turned to him. "I got to ask you something, Pastor. There have been rumors."

He touched his collar, sat on the edge of a pew, feeling cautious. "What's up?"

"That flower man, Jonny No Age, was he a member here?"

Eben knew what was coming. "Yes."

She went back to her polishing, spoke over her shoulder. "Brought along that bookkeeper, one that lived with him?"

"Joseph. He's an accountant, yes."

"Queer, weren't they?"

He wanted to respond, "We're all queer in one way or another," but dodged by asking, "What do you mean?"

"Oh, c'mon, Pastor. Sissies. I don't want that kind around my girls." She moved on to the next window. "He should have gone back to Raleigh when Jonny passed."

Mary stopped sweeping, paying close attention. Martha swept dust from the steps in front of the stage.

Mrs. Hucks got down from her stepstool. "I want nothing to do with the likes of Jonny's *girlfriend*."

She spat out this last word with contempt. Quotations came to him about casting the first stone, but this woman's life wasn't easy. Her family had been burned out in the fire and her husband hadn't had work in quite a while. How they made it was beyond Eben's understanding. The front door opened.

A stout man came down the aisle holding baskets of flowers. As if there *was* an all-knowing God, Jonny's friend had come by with arrangements for Sunday service.

Eben said, "Joseph! We were just talking about you. Come on in."

Mrs. Hucks said, "Mary, Martha, come here. We got to go."

Eben called out, "Girls, come see the flowers for tomorrow."

Joseph ducked his head to Mrs. Hucks and put the baskets on the stage by the pulpit and the choir benches. "We got some delphiniums today. They go well with the brown-eyed Susans and phlox, don't you think?"

Mary ran up to one basket, buried her face in the flowers. "Smells pretty."

Martha stayed with her mother.

"Mary, you come here right now," Mrs. Hucks said. "Right now!"

Mary obeyed, but called back to Joseph, "Real pretty flowers, mister man."

Mrs. Hucks took the girls in hand and left the church.

Joseph's mouth twisted. "Reckon I caused a ruckus."

"No need to apologize. Thank you for the bouquets. We count on you like the sun rising, I want you to know that."

Joseph looked at the floor as he spoke. "I'm returning to Raleigh. Going to close the shop and go back to accounting."

He turned to leave, tossing his last words over his shoulder. "She doesn't know any better, Pastor."

He watched Joseph leave, feeling as if he could have done more.

The unfinished sermon awaited him when he returned to his study, papers scattered on his desk, the Bible—his Revised Standard Version—still open to Proverbs, where he'd found a passage on doing godly works: "Commit your work to the Lord, and your plans will be established." That was his thesis, but he'd struggled to say outright something along the lines of, "Do good work, leave the rest up to your creator." As always, preaching about a creator he doubted felt false. But the language of the RSV wasn't quite right. He looked around for his office copy of the King James, realized he'd left it at the manse. Though he seldom removed the ancient King James from the pulpit, and as much as he didn't want to have to use the stairs again, he needed to compare the text, to see if differences between the two translations would help him focus.

Back at his desk with the elderly Bible, which was falling apart, he turned to Proverbs 16:3, saying "Ah-h-h," out loud as he read the ancient words, "Commit thy works unto the Lord, and thy thoughts shall be established." Thus, if we do godly works, godly thoughts will follow. Something like that. He pushed the King James aside, picked up his pen, and attacked the part of the sermon that had eluded him, glancing back and forth from Bible to sermon. Verse eighteen jumped off the page: "Pride goeth before destruction, and an haughty spirit before a fall." *Oh, for a way to present that to Sister Hucks.* He laughed aloud, reached for the King James, and knocked it to the floor in his haste. He grabbed it up, almost tearing off the back cover of the dilapidated Bible, caressing it as if to mend it. He looked at the spine to see if he'd broken it, noticed something he'd seen before, inside the back cover, but had never paid attention to. A list of names, numbers, letters. A record he'd assumed was pertinent back in 1842 when the Bible was dedicated to Second Presbyterian Church Colored. Those letters and numbers—could they be connected to the register?

He picked up the phone.

CHAPTER 26

Retta and me are sitting on orange crates in the alley when Mr. Griffin comes out of the prep room behind the serving line, his face telling me something's wrong. "Loraylee, your grandmother called. She sounded upset." My first thought is Hawk. Mr. Griffin tells me to use his office phone, for privacy. He must be thinking of Hawk, too.

Bibi picks up on the first ring. "Oh, Raylee, it bad, it bad."

I sink down in Mr. Griffin's chair. "What?"

She's crying. "Ray been arrested. He in jail."

Out the window in the alley, Retta stares back at me.

I say to Bibi, "I'll find out what happened, call you back."

I dial the emergency number for the police. A woman answers, gives me another number that rings four, five times before a man answers. "Chief Jailer's Office."

"My uncle, Raymond Glover, got arrested this afternoon."

"Hold on." I hear papers being shuffled, voices in the background. "Yes, indecent exposure, desecration of a burial site, resisting arrest."

"He did what?"

"Urinated on a grave."

The door opens, Mr. Griffin steps in.

"Can I come see him?" I ask the man on the phone.

He tells me to hold on again, more clicks, more silence.

Mr. Griffin sits in the chair across from his desk.

I put my hand over the receiver. "My uncle is in jail for peeing on a grave."

The man comes back on the phone. "Visiting hours tomorrow are ten till two."

"So he's gon spend the night there?"

"Yep. Judge will address bail in the morning. That all?"

I shake my head like he can see me. "What time tomorrow, the judge decides?"

"Court opens at nine." He hangs up.

Mr. Griffin comes around the desk, pulling the blinds shut on his way to me.

I prep the supper line and leave early, Mr. Griffin practically shooing me out the door. I get home to find Bibi on the sofa.

Hawk runs up to me. "Hey, Mama. Bibi's sad."

"Yes, baby." I touch his hair.

"Where's Uncle Ray?" he ask me.

Bibi say, "In jail."

I sit beside her. "Tomorrow I'll go downtown to hear what the judge decides. I might can visit Uncle Ray. No way he peed on a grave."

She sniffles. "He been having trouble. Sometimes he can't hold it."

"Yeah, but he would never go on somebody's resting place."

She sits up straight, wipes her eyes with the hankie she keeps tucked in her bosom. "You right. And he hasn't been in jail a day in his life. Tell the judge Ray is a good man."

* * *

I'm walking up Trade Street in my best dress, a white daisy print with a full skirt that swirls around my legs; got on a hat Bibi gave me, her pearl necklace and earrings, my shoes polished. The judge won't take me for trash. It's only eight-thirty but I'm sweating before I'm halfway to the courthouse, stopping to pat my face with Kleenex. My thighs rub together, starting to chap above the stockings I usually save for church.

I'm about to pass the Law Building when I get an idea: Uncle Ray needs a lawyer, and this building is full of them. The lobby is dim, cool, after the bright sun. Next to the elevator is a framed list of so many lawyers it makes me dizzy. I touch the glass. The name under my finger is Sidney Cruikshank, of Taylor, Taylor, and Wolston, Esq., Suite 304. Steel doors slide open and the elevator man say, "Going up?" At 304 I tell the girl behind the desk, "I'm looking for Lawyer Sidney Cruikshank."

She opens a black book. "Do you have an appointment?"

"No. I just need a lawyer."

"Your name, please? I'll go see if Miss Cruikshank is available."

"I'm Loraylee Hawkins." It comes to me what she said. "*Miss* Cruikshank?"

But the girl is gone. In a couple of minutes the door she disappeared through opens. A white woman comes toward me, dressed like a man in a suit jacket and long pants, a white blouse, gold necklace. "Miss Hawkins? I'm Sidney Cruikshank."

"Are you a lawyer?"

"I am."

She's sure of herself. "My uncle's in jail."

"Sorry to hear that. Why don't you come to my office and tell me what happened."

"How much do you charge?"

"Not a penny until I find out if it's something I can help you with."

"Okay." I follow her to an office with a desk in front of a window, shelves from floor to ceiling filled with books. She sits behind the desk.

I take a chair, looking at papers framed on the one wall without books.

"That's my diploma from law school, my license to practice, and my undergraduate degree."

Law school, university. "Not sure I should be here."

"Start by telling me what happened to your uncle."

Her long brown hair is twisted into a knot on the back of her head, one strand loose, which she tucks back over her ear.

"He got arrested for peeing in a cemetery."

She takes a writing pad from a stack of papers on her desk, picks up a pencil. "When?"

"Yesterday afternoon."

"Did he spend last night in jail?"

"Yes, ma'am."

She makes a note. "What's his name, age?"

"Raymond Elijah Glover. He's seventy-five, be seventy-six in September. My grand say he's got a problem that makes him have to go, can't hold it."

"Might be enlargement of the prostate, not uncommon in older men." She scribbles something. "And there's the scarcity of integrated bathrooms."

Her knowing this surprises me. "Yes, ma'am."

"Has your uncle been arrested before?"

"My grand say he's never been in jail. She's his sister."

"Your grandmother?"

"Yes, ma'am. We all live together."

"What's your address?"

I give her the number on Brown Street. "In Brooklyn."

She opens a box on her desk and flips a bunch of cards in

it. "Give me a minute, Miss Hawkins, while I see what I can find out." Her black phone is like ours, except for buttons across the bottom. She dials, then gives Uncle Ray's name, smiling into the phone like she's talking to somebody she knows. They chat back and forth until she say, "Thanks, appreciate it," and hangs up. "He's in the holding tank, where they keep people waiting for the judge to set bail. Far as I could find out, he's okay."

Relief comes over me. "When will they let him go?"

"He's on the docket for this morning, which means he'll be out this afternoon, given that his offense is a misdemeanor."

"A what?"

"A minor crime. He shouldn't even have spent the night there."

"What now?"

"If you hire me, I believe I can have Mr. Glover home before supper."

I look out the window, which faces toward Brooklyn. "Pay you, right?"

She pulls a paper from a desk drawer. "I'm recording today's date, your name, your uncle's name, and the charges." The piece of hair falls forward again, and again she tucks it back. "Do you have a dollar? I'll write here that you paid me. We'll both sign it, then go to the courthouse. I have to be back no later than one, so I hope things go smoothly."

"Only a dollar?"

"For now, and you're under no obligation for more."

I get my wallet from my purse. Two dollars. I give her one of them, and sign my name clear and careful beside hers.

We sit on a bench outside the courtroom. People walk up and down, talking loud. Across the hall a woman sits alone, crying. Miss Cruikshank goes to check on when the judge gon see Uncle Ray, and returns fast. "Let's go, Miss Hawkins."

In the courtroom she sits down with me, as uniformed guards bring a bunch of men through a door in the back. Uncle Ray's clothes are rumpled, he needs a shave, and his mustache got something caught in it. He tips his head to let me know he sees me.

A man calls out, "All rise." We get up, Miss Cruikshank telling me, "That's the bailiff. The judge is next."

A fat white man in a black robe comes through a door on the other side from where Uncle Ray entered, settles himself at a high desk. His hair is a reddish brown like Mr. Griffin's.

The bailiff calls out, "Oh yes, oh yes, oh yes. This honorable court for the County of Mecklenburg is now open for the dispatch of its business, the honorable Judge Jeremy P. Coley presiding. God save the State and this honorable court. You may be seated."

The judge picks up a wooden hammer, taps it. "First case?"

Other men in suits talk back and forth with the judge, and he takes care of two white men, pretty quick, fifty dollar fine for one, twenty-five for the other. What am I gon do if it's fifty dollars for Uncle Ray?

The next one up is a colored man charged with loitering and vagrancy. A lawyer explains things I don't understand and the judge say, "Dismissed."

This gives me hope that Uncle Ray will be coming home with me before long. Maybe without a fine. Maybe dismissed.

The bailiff calls out, "Raymond Elijah Glover. Indecent exposure. Desecration of a burial site. Resisting arrest."

Miss Cruikshank stands. "Your Honor, Mr. Glover's family retained me this morning. May I consult with my client outside the courtroom?"

"Is he a risk for flight?"

"No priors, Your Honor."

"Ten minutes, Miss Cruikshank. In the hallway." He

points to some police standing in the back of the court. "One of you go with them. Next?"

Miss Cruikshank motions to Uncle Ray. When he's close enough, I stare at his mustache, raking my fingers across my upper lip. He does the same. Whatever it was falls to the floor.

In the hallway Miss Cruikshank say to Uncle Ray, "Mr. Glover, I'm Sidney Cruikshank."

He ask me, "How'd you afford a lawyer?"

I glance at the cop, who turns his head, rolls his eyes, walks a few feet away but still in earshot. I whisper, "Only cost a dollar. So far."

We sit on a bench and Miss Cruikshank say to Uncle Ray, "Why don't you tell me what happened?"

Uncle Ray frowns. "I don't understand everything that man said, like about the desecration. I was visiting the cemetery. Then the need came on me to make water. The back door of the church was locked, and I couldn't get to the front, without I might wet myself. So I went behind a tree . . ." He stops, looks down at the marble floor. "Not on a grave."

"And then?"

"Policeman came up behind me, took hold of my arm, told me, 'I'm arresting you for indecent exposure.'"

She takes her pad and pen from her briefcase. "Did you resist him?"

Every once in a while, Uncle Ray gets mad. A look comes in his eyes telling me this is one of those times. "Yes, ma'am, I reckon I did. He grabbed me because I'm a colored man, doing nothing but what nature intended." He touches his head. "Bopped me when I tried to pull away." Uncle Ray shows us a cut under his thinning white hair. "I pushed him. He got me down, cuffed me."

"According to your niece, you don't have a criminal record."

"That's right. Drove a truck for Eckerd's for twenty-five

years, not even a parking ticket." He clears his throat. "Don't have a driving license anymore, don't need one."

Miss Cruikshank writes on the pad. "We're pressed for time, let me tell you what might happen. Having no prior arrests is very much in your favor. Do you have a prostate problem?" She pays attention to her pencil

He mumbles, "Yes, ma'am."

"Do you have a report from your doctor?"

"I could get one."

"I might have you do that, depending on the amount of the fine."

I hear somebody laughing nearby and see our cop talking to another police. Are they joking about us?

"So there's gon be a fine?" I say.

"Probably. There's been talk of punishing people who relieve themselves in public, when what we need is more integrated bathrooms."

Uncle Ray ask me, "How'd you find this lady?"

I smile for the first time that morning. "I went in the law building, picked her name. Thought she was a man because of Sidney." Makes me want to tell Pastor Polk that God brought me to her, even if she's a woman.

She laughs. The cop across the hall taps his watch. "Couple more minutes."

"Are you employed, Mr. Glover?"

"Retired. Started getting my social a few years back. Odd jobs. What you call a shade tree mechanic, a bit of carpentry."

"This judge feels bound to make an example of people he labels a nuisance to the general public." She clicks her ballpoint pen. "We can most likely get the indecent exposure charge removed. You obviously weren't exposing yourself for"—she stops—"for the usual reasons behind such a charge."

Uncle Ray nods.

"Were you near a grave when you relieved yourself?"

"No. That cemetery is at St. Timothy's Second Presbyterian, our church. Got family buried there." He means my cousin Lee, who I'm named for.

The cop heads for the door to court. "Let's go, Sidney."

Miss Cruikshank stands. "I might get two of the charges dismissed, if it's a good day for the judge."

"And if it's not?" I say.

"A fine. Should be less than twenty-five dollars. Will that be a problem?"

I start to speak, but Uncle Ray say, "No." He turns to me. "Not a problem, Loraylee. I got some put by." He frowns. "Never thought it would be for a thing like this."

Pastor Polk comes down the hall, almost running. "Ray, Loraylee! Livinia called me."

I tell Miss Cruikshank, "This is Reverend Ebenezer Polk, of St. Timothy's."

"Wonderful. I'm Sidney Cruikshank, Mr. Glover's attorney. If the judge wants to question you, are you willing?"

He pulls a handkerchief from his pocket, wipes sweat from his forehead. "It would be a privilege."

Uncle Ray say, "Pastor, that elm tree in the cemetery, any graves near it?"

"No. The roots make that impossible."

Miss Cruikshank makes a note, and we go back in. The judge is deciding on a colored woman charged with prostitution. She doesn't look like a whore. "Fifty dollars and thirty days," the judge tell her. "This is your fourth offense."

She stares back at him.

The bailiff calls Uncle Ray. "Indecent exposure. Desecration of a burial site. Resisting arrest."

Miss Cruikshank stands. "Your Honor, as to the exposure and desecration, Mr. Glover was visiting his family's graveyard yesterday and had a sudden need to relieve himself. A prostate problem. We can pursue getting a note from his doctor. At any rate, Mr. Glover concealed himself behind a tree and urinated. Not on a grave. The arresting officer happened to be passing the cemetery." She looks down at her pad. "As I said earlier, he has no priors. He's retired from long employment with Eckerd Drugs, receiving social security, works odd jobs as a mechanic and carpenter. Mr. Glover's minister is here, and willing to speak on his behalf."

The judge say, "What about the third charge, resisting arrest?"

"We'll plead to that. Mr. Glover was startled when he was approached from behind, tried to pull away. The officer struck him on the head, causing a laceration."

When they're done, the judge takes off indecent exposure and desecration, but he say, "As to urinating in a cemetery—consecrated ground—I caution you to use better judgment in the future."

"Yes, sir."

The judge makes a note. "Fifteen dollars, time served."

Pastor Polk takes out his wallet. Uncle Ray whispers to me and Miss Cruikshank, "He knows I'm good for it."

At noon the four of us are standing outside the Law Building. Uncle Ray tells Miss Cruikshank, "Send your bill and I'll pay you right away."

"I'll do that. Twenty dollars. Glad I could be of help."

I'm pretty sure she's only charging us because of Uncle Ray's pride. I say, "Miss Cruikshank, this morning I didn't like it you were a woman. Now I'm glad."

When I get home from work, I sit with Uncle Ray on the porch, him smoking his pipe, Little Sugar gurgling down in the gully. Evening, the sun giving up and the lightning bugs taking over.

"Must have been rough on you last night. Did you have a bed?"

"A cot, a pillow. It's noisy and they never turn the lights

off. Smells bad. Men who been there over and over tell me what I did was nothing." He takes a puff, then taps his pipe on the rail, staring up the street like he's looking for something. "Maybe nothing to them, but now I'm just one more jailbird nigger. That's what some folks will say."

CHAPTER 27

The day before the destruction of the graveyard was to begin, a cool Tuesday in June of 1965, Eben woke an hour earlier than usual, lying on his back in the double bed that felt too wide. He stared at the ceiling, a crack he hadn't noticed before. The manse showed its age. Next year a wrecking ball would split the ceiling in two.

After breakfast he walked to the cemetery, felt comfort in the familiar creak of the iron gate, the uneven pavers, the abundance of periwinkle at the peak of bloom, seashells on the most humble of graves, tombstones on others, the one soaring ornate marker. Small sites with rocks at head and foot where children were buried during the polio epidemic.

He walked to Nettie's marker: NONETTE SERENA HASTY POLK, BELOVED WIFE, NOVEMBER 5, 1910, AUGUST 29, 1958. He settled on the iron bench beside her grave, where he'd sat at least once a week for six years. "Dear girl, this may be our last visit here." When he'd first come to her grave shortly after she died, he'd sat in silence. Then one Sunday, he'd spoken softly to her as if she were sitting beside him, told her about having lunch with a church family who'd squabbled all through the meal, that he felt he'd failed by not soothing ruffled feathers. He got great comfort in sharing the story with her, though he kept looking around to be sure no one could hear him. After a while he realized that this worry was needless. Anyone who saw him sitting in the graveyard stayed at a respectful distance. After that he avoided going to her grave on Sundays, when families most often visited their dead, and came to appreciate the solemn silence of weekday mornings.

"Well, old girl"—he took a deep breath, let it out slowly—"tomorrow it begins. I've taken to praying again, really and truly praying, because I cannot stop them from disturbing you. All I can do is seek peace, given that I'm not one for prayers of intercession. But peace is not easily won, Nettie." He sat in silence for a few minutes, as if waiting for the ground to respond.

"We've taken some comfort from breaking the code, Marion, Georgeanne, and I. Connects us to Second Presbyterian Church Colored in a way I never realized I needed. My, my, can you imagine what a hard life they had back then? Had to keep silent about those who could read and write, even the freedmen, and Lord knows what would have happened to gifted slaves." He heard the rusty gate, looked over his shoulder.

Georgeanne walked up, touched his back. "Talking to Nettie?" She seemed to find this perfectly normal.

"Yes, telling her about the register, the code."

"Do you mind if I join you?"

"I welcome the company."

She sat down beside him. "Wanted to share one last piece of the mystery, if now's okay."

"It is." *Now that you're here.*

"After we saw that the code identified literate members of

the church, named the whites to be avoided, Klan and all, I got so caught up in it that I forgot the remaining puzzle."

"Which is?"

"JTQ." She pointed to the stone at the edge of the graveyard.

"Oh, yes, slipped my mind, too."

"I wondered why a stone as recent as 1926 was at the back of the cemetery. Didn't make sense. It should have been at least in the middle." She took folded papers from her purse. "Here's what I found."

The name "John Thomas Quarry, 1860–??" was centered at the top of the first of three typewritten pages.

"This is the man's history, gleaned from several sources. Fascinating what it reveals. You can read it now, or I can synopsize it for you."

She'd done a huge amount of work. He said, "Please give me the essence, then I do want to read this."

"Oh, good!" she said with obvious pleasure. "He was born a slave in 1860, as noted, in Pineville, on what had once been the Polk plantation." She looked up from her notes. "Have you ever wondered about your connection to James K. Polk?"

"It's crossed my mind, but I haven't wasted a lot of thought on how I might be connected to a white president."

She laughed. "Understandable. What do you know of your ancestry?"

"My parents were both free; my grandparents were slaves."

"Mecklenburg County?"

"Yes. So you're guessing I'm related to President Polk?"

"It's possible. His father was a slaver, had large land holdings in Pineville before he moved his family to Tennessee. So . . ."

"Doesn't interest me. What about Quarry?"

"I kept thinking about what Reverend Tilley said, that

slaves ran off and those left behind said they'd died and were buried, the evidence being a gravestone."

"Yes, something like that. I didn't doubt it."

Georgeanne said, "He also told you about things that seemed important—"

"Vital, that was his word."

"Yes, vital, didn't matter after enough years had passed."

"That's what he said."

"I wager you that the stone marked 'JTQ 1926' sits on an empty grave. A child named John Thomas was born in 1860; that's in the register. In 1890 he worked in the town of Hillsborough, cutting stone for buildings being erected on the Duke campus. At some point in the early 1890s, John Thomas became John Thomas of the quarry, then John Thomas Quarry, a name apparently chosen by the man himself when he signed up to receive paychecks at his permanent address of 809 East First Street, Charlotte." She paused. "Brooklyn."

"Returning home to St. Tim's Second Presbyterian."

"Exactly. Oh, and by the way, I forgot one other detail about the Polk family. Presbyterian, all the way back to Scotland."

"Hmm, maybe there is a connection. Imagine that."

She went on. "In November of 1898 a John Thomas Quarry was arrested for assaulting a white man during the riots in Wilmington, but managed to escape in the confusing aftermath when dozens were jailed, poor records kept, many buildings burned to the ground. Quarry was not heard of again until a policeman tried to arrest him in Charlotte, in December 1925, for the crime of insubordination."

"He would have been an old man."

"Sixty-five, not much older than you are now."

"Well, yes. I wonder what he'd done, insubordination."

"He walked down Trade Street at ten in the evening, which was frowned on by the local constabulary. A scuffle ensued. Quarry got a billy club from the policeman and hit him with it, rendering him unconscious. The story in the *Charlotte Observer* indicated that he fled on foot and was being sought for inflicting bodily harm on an officer of the law."

"And died shortly thereafter?"

"From the date on the rock, you'd gather that, but no, what I think is that his family helped him get away, said he'd died and was buried here. Chiseled in his initials and the date, put the stone where it's likely no one else was buried." She pointed to the back fence. "Apparently, he and Younger Tilley were lifelong friends, so Tilley may have taken part in the deception."

"Which is why he'd have said, 'Not his grave, just his marker.'"

"Exactly."

Eben stretched his leg, rubbed his knee. "Tilley really was trying to tell me something that was of great importance to him. I guess we'll soon know whether there's a body in that grave."

"If there is, it's not John Thomas Quarry."

"No?"

"Quarry was reported as participating in the protests in Durham in the 1940s, when he'd have been well into his eighties. According to a story in the Durham paper, the report was bogus, given that Quarry was buried in Charlotte in 1926."

"My word, was all this in the papers in the library?"

"Good Lord, no. But I took what was there and ferreted out other facts, connected the dots."

"You must be good at research."

"How else would a colored girl get into law school in the 1930s?"

Eben laughed. "I tell you, I am impressed. All these years, when I've seen Quarry's stone, I've wondered."

"We've connected most of the graves to those still living in Brooklyn," Georgeanne said. "The register—or what remained of it, after the water damage—gave us that. But I wish we could have linked families of Negroes here to the founding fathers. For instance, Brooklyn has many Alexanders, and I'd wager they go back to Hezekiah himself, the glorious patriarch of Mecklenburg."

"No doubt. In fact, one of my favorites at St. Tim's is Loraylee Alexander Hawkins," Eben said.

"Of course, her boy is a perfect example of how white genes can skip generations."

Eben rubbed his chin. "Hmm, perhaps." He wished he could tell Georgeanne what he suspected about Hawk's genes, after he met Loraylee's boss at the S&W. He said, "A while back you mentioned a husband, but I don't see a wedding band."

She smiled. "He's no longer in the picture. A long story. But I'll ask you a variation on the same theme. Why, after six years, are *you* wearing one?"

The next day the crew arrived on schedule, eleven Negro men with shovels and pickaxes against their shoulders as if they were marching to war. No sign of the dreaded backhoe. A white woman with a clipboard accompanied the workers. Her sole task seemed to involve sitting on the brick wall that ran around three sides of the graveyard, writing on a legal pad, recording names from gravestones as they were removed.

Marion Lipscomb was there before the work began, promising Eben, "I won't interfere, haven't that right, but I do want to be sure the dig is conducted properly. I hope we can further connect the history of St. Tim's for those still living."

True to his word, Marion helped discriminate between dirt and artifacts as the graves were unearthed. During the first afternoon, a shovel brought up what Eben saw as a large clump of dirt; it turned out to be a small oval box, wrapped in a woman's housedress in the style of the 1890s, flower print still distinct. Inside the box were the bones of a tiny infant who must have been born prematurely. After this discovery, and with careful direction from Marion, the gravediggers proceeded with great caution, moving slowly. In the second week a supervisor from the city showed up to ask why there wasn't greater progress. At that point Eben stepped aside, let Marion speak for St. Tim's.

"If you'd like, sir, I can halt the removal completely, given that several statutes have been violated or ignored," Marion said to the city official.

Eben didn't know or care whether that was true.

Marion continued, "Or we can proceed with the caution necessary to honor the remains we're disturbing."

"Okay," said the supervisor. "But get on with it. The city has a schedule to keep." He left, shaking his head.

Marion had spread a piece of canvas in the lawn behind the manse where relics unearthed could be examined and cataloged: pieces of pottery, handles from coffins, buttons, dresses, hats, long bones and skulls, an entire upper plate, teeth intact. A cook pot. A glass without a chip, which Marion explained, "May have been filled with water, placed in the grave in case the deceased should wake up thirsty."

"Are you joking?" Eben asked.

"I've seen stranger things."

Where caskets had disintegrated, new boxes were provided, the remains identified with great care.

On Wednesday of the second week Marion knocked on Eben's back door. "Eben, we'll be disinterring the grave of Nonette Polk this afternoon."

He believed he'd been prepared for this, but he was not. "Thank you for telling me, Marion. I'll be there."

He went back inside, sat on the sofa in the living room,

thinking that he should call someone, feeling Nettie knew, that her spirit was in the wingback chair where she'd sat many evenings by the fireplace. "My goodness, Nettie girl, what am I going to do? They're taking you away." He felt as alone as he ever had. As if she had spoken to reassure him, he realized that he didn't want anyone besides Marion, with his professional detachment, during this awful duty. He told her, "You'll be with me and that's all I need." He stood, touched his collar, brushed the front of his black coat.

Marion nodded to him as he arrived at the cemetery, then stood a respectful distance from Nettie's grave.

Her tombstone was propped against the wall. "Where's my bench?" Eben asked Eli Patterson, who stood nearby, shovel at the ready.

"We set it by the back door to St. Tim's, Preacher," Eli pointed.

He saw it and felt an almost foolish relief. "Okay. Well, I guess we should get started." He touched the man's shoulder. "Glad to see you've got work, Eli."

"Yeah, been tough on me, getting fired after all those years at the Liberty Life."

"Is it permanent, as a gravedigger, I mean?"

"General laborer for the city, doing what needs doing. This week it's here." Eli hoisted his shovel.

Eben sat on the cemetery wall as the digging started, looking anywhere but at the grave. Nettie would be moved to Pinewood, where her parents bought plots before the last graves were sold in 1947. He almost couldn't bear to think that he wouldn't be buried next to her, and had decided on cremation, for his ashes to be scattered on her grave. He'd added a codicil to his will, hoping that someone would carry out his wishes. Oscar, if he could stay out of jail.

He caught the gentle scent of the honeysuckle Nettie had planted at the back of the cemetery along the fence. Her efforts were so successful that the thick green vines had become a wall of flowers all through the summer.

The crew dug down into the grave with a steady rhythm. First the pickax, then the shovel. Pickax, shovel. He remembered when Nettie's coffin was lowered into her grave, the finality of that, wanting to touch her once more, how reluctant he was to toss dirt in after her as Brother Westmoreland intoned, "Ashes to ashes, dust to dust."

The muffled thump of metal on wood brought him back, a sound he'd heard over and over in the past week. As the top of Nettie's coffin appeared he wanted to tell them to stop, that they had no right to disturb her. The men lifted it out of the grave and set it on the broken ground. He focused on a scratch that ran down the side, showing dull yellow wood under the mahogany finish. The phrase, *mahogany finish,* came back to him in a way he hadn't understood when he'd arranged her burial. He wanted to go to the kitchen, scrabble through the cans and jars under the sink, find the brown scratch cover that Nettie had used on their furniture. The shining coffin he'd buried her in was nothing more than a painted pine box. And she was inside, in the blue dress she'd worn to Noah's christening. "Easy, now," he called out as the men tipped the coffin to get it up onto the truck bed. "Easy."

He turned away. What was left was only the husk of his Nettie. He lifted his hand to Marion and walked back to the manse, head down.

In the seventeen days it took to remove, catalog, and transfer the remains from sixty-three plots that ultimately gave up seventy-seven corpses, Eben made certain that the relocation of every grave—dispersed to five cemeteries around the city and county—was duly recorded. He did what must be done, continuing the century-old register in his own hand, not caring that he might be duplicating the city woman's work.

The old book had helped put names to all but three shrouded corpses, and Eben had finally accepted the futility of trying to identify those. The unmarked remains would be reinterred in a common grave with a single marker: THREE SLAVES OF MECKLENBURG COUNTY, CA. 1845, REST IN PEACE. The year chosen was the earliest date found on the stones in the cemetery.

Marion said, "We'll never know who those three were, whether man, woman, or child, but they were of your community. They lived and died here, and the marker honors them, even if anonymously." As he often did, Eben wondered whether those unknown souls were living again in God's heaven. And truly, it didn't matter to him what the headstone said, as long as the remains of those three were given the proper respect.

Gideon Rhyne showed up on the last day of the destruction of St. Tim's Cemetery, as Eben and Marion surveyed the barren ground. In his usual way, Rhyne spoke as if for the community, clapping Eben on the back. "We can't know the ways of the Lord, of course, but we've learned that acceptance is the only way to a calm mind." His habit of speaking in the plural had long bothered Eben, but he'd chosen to ignore it. Rhyne pulled out a paper from an inside pocket of his coat. "We trust this will give you consolation." He read aloud a quote from Ezekiel: "And you shall know that I am the Lord, when I open your graves, and raise you from your graves, O my people. And I will put my Spirit within you, and you shall live, and I will place you in your own land; then you shall know that I, the Lord, have spoken, and I have done it, says the Lord." A gold ring on Rhyne's pinkie gleamed as he waved toward heaven, folded the paper, and put it in his pocket. "We think it's a fine job you're doing here, Pastor Polk." Rhyne left the cemetery, a whiff of bay rum trailing him.

Marion watched Rhyne drive away. "That's one pompous son of a bitch."

Eben laughed. "Agreed. At least he's solidly ensconced at the House of Prayer. I feared he might join St. Tim's."

They stood by the wall that embraced the remains of the cemetery. Piles of dirt beside ragged holes, pieces of brick, a crumbling headstone, a distressing odor that made him think of rust, blood, mud. The upturned earth was dotted with the pinks and purples of dying periwinkle, bits of seashell. The city had promised to leave a smooth field when the graves were all relocated, but Eben had come to doubt anything the city said.

He bent, picked up a piece of brick that bore the impression CMBW, 1875. He brushed dirt from it, showed it to Marion. "Charlotte Mecklenburg Brickworks. Every single one of these was made by hand." He ran his finger over the letters. "They shut down before the turn of the century. I'll keep it as a paper weight."

"Do you know where you're going?"

"I'm talking with a church north of Graham Street, near Smith. If we can combine the two congregations, it might work out. There's a house for sale that could serve as the manse. I'm optimistic."

"Will your flock move with you?"

"Some will. The AMEs are staying in Brooklyn, so there's that."

Within a week, the graveyard was a smooth field of red clay. Seashells retrieved from the graves dotted the top of the brick wall. Eben had the wrought-iron bench returned to approximately where it had been, beside Nettie's grave, where it stood alone in the barren ground, purposeless. He sat on it, missing Nettie more than ever, realizing how much consolation he'd gotten talking to her over the years. He'd gone over to Pinewood only once since her reinterment and had no desire to return. His connection to her had been at St. Tim's, and when he'd tried to talk with her at Pinewood he'd had the strange sensation that her parents were listening. He pounded the arm of the bench with his fist, as if it could explain things. Nettie was gone. Gone from this ground, from the earth. Even his memories of her were fading. He decided to have the bench moved to the front yard of the church, where people could sit on it after services. He stroked the iron seat.

Until grass began to sprout, he didn't realize that the city had scattered seed in the empty field where the cemetery had been. Why had they done that, knowing that the whole block of McDowell would be leveled? The manse and the church itself were slated for demolition in the spring of 1966, giving him eleven months to relocate. What was coming was another funeral, though without services, no raging at the dying of the light of what had been Brooklyn. Rather, he suspected that one by one his followers and their neighbors would find new homes. New churches. Lifelong members of St. Tim's would be replaced by strangers. He felt a softening of his grief for Nettie, and a connection to the bench where he'd sat talking with her. No matter what, he would take it with him to the new St. Timothy's Second Presbyterian, wherever that might be.

CHAPTER 28

"Them!" Hawk shouts, listening to a football game on the radio.

"Watch your language, boy." Uncle Ray's voice is sharp.

"He said 'them,' " I call from the kitchen. "What's wrong with that?"

"Thought he said 'damn,' " Uncle Ray mumbles. "Sorry."

I push Bibi out of my way and put a plate in the cabinet. Uncle Ray does his best to correct Hawk's speech, makes the boy toe the line, he tells me more than once. "Got to put his best foot forward, the way things are today." He never corrects me.

"Tell you what, Hawk," he say, "how'd you like to see real football?"

"Yay! When we going?"

"When *are* we going. How about next Saturday, the Queen City Classic?"

I say, "I want to go!"

Bibi's at the sink. "Me too. What's a classic?"

We all laugh.

The next evening Uncle Ray say he got four tickets. "We can walk to the parade on McDowell and catch a ride to Memorial Stadium, somebody'll take us."

"Walk to McDowell, even Bibi?" I ask him.

"You can walk four or five blocks, can't you, Livvie?"

"Sure I can. I get tired, there'll be somebody stoop to set on."

By two on Saturday Hawk is dressed to go. He climbs into the rocking chair on the front porch, sits a minute, runs back into the house. "I'm ready, Mama."

"The parade doesn't start till five. I'm gon take a bath."

"A bath takes too long."

Uncle Ray say, "Tell you what, boy, let's walk down to the creek, see what's happening there."

"Be back soon, Mama."

The screen door bangs behind them, giving me peace for things I like doing on my almost-never Saturday off. Washing my Sunday stockings in the kitchen sink, then Shushu's white gloves, putting them on a stretcher to hang in the sun. My favorite thing is a soaking bath. I shake Ivory Flakes in a tub of hot water, ease myself into it, settle down with the whole of an hour in front of me, turning the hot faucet with my toe when the water gets too cool, lying back to think about Mr. Griffin, how little time we have together. The book he gave me—*Stranger in a Strange Land*—I've been reading every night before bed. It starts out, "Once upon a time . . ." making me think it's a fairy tale, but by the second paragraph I know that's not so: ". . . the greatest danger to man was man himself." This is no fairy tale. I read that and go off in my mind thinking about how people are mean to each other, and dangerous, making some folks homeless.

Mr. Griffin say the book is science fiction. "It's maybe going to be confusing at first, but if you stick with it . . ." He often does that, starts telling me something then stops in the middle.

I scrub my feet with the brush that's got bristles on one side and pumice on the other, especially my heels, which get cracked in winter. This doesn't bother me except for Mr. Griffin seeing them. I pumice away. Every night I put Vaseline on them, socks over that. Helps. When I wash the socks, I have to scrub the Vaseline out. Stubborn stuff.

The bath calms more than rough skin. I start feeling like not a problem in the world can't be fixed with a warm tub on a Saturday afternoon. But too soon a pounding on the door brings me back to what's going on today. "Mama!" Hawk shouts. "Get outta the tub and get ready!"

"I'm about done. Go look in the closet and see what I should wear."

Silence. "Me?"

"Yeah, you. Pull out something you like."

"I like the sparkly one." He's talking about a blue dress with sequins on it that I wore once, to a school dance all those years ago.

"Not for a football game. Something else. And remember it's cool today."

When I walk into our bedroom, wrapped in a towel, I see my plaid wool skirt on the bed. Hawk's put out my black high heels and the Keds I wear walking to work, changing to my S&W shoes when I get there. I hear a noise and turn to see his hand sticking out from behind the open closet door, holding a blouse on a hanger. "This?" There's a sigh in his voice. He's not too fond of our game.

"The skirt is fine, and the Keds. I'll get me a top. You did real good." He gives me the wide grin that reminds me of his daddy, races out the door hollering, "She's getting dressed. Mama's getting ready!"

Late afternoon on a fall day, the four of us head up to McDowell. Bibi has on a dress she favors, a beige corduroy button-up, with her orange sweater that makes her skin glow.

She's got her straggly white hair in a bun, curly wisps framing her face, a sparkle in her eyes. She doesn't get out enough on fun stuff like this and I'm tickled she's with us. Uncle Ray walks a step or two ahead in his eagerness, Hawk's hand in his, both of them almost skipping they're so excited. Hawk looks over his shoulder. "Y'all c'mon, don't lollygag." Lollygag, a Bibi word.

Brooklyn is a ghost town, the laundry shut up tight, the drugstore with a sign on the door, GONE TO THE QUEEN CITY CLASSIC. Two doors up First Street is a blank space, like a missing tooth, where Steadman's Flowers use to be. I will never forget Jonny No Age and the bouquets he brought Bibi. She looks at the dirt lot where his store was, shakes her head but keeps on walking. More and more buildings have been torn down, and empty houses look haunted where folks have moved out.

Before we even see the marchers, we hear the band music, start stepping in time to it. A thick crowd stands at the corner, but folks part to let Hawk get in front. He grins back at me, letting me know he's okay alone. I wouldn't worry anyway. Most everybody knows Hawk, gon watch out for him.

It's a chilly fall day, the sky gray blue, streaky clouds, but nothing to make me think it'll rain on the game tonight. Here comes the Second Ward High School band in blue and white, the drum major out front, twirling. I get chills listening to the school song, start singing out loud, *"Dear Second Ward, our alma mater, we pledge ourselves to thee."* Several people around me join in, voices rising as the band marches down the street, the cheerleaders high-stepping in saddle oxfords.

What's it feel like to be seventeen and popular? Back then I had cares. My mama long gone, my daddy long dead. End of my sophomore year, I drop out, start working, first at the pharmacy, then for the Stones at the grocery, then the S&W. Too busy to march in a band.

Bibi grabs my hand. "Look, there goes Dooby's grandboy, playing that horn." I see the boy with the trombone, the slide going in and out, and wish Dooby could have lived to see him. A bit of wind stings my eyes and I look down, see Bibi's toe tapping. Across the street is Pastor Polk, waving to the band, standing next to Mr. and Mrs. Stone. Such fine folks went to my same high school thirty-forty years ago.

"Mama!" Hawk's voice, shouting over the crowd. "A princess!"

People step aside to let me get to him. He's pointing up the street and here comes what does look like a princess, sitting on the back of a convertible in a white gown, waving. I'm thinking she's got to be chilly, nothing on her shoulders, but she looks like she hasn't a care in the world. Then someone's reading my mind. A man holds out a coat. She takes it, waving all the while, and puts it on.

"She's from West Charlotte," somebody say, "and behind her, here comes the Second Ward girl."

"See, Mama," Hawk say, "princesses."

Right behind the convertibles with the pretty girls come the West Charlotte band in maroon and gold, roars coming from the crowd. Maybe more lions here today than tigers, but we hold our own.

We stop at Jimmie's Burgers, where our ride is gon pick us up, and Uncle Ray orders two hot dogs. Hawk say, "Me too," and for once I don't argue. He wants the same thing Uncle Ray gets, no matter what. If Hawk doesn't eat the second one, I will. When she brings our order, the waitress yells over her shoulder, "We low on dogs!" Makes me chuckle and Hawk ask, "What's funny?" I say to him, "We low on dogs." He laughs so hard.

At the stadium Uncle Ray takes charge. "Don't need to be in the ticket line. This way." We follow him like he's a mother duck, and he sure enough knows where to go. Hawk stops when he sees a girl selling popcorn, his eyes asking for some. Uncle Ray buys us all a bag and I decide not to think about money this evening, or my hips.

We sit a few rows behind the Second Ward band, facing West Charlotte on the other side of the field. The bench is hard and cold. Some people brought pillows to sit on, wish I had.

Down on the field, the cheerleaders are moving around in bunches in hand-me-down uniforms from white high schools—ours from Central and West Charlotte's from Harding. Hand-me-down colors, too.

Both bands play the national anthem and folks stand, hands over hearts, to sing. Second Ward people stay standing while our band plays the school song. Everybody joins with me singing it, even Hawk; he does well for someone not knowing the words. Soon as West Charlotte is done with theirs, the bands break into a fast tune. The cheerleaders run to the end of the stadium and form two lines for the Second Ward Tigers to charge onto the field. The whole place goes wild. Hawk jumps up and down, clapping. Same thing happens for the West Charlotte Lions, and the game gets going.

Hawk already understands football in a way I never will. He follows the ball, yells, "Pass it, pass it!" before I even knew who has it. He shouts, "Yay! Flag!" I look around to see it before realizing he's not talking about the Stars and Stripes. A bit later he say, "That's what I'm gon play."

"Football?"

"No, him." He points. "Number four. I'm gon be the quarterback."

I watch number four start to run with the ball, then get tackled. He hits the ground hard. I'm not too sure about football.

The halftime show starts with those same pretty girls from

the convertibles walking out onto the field wearing long capes, other girls walking behind them holding the capes to keep them from dragging through the grass. Boys in suits and ties walk beside the princesses, proceed to the middle of the field. The bands go quiet and the loudspeaker announces, "Please stand for the crowning of the Queen City Classic Queen of 1965, Miss Bree-Anne Allred of Second Ward High School."

The shouting becomes a roar. A sparkling tiara is put on the head of one of the girls. She waves and waves in her beautiful white dress as they all walk off the field.

Hawk say, "Now the princess is a queen."

"You right," Bibi tell him. "That's something, those pretty girls."

The loudspeaker again, "Ladies and gentlemen, let's have a big hand for the battle of the bands!"

The bands march onto opposite ends of the field. The drum majors and majorettes for both schools meet in the middle, holding batons with rags on the ends. The lights go down, there's a long roll of drums as the rags get lit, then the majors and majorettes begin to dance, swirling the fiery batons, tossing them in the air, catching them, circling themselves with fire, running around each other. One of them throw hers high in the air, does a flip, catches it. "Oh, my," say Bibi, "oh, my."

The lights come back on, the bands break into the same tune together and march off the field. Smoke drifts up into the stadium.

My bottom hurts from the bench and I wiggle as the game starts back up, trying to get comfortable. Couple rows below us is a family, the man on the aisle, stretching his long legs. Two children, a boy and a girl about Hawk's age, between him and the woman I reckon his wife. She's got on a brown coat with a fur collar, a hat, a plaid pillow under her, a Co-Cola in her gloved hand. I look away, remember what Bibi always telling me about not knowing somebody's life from the outside looking in. Right then I don't believe that one bit.

It almost breaks Hawk's heart when West Charlotte wins the game. Only one point, but he's so disappointed. "A point after kick, right there at the end," he tells Uncle Ray on the way home. "Stupid one-point kick. But Second Ward gon win the next one, right, Uncle Ray?"

"You got that right."

We come through the front door and Bibi's on the couch before I can stop her. She stretches out, closes her eyes. I go for a blanket to put over her, wishing I'd got her to pee first, hoping she won't wet the couch the way she does the bed too often now. Oh well, I say in my head as I go with Hawk to our room. It's been a fine day.

CHAPTER 29

"Raylee!" Bibi shrieking wakes me up. Something roars, like it's in the house. The clock on the bureau say seven forty-five. I stumble from bed, run to the kitchen. Bibi's in her nightgown, pointing out the screen door, her finger trembling. A bulldozer's pushing itself into the house where Hawk's friend Desmond use to live, behind us on Watts Street all these years. The floor throbs under my bare feet and the kitchen smells like gasoline.

"The end is here!" Bibi grabs at me. "Oh, child, the devil is eating up the Whitin house."

I pull her close. "Sh-h-h, Bibi, not the devil, just a bulldozer." She's frail under her gown. "We knew this gon happen. Sh-h-h."

Her eyes are wild like she's seen a haint. "You wrong. The devil fooling us, looking like a bulldozer."

The machine backs away, comes at the house from the side. Its jaws take a bite from the roof. The gutter falls away, the chimney breaks up in a shower of bricks.

"Mama!" Hawk slams into the kitchen, runs to the door. "Pow!" he yells. "Wham!"

I stop him from going outside. "They're tearing down Desmond's house. I told you last week the city would do that, remember?"

"Yeah. His family is staying at his auntie's until they find another house." There's a button missing on his pajama top, makes me want to fix it right now.

"That's right," I say, "and we hoping we'll be neighbors again."

"Yeah," say Hawk, "that's what Mr. Whitin told me."

Timbers split with loud cracks. A sink thuds to the ground, followed by a toilet. A roll of paper bounces across the grass.

Hawk shouts, "The bathroom's in the backyard!"

Siding falls on the cab of the dozer. The white man driving it turns off the machine, calls to the dump truck sitting on the street. "Harry, back it on over here."

A week ago kids started throwing rocks at the windows of the deserted house, busting out the glass, leaving empty squares. The last official thing we heard say it would begin behind us, and Uncle Ray said we lucky to be on the edge of Brooklyn. "They'll eat up the middle before they take down the border. Folks passing by won't know it's happening."

I touch Bibi's shoulder. "Sit down, calm yourself. Nothing we can do."

She takes her place at the table. Hawk stands beside her, excited, not wanting to sit. "Oh, Lordy," she say. "Oh, Lordy."

Hawk keeps looking into the yard. The bulldozer opens its mouth and picks up a pile of broken house, drops it in the truck.

Uncle Ray comes up behind me. "No matter. Let's eat." He closes the back door, dulling the noise.

I take the percolator to the sink, start filling it.

Uncle Ray say, "I'll set the grits to boil. Hawk, put milk

and juice on the table. Livvie, see about the bacon." He's bossy, not like him, but it's what we need.

Hawk ask, "What if the dozer comes to our house?"

"We'll be living here awhile yet." I touch his cheek, and he pulls back, too old for such things. "Do what Uncle Ray tells you . . . milk and juice."

"Yes, ma'am." Hawk goes to the icebox, looking over his shoulder at the closed door.

Bibi stands, smoothing her gown. "You right, Ray. Even at the end of the world I want breakfast." She makes me laugh, she always does. "Raylee, why you not dressed for work?"

"It's Monday, Bibi."

"Oh." She looks blank but she say, "I know that."

We sit at the table eating like it was ordinary to have men yelling out back, the dozer rumbling. A normal breakfast except for a loud bang that makes Bibi drop her fork, except for Hawk eating too fast so he can look outside again.

Soon as we done, he jumps from his chair and opens the door, staring through the screen at the machine moving back and forth. He's nearly eleven, getting tall like his daddy, growing so quick.

After he leaves for school, I do the dishes, watching out the window as the dozer pushes against the two remaining walls. A kitchen light breaks off, slides down the crooked floor. The house collapses, empty window frames crumbling. The dozer moves in, tossing stuff in the dump truck, one mouthful, then another.

By eleven o'clock it's a mound of boards, brick, shingles. A flap of linoleum, blue and white, lying on top. The dozer climbs over the heap, rolls back and forth, flattening it.

Uncle Ray looks out at the mess. "Thing I'm gone miss the most is Boyce's garden." He sits back down at the table. "Helping him turn the ground, planting potatoes in the fall, beans and such in the spring."

I look through the window. "I'll miss the vegetables." Amazing what came out of a scraggly patch of ground. Tomatoes, peppers, summer squash, bright colors like Christmas.

It's happening, and we can't stop it. Bibi is right, the devil has come to Brooklyn.

Tuesday morning I'm back at work, filling a metal basket with eggs from the fridge. The S&W is a world apart from Brown Street. Bustling with busy people, who say hello, make jokes, laugh while doing what they do every day. The kitchen smells of breakfast cooking to feed a hundred or more by the time the door opens at seven-thirty. Dishes rattle, water runs into pots, ham and bacon sizzle on the fry top.

Retta sees me. "Hi, Loraylee, how's it going?" She's chopping cantaloupe, strawberries, bananas, her hands flying with the knife barely missing the tips of her fingers, making a chunk-a-chunk rhythm. She's the best chopper at the S&W.

"Going good," I lie.

Mr. Griffin comes up beside me while I'm whipping cheese into a bowl of scrambled eggs. "You all right?"

I get a whiff of his Old Spice aftershave, and I almost crumble. Feel tears coming. I swallow them away. "They started the tear-down yesterday behind us." I whisper, looking into his gray eyes. Hawk's eyes. "The house was pretty much gone by noon."

"And your house, is it . . ." He turns away, pretending we not talking personal, careful like he always is.

"We lucky to be on the edge. It'll be another six or eight months before they get to us."

"Half hour!" the fry cook calls out, and I go back to whipping up the omelet. Mr. Griffin walks over to the chalkboard where he keeps track of the meal prep, scribbles on it. He puts the chalk down, looks over his shoulder at me before he goes into his office, a tender look that gets me through the morning rush.

Retta and me go to the alley for our ten-thirty break, like we always do now, with Cokes and her Chesterfields. After she lights up, she say, "What's going on with you and Archibald?"

For a second I don't know who she mean, but remember that when she teasing, she say Archibald instead of Mr. Griffin. I go hot all over, thinking somebody know something, but I say, "Don't know what you're talking about."

"I'm talking about how he always speaks to you." She tilts her chin up, stretches her neck, and I know what's coming. A smoke ring. Then another one inside the first. Amazes me she can do such a thing.

"He's always checking on everybody, you too."

She looks sideways at me, sly like. "Okay." She swats at the smoke with one of her chapped hands.

"Okay?"

"Yep. Okay if you don't want to talk about it. But I know something's going on between you two."

She doesn't say anything else as a truck turns into the alley off Church Street, slow. It doesn't quite make it, has to back up, try again. On the second try it gets all the way into the alley, comes rolling toward us, stopping at the shoe store.

The back door to the paint store opens, and I say, "Here he comes. Watch."

Retta laughs. "That man wastes a lot of energy."

The man from the paint store raises his fist, shaking it at the truck driver, who has started unloading boxes from the back of the truck. "Move the goddamn truck, you hear me? I got a delivery coming any minute."

The driver hollers back, "Cool it, Joe. You don't own this alley."

Same thing happens once or twice a month, fun to watch.

When I get home I walk around to the back instead of going through the front door like usual. I touch our clothesline as I pass it and see nothing but mud where the Whitins use to live. Something catches my eye, part of a bowl sticking out of the dirt, bright blue on the outside and white where it broke. I rub the mud off with my thumb and think of Veola Whitin mashing potatoes in that blue bowl, making supper for Boyce and Desmond. The same blue was in the linoleum that went away on the dump truck. Veola kept a good house. They're living with her sister in Third Ward until they find their own place, and Veola say it's awful crowded. The day they moved we promised we'd figure out a way for Hawk and Desmond to see each other.

I go up the back steps into the kitchen. Bibi has beans baking, filling the house with the smell of molasses and fatback, the way Uncle Ray and Hawk like them. Hamburgers frying in a pan, baked apples and slaw in bowls on the table, rolls ready to go in the oven at the last minute. She's all right today, not burning anything, moving around with a ladle in her hand when I come in. She puts it in the spoon rest on the stove. "Everything okay at the S&W?"

"Good. Real good." I close the back door. This evening I want to pretend that the quiet across the backyard is like always, people sitting down for supper after working all day.

"Hawk's with Ray. You tell them ten minutes."

"Yes, ma'am, I'll do that." Everything's back to the way it's supposed to be. I call out, "Hawk? Uncle Ray? I'm home."

CHAPTER 30

The phone was ringing when Eben came in the front door but stopped before he could get to it. He stifled his frustration, thinking of how he'd advise others, "Don't worry, if it's important, they'll call back." An hour later he was fixing lunch when it rang again, and he answered. A man said, "I'm calling about Oscar Simpson Polk. Are you a relative?"

What has Oscar done now? "Yes, this is Eben Polk, his brother."

"Oh." A moment of silence, then, "I'm afraid I have some bad news."

"Who's calling?"

"Harvey Wiggins, in administration at Charlotte Memorial Hospital. Mr. Polk, I'm sorry to tell you that your brother passed away early this morning."

"Passed away?" Eben sank into a chair by the wall phone.

"Yes, apparently he was near death when he arrived, and could not be resuscitated."

He couldn't speak.

"Mr. Polk? Are you there?"

He wanted to hang up, but mumbled, "I'm here."

"In cases like this we hold the body in the hospital morgue until . . ." The man stopped.

"Cases like this?"

"When police are involved."

He was nauseated, felt faint, wanted to lie down. "May I take a number and call you back?"

Another hesitation. "I'm not sure I can tell you anything else. You need to come to the morgue to identify your brother. Officially, I mean. We ID'd him from his wallet, but until a relative has—well, that's why I called."

"Okay, I'll come right over." He hung up, sat at the table, stared out the screen door into the backyard and saw the field that had been the cemetery. There'd never be another burial at St. Tim's.

At the hospital, he was taken to the morgue where a white man working at a desk glanced up, then back to a pile of papers. "Yes?"

Eben cleared his throat, took a step back. The man saw Eben's collar. "Sorry, uh, Father?"

"Reverend Polk."

"Polk? Yeah, you must be here about"—the man shuffled papers, read from one—"Oscar Polk, is that right?"

He'd been hoping Oscar wouldn't be here, that it was another black man, that someone made a mistake. "Yes, Oscar Polk."

"Okay, Reverend. Come with me." The man got up, led him into a chilly room. "We got him a while ago."

"How did he—" He stopped short. "What happened to him?"

"Sorry, I don't have that information. They can tell you upstairs. I just need you to make a positive ID. Then sign some papers for me." The man walked to a wall with rows of rectangular drawers. He consulted a list on a bulletin board and pulled open a drawer that held a sheet-draped body. "You ready?" he asked.

Eben wasn't, but he nodded.

The man pulled back the sheet.

"Oh," was all he could say.

"Is this Oscar Polk?"

"Yes." Funny Oscar, reckless Oscar, troubled Oscar. His brother's familiar face, a bloodless charcoal gray. Eben stood there, felt helpless, useless. What was he to do now?

Noah. He had to tell Noah.

Oscar had gotten out of jail a month ago, rented a furnished apartment on Congo, over in what was left of Blue Heaven, asking if Noah could stay with Eben, "Till I get back on my feet, okay?" Again Eben hoped that Oscar would become the father Noah needed. That was up to Eben now.

Noah was pushing the rattling lawnmower across the front yard of the manse with an ease and grace Eben envied, given his own struggles when he tried to mow the lawn. In the past some member of the church showed up to cut the grass, but since Noah moved in last spring, he'd taken care of it without being asked or reminded.

He could almost see Noah growing. Strong arms, big feet—the last pair of shoes had been a twelve.

Noah stopped mowing as if he could feel his uncle looking at him. Eben walked across the grass. "Hey, Noah. The lawn's looking good."

"Thanks, Uncle Eben. I got a ways to go yet."

"I'd like you to take a break. C'mon inside."

Noah pulled a rag from the pocket of his jeans, wiped his face, hung the rag across the handle of the lawnmower. "Okay."

In the kitchen, Eben pulled out a chair, motioned for Noah to sit. "How about a glass of tea? That's hot work you've been doing."

"What's going on?"

Eben took glasses from a cabinet, got out a tray of ice, poured the tea. He sat down across from his nephew. "I'm sorry, Noah, but I've got some bad news for you."

"Daddy, isn't it?"

Noah had been calling Oscar Dad for months. But now he was a scared boy.

"Yes. He—" Eben didn't know where to start. He rubbed at a smudge on the table. "You know your father had a drinking problem."

"Still does."

He took Noah's hand. "He's dead, son."

Noah paled. "I knew that's what you were gon say." He got to his feet, drained his glass in one long drink. "I'll go finish mowing."

Eben stood abruptly. "No, no. Stay with me."

Noah stopped, turned back. "How'd you find out?"

"A phone call this morning. The police got a tip about a fellow selling moonshine—that man Mash. Seems he got Oscar involved in a still on Second Street, behind one of the burned-out houses. The cops raided the place. I don't know all the details, but guns were drawn. Your father was shot."

"By the police?"

"I don't know."

"Was anyone else killed?"

"Not that I know of. But Mash is in jail."

Noah slumped back into his chair, began to cry. "Good. That's good."

Eben put his arms around his nephew, smelled sweat and grass, felt the boy's shoulders shaking. "I'm sorry, Noah. So very sorry."

Two days later as he entered the crowded sanctuary, all Eben could see was the open coffin on a stand in front of the two steps that led to the choir pews, the plain oak pulpit. He walked to the coffin, stood looking down at his brother. Oscar had tried over and over to grow a mustache. The straggly graying hairs on his upper lip brought Eben to the edge of tears, but he collected himself, took in a deep breath. He touched a cold hand. "Goodbye, Carman, gon see y'soon. You got that?"

He turned and took a seat next to Noah, slumped in a corner of the front pew. His nephew hadn't cried since he first heard of his father's death, but had been silent, withdrawn. Now he put his face against Eben's shoulder, took his arm.

The Reverend Dr. McMillan of the AME Zion, who'd offered to conduct the service today, nodded to him from a seat on the stage. The choir filed in, lined up facing the mourners as they sang, *"Precious Lord, take my hand, Lead me on, let me stand, I am tired, I am weak, I am worn." Yes,* he thought, *I am worn.*

Reverend McMillan opened the service, led the congregation in prayer, and spoke briefly of Oscar's life: the athlete, the father, the brother.

As the service proceeded, Ben Stone, who'd known both brothers since childhood, walked slowly to the front of the church, stood in the center of the top step, his hands folded in front of him, his long legs spread. "Oscar, Eben, and I—we fancied ourselves the three musketeers of Brooklyn, back when we sat side by side in the sixth grade at Myers Street Graded School in 1918. Oscar was two years older, but in the same class as we were because, as he put it, 'The teachers liked me, kept me back so they could have another year with me. Did that twice in fact.' " Scattered laughter.

"Carman, Neezer, and Benjy, those were our brands, our street names."

Eben remembered when Oscar had told him that Carman would be his brand, lying in the bed they shared in the shotgun house on Second Street. "Get it? Os-CAR, Carman. I'm gon have me a hot set of wheels, gon drive all the way to New York City in it, find me a fine lady there. 'Carman,' she gon say, 'take me for a ride.'"

In a few words Ben captured a man who few knew as well as he did. "Oscar Polk had a wild streak, but he also had a kindness that many in our neighborhood know from personal experience. After the fire swept through Brooklyn two years ago, Oscar helped clear the rubble, found beds for the homeless, worked in my store setting up a soup kitchen." Ben cleared his throat, touched his eyes with a Kleenex, looked at Eben and Noah. "And Oscar Polk loved his son Noah with all his heart.

"So I don't want to hear a word about his trouble with the law. We're gathered here to lay to rest a man who did the best he could, which is the most we can ask of anyone." In the hushed silence that followed his words, Ben returned to his seat.

Pricey Hubbell, another friend from childhood, rose with the choir, began to sing in a rich baritone, *"Deep river, my home is over Jordan. Deep river, Lord, I want to cross over into campground."* The choir joined in behind Pricey, and Eben finally let the tears fall that he'd been holding in since he'd stood next to Oscar's body in the morgue.

As the hymn came to a close, Reverend McMillan stood to lead the mourners in prayer. It felt so strange to Eben to be sitting in a pew looking up at another preacher at his pulpit.

Together Eben and Noah cleared out Oscar's small apartment. In the bedroom Eben folded a faded chenille bedspread he remembered from when they were boys, put it in a cardboard box. He looked around. "I can tell the Salvation Army to come get what's left. Is there anything else you want?"

Noah shook his head. "I got some sweaters, ties, couple of

suits. His trophies. He was a great football player." He held a framed photo of his mother.

"Coach said he was the best running back he'd ever seen."

Noah's face clouded. "There was a picture of Daddy in his football uniform, from the *Charlotte Post,* but I can't find it."

"It's in one of the boxes."

Noah smiled. "Good."

It only took two trips in Eben's car to remove everything that was left of Oscar Polk.

Eben opened his bedroom window, crawled into bed in the dim glow from a half-moon high in the sky. Faint music drifted in. Noah must be playing the transistor radio Eben had given him for Christmas. Should he go to him? Would Noah come to him if he got too sad? It was difficult to know how to help a sixteen-year-old, close to manhood but still a boy.

Eben and Nettie had loved lying in this bed on moonlit nights, talking. He spoke softly to her, "Well, old girl, looks like we've got us a son after all these years." A memory hit him of her climbing on top of him, kissing him, her face awash in the hazy light. "So we have," he was sure she said.

CHAPTER 31

Bibi is in Hawk's bed again. What makes her do that? Once or twice a week I come home to find her there, snoring. She sleeps through the day more and more lately, keeps us up at night. I'm thinking I should take her to see Dr. Wilkins, but she doesn't want to. "He gon poke me, say I got high blood, give me medicine."

Last week she told me something I didn't pay much attention to. "What that ringing?" she asked as we left church. I thought she meant the bell at St. Tim's. Then, couple blocks away she said, "Whistles, bells. Hear that ringing?" She stumbled.

I took her arm. "Bibi, you not feeling good?"

She stopped, her silver hair fuzzy around her wrinkled face, her brown eyes almost hidden by flaps of skin. "You gon get my hankies. Some of 'em was Bibi."

"Okay." Made no sense to me.

I push that memory from my mind, get a brown work shirt of Uncle Ray's, so worn it feels like Kleenex, perfect for a robe for Hawk to be a shepherd in the Christmas play. I'll fix him a beard from cotton balls and shoe polish. He can wear his sandals, hold a staff Uncle Ray's making from a cane. I get the shirt all laid out on the living room floor, long sleeves cut open, just enough material for a robe for Hawk, even as big as he's getting.

The wind's picking up, knocking the limbs of the magnolia against the roof. At work this morning I hear it's gon snow today. I go to the porch to check the temperature, and find it has started, blowing white across the yard. Only sound is the clacking of tree limbs already got ice on them. No birds. No cars. Uncle Ray's Esso thermometer say twenty-seven degrees. Sleet stings my face. A neighbor fetching the afternoon paper waves, "Got a regular blizzard coming, what I hear."

"I believe you're right."

He goes in his house.

Charlotte is not quite south enough for snow to be rare, and not quite north enough for it to be regular, but we get one or two snowfalls every winter, enough that folks get excited at a few flakes in the air. Every time the weatherman say it's coming, Bibi tells me about the heavy storm in 1940. "Snowed least a foot. You were three. Your daddy wrapped you up, took you out to build a snowman, then y'all went sliding down the hill over on Morrow." She has told me so many times I feel like I remember it.

I sit in the rocker, watching the grass turn white, wishing my daddy was here to take me and Hawk sliding on that hill, using the lid off the garbage can for a sled. Uncle Ray and I could go down there with Hawk when they get home. I smile thinking about it, sitting on the porch till my feet feel like they are frozen to the floor.

Inside I stand by the stove, warming myself, wondering do we need any groceries. There's milk in the refrigerator, fresh rolls I brought home from the S&W, eggs, butter. It's getting late for me to get to a grocery, but the snow coming down makes me feel like storing up on food. What I do instead is get back to the shepherd costume, cutting off the lapels from the shirtfront, saving the buttons.

I think about work while I sew pieces together. Mr. Griffin put me and Retta side by side this week, me on bread, her on dessert, knowing we friends. The hours fly by, us passing dishes to customers, greeting our regulars, talking about Becky and Hawk when the line is slow.

Uncle Ray comes in, Hawk behind him, dusted with snow, excited. "Guess what, Mama? No school tomorrow."

"It's a mess out there." Uncle Ray helps Hawk take off his coat.

I hold up the cloth, show it to Hawk. "Almost got you a shepherd robe."

He grins. "Yay!"

Uncle Ray ask, "Where's Bibi?"

"Sleeping in Hawk's bed."

"I'm gon wake her, time to start supper." He comes right back. "She's not there."

"Bathroom?"

He shakes his head. "Not in our room, either."

I can't think.

He gets his coat. "Maybe she went out back. I'll go look." The kitchen door opens and closes.

In our bedroom the sheets and covers from Hawk's bed are on the floor, his dresser drawers open, the clothes all tossed around, not neat like he keeps them. What was she doing? She's not in her bedroom, not in the shower. Her coat is hanging in the hall closet.

Uncle Ray comes back with our money jar. "This was in the yard, the lid off, cash still there. You seen my garden boots? They're not on the stoop."

I open the back door. The frigid air hits me. Bibi's out there in nothing but a nightgown.

"Sit tight," he say. "If I don't find her soon, we'll get help." He pats my shoulder. "She probably got it in her head to visit someone." He heads out.

Hawk has turned on the radio in the living room, singing to a song he likes about a magic dragon. Few minutes later he comes in the kitchen. "Where's Uncle Ray?"

I start putting away dishes. "Bibi's visiting someone and he's gon bring her home."

I don't think he buys that. "Can I bring my homework in here?"

"Sure." I open the refrigerator, take out collards and fatback, last night's leftover cornbread, a wedge of cheddar to make macaroni and cheese, Bibi's favorite. For the greens I cut up "the littlest bit of sweet onion," the way Bibi taught me, saying it was her grand's secret. When I wipe my eyes, I tell Hawk it's from cutting the onion, and I go to make his bed. One of the sheets is damp. Bibi must have stripped the bed because she wet herself. I gather them up and smell the urine along with a faint whiff of vanilla, which Bibi dots behind her ears after she bathes. Sugar cookies baking in the oven at the S&W always make me think of her.

I take the laundry to the kitchen. Uncle Ray is shaking snow off his hat, brushing it from his shoulders. His nose and cheeks are red.

Hawk say, "Where's Bibi?"

"I couldn't find her. Checked with neighbors up and down the street. Nobody's seen her."

Hawk stands up fast, his pencil hitting the floor. "Is she lost?"

Uncle Ray takes him by the shoulders. "She's out and we don't know where. We'll get help to look for her." Hawk buries his face in Uncle Ray's chest and they stand there, hugging each other.

I touch Uncle Ray's hand. "I'm gon call the police."

"Yes, I believe we should." He say to Hawk, "C'mon, boy, bring your homework to the living room, let me see what you're doing. Your mama's got to use the phone."

A man answers, "Police Department, Sergeant Hollins."

"My grandmother's missing." My voice breaks. "She's outside in her nightgown."

"Name, please."

"Livinia Hawkins. She's eighty-one and not well."

"No, *your* name."

I feel stupid. "Loraylee Hawkins."

"What's that? Lorelei?"

"Loraylee." I spell it.

"Phone number?"

I give it to him.

"Address?"

None of what he's asking for is going to find Bibi. "1105 Brown Street, Charlotte 2, North—"

"How long has she been missing?"

The kitchen clock say five-fifteen. I try to think when I saw her in Hawk's bed. "A couple of hours."

"Hold on." I hear men talking, a phone ringing, a typewriter. I wait and wait in the empty kitchen that smells of collards.

He comes back. "We got nothing on her. Can't do anything until she's missing for twenty-four hours. She'll be back soon, probably went to the store, didn't tell you."

"No, sir, not Bibi. She's off in her head."

"Call us tomorrow if she hasn't turned up."

He's not gon do anything. "Yes, sir, goodbye." I hang up before he can say another word.

I stand there in the empty kitchen wishing with all my heart that I could call Archie. Lately when I think of him he's always Archie, not Mr. Griffin, and sometimes I whisper his name out loud. There's not a single thing he could do about Bibi being gone, but if he was here, he'd hold me and let me cry.

There's a paper under a magnet on the side of the refrigerator. Not on the front, where we leave notes. Bibi's shaky writing: "Mess myself. L." The *L* is scrawled large, two wobbly loops. She use to have such a smooth hand

I stare at the note. "Uncle Ray!"

He comes in the kitchen fast, reads it. "Mess myself?"

"She wet Hawk's bed. That's what she means." I fold the paper over and over. "The police won't do anything till at least tomorrow. Oh, Lord."

"I'm calling Pastor Polk."

"Yes."

I go to the living room, sit down next to Hawk. The radio is playing a song I like. I listen to it, telling myself, she loves me, yeah, yeah, yeah.

Uncle Ray calls from the kitchen. "Pastor is going to get folks out to look for Livvie. I called Ben Stone, too. The macaroni's done."

Georgeanne Wilkins knocks on the front door as Hawk and I are finishing supper. "Eben Polk called me," she say, pulling off her boots. "My car was skidding all over." Her Buick is parked on the street.

Right behind Miss Wilkins is Hildie Stone, carrying pies in cardboard boxes. "One apple, one peach. They're real good, warmed up." She sticks the pies in the oven and pulls out a chair at the kitchen table. "Ben, the pastor, half a dozen men from the church are out talking to people, walking the streets."

The wind is howling, not at all the quiet snow we usually get.

Another knock at the door, and there's Veola Whitin, carrying a big pot of soup, Desmond behind her with a platter of cornbread. "Boyce is out with the men, and nothing would do but Desmond come over to be with Hawk. Y'all heard anything yet?"

I am glad to see Desmond. This is a hard night for Hawk. "Hey, Desmond." I give him a hug. "He's in the living room." Desmond runs from the kitchen.

Veola puts the soup pot on the stove. "Vegetable beef. Enough here for a couple of meals." We sit at the table with Mrs. Stone, and Miss Wilkins joins us. Here she is, caught in a snowstorm, and dressed uptown like. Necklace, earrings, a silk scarf at her neck. She ask, "When did you see Livinia last?"

I feel tears coming on. "I found her sleeping in Hawk's bed about three. When Uncle Ray and Hawk came home an hour later she was gone."

"How could she have left the house while you were here?"

I've been dreading that question. "I went out front to watch the snow, check the thermometer. She must have left by the kitchen door before I came back in." My legs shake against the table.

Mrs. Stone say, "You've had a time taking care of her. I know how bad her memory is."

The four of us sit while the wall clock ticks. Hildie tells us about a new magazine rack in the grocery store, and Miss Wilkins say she's got a student disrupting her classes. Veola and Boyce like Third Ward, but Desmond misses Hawk a lot. We talk about everything but the sleet clicking on the windows.

It's after ten when Uncle Ray comes through the front door, shivering, rubbing his hands, Preacher, Mr. Stone, and Boyce Whitin behind him. The icy air comes in with them. Mr. Stone looks at his wife, shaking his head.

They stamp their feet, brush snow from their coats.

Uncle Ray pulls off his hat. "We've been all over, got people on the lookout. Went up and down Plum and Long. She couldn't have gotten more than a couple of blocks, bad as it is out there, but we went all the way to Myers Street School, checked the tunnel, too."

"We're not giving up," Pastor Polk say, "We just needed to get warm, have something to eat, before we go back out." His nose is red, his eyes are lined with wrinkles, more gray in his hair than I've noticed before, but having him in our kitchen makes me feel better. He hasn't given up on Bibi.

Uncle Ray sits at the table. "We're gon check Watts and Morrow when we go back out, all the way to what's burned, then down by the creek."

I feel weak, thinking about Bibi slipping into Little Sugar.

Mr. Stone holds his hands in front of the stove. "Had to put chains on my tires. Streets are slick."

Mrs. Stone gets up. "There's macaroni and cheese, collards, a couple of pies. Veola brought soup and cornbread."

"Sounds good, thanks." Pastor sits at the table in his heavy coat.

I dish out some macaroni but I'm shaking so bad I spill it.

Uncle Ray takes the plate and spoon, puts them on the table, holds me close. I can smell the cold on him. Pastor gets up and puts his arms around both of us. "The Lord is with you. He is with Livinia, your Bibi."

At five in the morning Uncle Ray comes back. I'm in bed, finally. Hawk and Desmond are in Hawk's bed across the room, not knowing all that's happened during the night. Veola went to a neighbor's house, but let Desmond stay here. Miss Wilkins is on the sofa in the living room, Mrs. Stone's in Bibi's bed. I'm not asleep but I'm not awake, either. I'm seeing Bibi in my mind, wandering around in her nightgown, confused, asking me how to get home, saying she wants some breakfast, telling me—Uncle Ray touching my shoulder brings me back.

"We found her. She's alive." He sits on the edge of my bed. "A couple of hours ago. In the tunnel, glad we checked it again. Somebody had covered her with newspapers and cardboard. Lots of homeless in there, especially on such a night." He straightens, puts his hand on the small of his back, stretching. "We put her in Ben's car, didn't wait for an ambulance. Took her to Good Samaritan. They got her warmed up, but she hasn't come to yet. . . ."

"She going to die?"

His voice is weak. "Doctor said exposure, hypothermia, frostbite, things like that. She's got no fight left in her."

I can't imagine Bibi not fighting anymore.

"Pastor called the police to tell them about the other people sleeping in that tunnel, and he say they know. They know and not doing a thing."

Hawk rolls over, mumbles. "Did Bibi come home?" Desmond sits up beside him, rubbing his eyes.

Uncle Ray goes to Hawk. "We took her to the hospital to get her warm. Folks there are taking care of her."

Hawk sits up, leans against Uncle Ray, his voice muffled. "When will she come home?"

"Soon as she's better."

The power fails while we making breakfast, leaving the kitchen in shadows, the scrambled eggs not quite done. Uncle Ray goes to the living room to put more coal in the stove, taking the percolator with him to keep it warm. When he comes back I'm spreading jam on bread for Hawk and Desmond. "You need to get dressed, Loraylee," Uncle Ray say. "Go with me to the hospital. Hildie and Georgeanne can stay with the boys."

★ ★ ★

"Livinia Belle Glover Hawkins has left us." Pastor Polk's voice rings out from the pulpit. "She was Bibi to her family, Livvie to all who knew her during her eighty-one years on this earth. We gather to mourn her passing, to comfort her family, to share our memories of a woman who touched many of us."

We have always sat in a pew in the middle of the church. Now here I am, up front, feeling like all eyes are on us. Archie and Retta are on the last row. We were still in the vestibule, waiting to be seated, when they got here. Archie gave my hand a squeeze—quick enough not to be noticed—and they took seats in the back. I saw them again when we followed the usher to the front, and it was all I could do not to stop. I wanted to have Archie with me, wanted that so bad.

Uncle Ray put his arm around my waist as we walked toward the white casket covered with roses. Soon it would go in the hearse parked out front, then to the new cemetery off Beatties Ford, north of the interstate.

The casket is locked up tight. Bibi told me more than once to be sure her box was closed. "Don't want people gawking at me after I'm gone." She told me, "I want a white box with roses on it, and not just red. All colors of roses." The last few times she talked about it, she said for me to get Jonny No Age to do the flowers. I didn't remind her that he passed. With his shop gone, I had to call a florist over on Morehead, somebody I never knew about before. They said I was asking the impossible, so many different roses in the dead of winter, but when I explained the situation, a kind woman said she'd do her best. It was expensive, but it was worth it, and there they are: red, white, pink, lavender, and what Bibi would have loved the most, a bright orange.

She died with Uncle Ray and me beside her at Good

Samaritan. Never woke up again but she knew we were there. She squeezed my hand and her breathing stopped. We sat there quiet, Uncle Ray and me, letting her go.

A woman took us to an office where we signed papers. She gave me a bag. "These are her things." I couldn't think what she meant, then I saw Bibi's nightgown all folded up. Something heavy in the bottom of the bag. One of Uncle Ray's gardening boots. He tossed it in the waste basket.

We went to the elevator, stood side by side in the long hall, busy people passing us by. A baby cried somewhere way off.

"Livvie's soul has found a new home." Uncle Ray's eyes filled with tears. "Like I always say, death is birth."

Mr. Stone drove us away from Good Samaritan in the thin gray dusk, a few flakes still falling. Mrs. Stone was at our front door when we came up the steps. "She's gone?"

"Yes." The electricity was still off, but the living room was warm from the coal stove. I knew the rest of the house would be icy. "Where's Hawk?"

He came into the living room, his winter coat on over his pajamas.

I walked with him to the sofa.

"Bibi gone to heaven?"

"Yes." He let me hold him for a long time. He already knew.

On the way to church this morning he say, "Bibi won't be sleeping in my bed anymore."

"That's right."

"I didn't mind when she did. I like sleeping in her bed, behind the curtain, talking to Uncle Ray."

"You can do that when you want."

He was quiet for a few minutes. "I've been thinking about that. I want to move in with Uncle Ray."

"That'd be all right," I say and Uncle Ray say, "Fine by me."

Now he's between me and Uncle Ray in his Sunday suit that was too short until I let the hems out. The choir sings, "His Eye Is on the Sparrow." Bibi sang that hymn while she did dishes, mopped the floor, hung out the clothes. *"I sing because I'm happy. I sing because I'm free. His eye is on the sparrow, and I know he watches me."* I hum along until my throat closes up, the tears starting again. I've been crying most of the four days since she left us.

With Hawk snug by my side, Uncle Ray next to him, Grand and Pap in the pew behind us, I'm grateful I have family. During the service, Reverend Polk talks about Bibi, how she's been like a mother to me. Makes me think of Candy Shumaker Hawkins, who I wouldn't know if she walked in the door today. I favor her, at least in the one photo Grand gave me, taken right after I was born. In that picture Shushu is half turned, like she's fixing to run. Her head's tilted forward a bit, peeking at the camera from the corners of her eyes. Seemed to me she was saying, "You not gon get no picture of me." When she left me and Daddy, I was still on the breast. Bibi say I cried for a week. "You near about starve before I could get you to take a bottle."

Bibi was my mama.

CHAPTER 32

Persy followed the teardown of Brooklyn through stories in the morning and afternoon papers, occasionally buying copies of the *Mecklenburg Times* and the *Charlotte Post,* though she didn't share the latter with Blaire. It had been four years since she'd met Loraylee Hawkins and her son at the beach, but she still thought about them. The most recent article outlined Phase Four of the redevelopment, which included Brown Street, and which was scheduled to start soon.

Persy set aside an area in the attic, where Blaire almost never went, and began to collect newspapers, sturdy paper bags, anything that could be used to wrap a teacup or a drinking glass. At the hardware store she bought a retractable tape measure, a box of marking pens, rolls of twine, masking tape, and labels. She got cardboard boxes from dumpsters behind grocery stores, collapsed and stacked them. As further ideas occurred to her, she added to her stash: a can of Dutch cleanser, Pine Oil disinfectant—she loved the smell of it—rags, a scrub brush. She'd been through enough moves to know what was needed, the last in the winter of 1954, into this house, right before she'd found out she was pregnant again.

Several times over the next few weeks she drove to Brown Street. The houses in Loraylee's neighborhood began to empty, the windows blank, grass growing wild in untended yards. On one visit Persy had seen Hawk walking toward home, a book satchel in his hand, taller, but his hair still the rusty color she remembered so well.

In May another announcement appeared in the *Observer*: "Phase Four of the Brooklyn urban renewal project is underway. Forty acres bordered by Independence Boulevard, Ridge Street, Kenilworth Avenue, and South McDowell will be cleared in uptown Charlotte, making way for on-ramps to the new beltline. The Department of Transportation . . ." Persy stopped reading, pondered the term *uptown*. She asked Blaire about it.

He said, "Makes sense. The Square is on a hill."

"It's marketing. Uptown is posh; downtown is hayseed." She showed him a small article on page two. "Laird Carson is getting out."

Blaire glanced at the story. "Yeah, Jerry told me."

Carson, who'd tried to collect double on the forty-thousand-dollar lien, had been sentenced to three years in prison; the restraining order was lifted and the sale to the city went through.

"Did you know about the change in zoning, twenty years ago?" Persy asked Blaire.

"It was common knowledge."

"Yes, common among those who did it. Rezoning from residential to industrial doomed Brooklyn, long before those who lived there knew what was coming."

"Brooklyn has to go, Persy. You'll understand when you see the results, a revitalized downtown Charlotte."

Persy folded the newspaper and handed it to Blaire. "Uptown." She went to their bedroom to check the list of packing supplies she'd stored in the attic, made up her mind to carry out her plan tomorrow. There was nothing she could do to stop the bulldozers, but she could make a small difference for Loraylee and her family.

CHAPTER 33

"Misery is when you heard on the radio
that the neighborhood you live in is a slum
but you always thought it was home."

—Langston Hughes

Home will never again be 1105 Brown Street, Charlotte 2, North Carolina, where I was born in 1936, where Shushu left me when she went to Chicago, and where Bibi and Uncle Ray brought me up from a baby to the mother I am now. I'm glad Bibi never saw the day when the city say we got to move. She bought and paid for our home working forty years as a maid, but that came to nothing when the city say Brooklyn is blight. That which withers our hopes.

We get the check from the city, settle the taxes due on Brown Street, and have seven thousand dollars left to find a new place to live. Uncle Ray say he wish Bibi could know, proud as she was to have paid off the mortgage. With Archie's savings added in we have enough for a place north of the interstate, where folks might not mind us being mixed. But the first few we see are in neighborhoods that make me nervous, like eyes are studying us from the windows. Archie doesn't notice.

Day after day we go looking, hopeful, excited, but pretty soon I'm feeling like we never gon find anywhere we fit in. I have to keep reminding myself what Uncle Ray has told me time and again, "We can't know how a thing gon turn out."

If Hawk is with us and we stop at a place, he ask me every time if Desmond gon live close by. Those two boys have been together since they learned to crawl, and I tell him all of us are hoping for that. I talk with Veola every couple days.

Uncle Ray say his head's swimming from the possibilities, but mine's not because in three weeks of seeing first one, then another, not a single one is even close to what we need. Some we like are in all-white or all-black neighborhoods where one of us isn't welcome. Like yesterday. A woman called to us from the yard of a house next door to one we were considering.

"Hey." She beckoned Archie to come to her yard, talking loud, had to know I could hear every word. "You must be the Realtor." Before he could set her straight, she say, "Not that I have anything against nigras, but since you're in the business, you know how values go down when they move in." She gestured to us with a broom, started back sweeping while she talked. "We have lived here twenty years, got a lot invested in it."

He finally got a word in. "I'm not a Realtor. I'm with them. We're looking at the house with a mind to buying it." He walked back to us. She frowned, went into her house, shaking her head.

Hawk pulled me back toward the car. "This is not it," he say. That made Archie laugh.

We finally find a house Uncle Ray say he wants to live in. A duplex, like Auntie Violet's place at the beach. He looks around at the front yard, say to Hawk, "Could take out one of the hedges, plant a magnolia right there. Let's go to the back, see is there room for my roses and tomatoes, a swing for you. Maybe even a chicken coop."

Across the street a black man's on a ladder, cleaning the gutters. "He could be a hired man, or he could live there,"

Archie say. Then a colored woman comes out the front door carrying what look like a glass of tea, which she hands up to the man on the ladder.

Archie laughs. "Pretty clear they live there."

As run-down as it is, Archie is excited. "In a duplex I could live on one side and y'all on the other." I don't like this idea one bit and am about to tell him when he say, "We can cut a door in the living room wall, an archway that'll open up the breakfast nook, too, give us a dining room."

A thumping sound comes from the back of the house. Hawk's on the floor in one of the bedrooms, kicking the wall.

"What's wrong?" I say.

His face is a storm. "There's a bug in the bathtub. A big one."

Archie sits down next to him. "This place has been empty for a long time. We'll get rid of the bugs, don't you worry."

Hawk kicks the wall again. "I peed in the toilet, but it won't flush."

I have to bite my lip not to laugh. "I reckon the water's not on."

He wipes his nose with his sleeve. "Are we gon live here?"

Archie and I look at each other. "Maybe," I say. "It's the best place we've found."

"What about Desmond?"

"We working on that, his mama and daddy, too."

Hawk gets up. "I'm going out back. Uncle Ray's talking about a vegetable garden."

Archie and I walk to the living room where he pulls out the measuring tape he carries for house hunting, starts running it along the wall, jotting down numbers. "We could put an archway right here."

I'm starting to feel better about this house.

He say, "We could get married in Pennsylvania, did you know that?"

I shake my head meaning I didn't know that, but he takes it the wrong way.

"Is that a no?"

"No."

"So is it a yes?"

I nod. I can't talk.

He tips my face back, smiles his handsome smile. "It won't be legal in North Carolina, of course, but you and I will know."

The kitchen door slams. Hawk and Uncle Ray come in from the backyard. I find my voice. "We getting married."

Uncle Ray frowns. "Not around here."

Archie say, "No, sir, in Pennsylvania. I have a cousin lives in Allentown and we can stay there." He's been saying "sir" to Uncle Ray since they met. I can tell how much that pleases Uncle Ray.

Hawk ask, "Would that make you my daddy for real?"

"Yes, for real."

Hawk hasn't had much to say about Archie since we told him last month.

"Needs a lot of work," Archie say.

I've been knowing that. Peeling paint, weeds growing through cracks in the front walks, one of the back stoops sagging. There's brown rings in the toilets, stains on the kitchen counters. Makes me itch to get to work.

We don't have to check out the neighborhood, knowing one black family lives across the street, and we've seen a white man cutting grass in the next block. It's enough that the house has what we need and we can afford it.

Archie goes to the bank, and two weeks later we tell Ray and Hawk.

"We got us a place to live," I say.

Hawk ask, "The duplex?"

"That's right," say Archie. "You like it, don't you?"

"I like the backyard. Are we getting a swing?"

"Yes, we are, soon as we move in."

"Where's Desmond going to live?"

I'm ready for that question. "His mama and daddy are looking at a place not too far away, same school for certain."

"Yippee!"

I take a week of vacation to fix up the new house before we move in, and the more time I spend there the more I know how different this part of Charlotte is from Brooklyn. If I get hungry, there's nowhere nearby I can walk to for a soda or a sandwich. I can't look out the kitchen window and see Boyce Whitin working in his garden. There'll be no more parades on McDowell. Pastor Polk found a new home for St. Tim's, over near Smith, too far to walk.

There's not a soul I know in this neighborhood nor anywhere close by. The more I think about how far I am from what I've always known, the worse I feel. Archie comes to pick me up and finds me sitting on the back stoop, crying, a scrub brush in my hand.

"Sweetheart," he say as he comes through the kitchen door. "Whatever in the world is wrong?"

"We have made a big mistake." I see the confusion on his face but I can't stop. "I wanted a sandwich. You weren't here and there's no place I can walk to. Can't even go to church if you're working on Sunday mornings. What have we done?"

He sits on the step next to me, pulls me close. "I know, I know. I promise you it'll be better."

"Are you gon open a grocery on the next corner?" I sob into his shoulder. He can't promise me anything.

I wake to hear the screen door on the front porch scraping over and over. I get my robe on and walk barefoot to the living room. There's piles of stuff on the floor, the sofa, Uncle Ray's chair. "What's all this?"

Uncle Ray puts a bulging grocery bag on an end table. "Thought maybe you could tell me."

Hawk say, "Boxes and pens and tape." He calls to Uncle Ray, who's gone back out. "Where's the letter?"

Uncle Ray comes in, hands me an envelope: "To the Hawkins Family." I open it. "I hope this will make your move a little easier, and that your new home is as nice as your old one." It's signed, "A friend." I look in the envelope. Empty. "Who would do such a nice thing?"

Uncle Ray shoves aside a stack of boxes and sits on the sofa. "Beats me." He's tired, looks older than his seventy-six years. "Dozer showed up this morning, just sitting out there. Glad Livvie didn't see it, would have broken her heart."

He's not home the next day when men arrive with a chainsaw to take out the magnolia. Something goes wrong with the motor and they have to leave. They'll come back next week to finish. So the tree's still there, branches across the front walk. I get one of the last blooms, keep it in a bowl of water till it turns brown, then let it go.

We're gone before they come back for the magnolia, so Uncle Ray won't see it come down. If the house would of broken Bibi's heart, the tree would break his.

We moved a couple days ago, and I'm getting to know the new place. Don't think of it as home, not yet, but it does have some advantages, like two bathrooms, two yards, and two fireplaces, more room than I ever thought I'd have. No more mildew. Pretty curtains, wallpaper, new sinks and toilets. Archie's bookcases are along the wall on either side of the new door, full from top to bottom. The furnishings from Brown Street look tired here, but Archie say let's take one thing at a time.

We are close enough to walk to the new cemetery where Bibi is buried. After we finish unpacking, we go visit her, taking roses to put on her grave. This is the first time we've seen her marker: LIVINIA BELLE GLOVER HAWKINS, 1884–1965. OUR BIBI.

We head down the street toward home, Hawk and Archie in front, Uncle Ray and me walking along behind. Hawk's gon be tall like Archie, already my height and not quite twelve.

After supper Uncle Ray and I sit on one porch, Archie and Hawk on the other. I'm in the rocker from Brown Street, Uncle Ray in his straight chair, puffing on his pipe. The air is damp, a light rain falling.

A car comes down the street, slow. I close my eyes and listen to the swishing of tires on wet pavement. Sounds like Little Sugar.

Acknowledgments

For thirty-two years Laurel Goldman has helped me find my way through several novels; thanks to her and to members of our Thursday morning writing group: Mia Bray, Claire Locke, Betty Palmerton, Maureen Sladen, Cat Warren, Fabienne Worth, and the late Lucinda Paris. John Manuel, Carter Perry, and Eve Rizzo helped with early drafts.

My number one researcher is my number two child, Teresa Colleen Faw. Reesy brought me treasure-troves: the Brooklyn Oral History Project and the digital collections at the J. Murray Atkins Library, both at UNC-Charlotte. She also found an abundance of contemporaneous planning commission minutes and news stories on the "renewal"—read: destruction—of Brooklyn.

One book was a major resource: *Sorting Out the New South City: Race, Class, and Urban Development in Charlotte, 1875–1975*. My thanks to the author, Thomas W. Hanchett, PhD, who also gave me last-minute editorial assistance.

Roderick Kevin Donald, PhD—Tribal Archaeologist for the Colville Reservation in Washington State and family friend since he was a boy of sixteen—was a rich source of knowledge about old graveyards.

My appreciation to: Kelly Wooten, at Perkins Library, Duke University. Marilyn Schuster, at J. Murray Atkins Library at UNC-Charlotte. Leon Gill, for feedback that changed Loraylee's voice. Friends in Atlanta: Jackie and Jeffrey Tony, for help with courtroom details, and David Bottomly, for correcting an evidentiary scene. Brandon Lunsford, University Archivist, James B. Duke Memorial Library, Johnson C. Smith University. Shelia Bumgarner and Tom Cole, librarians at the Robinson-Spangler Carolina Room of Charlotte Mecklenburg Library. Dr. Vernon M. Herron, for his scholarship and a thick folder of documents about Brooklyn. Ellen Weig for help with researching urban renewal. Elizabeth Woodman, editor of Eno Publications, Hillsborough, NC, for including the first chapter of my novel in *27 Views of Charlotte: The Queen City in Prose & Poetry.* Pat French, who got Jean-Michel out of the house for countless hikes on Occoneechee Mountain. William Droegemueller, MD, who understood my need to be away from the green journal office on Thursday mornings for twelve years. My agent, Robert Guinsler, and my editor, John Scognamiglio, for their continued belief in me. Cliff Staton, for explaining writers' notes and relieving me of the burden of sticking to the facts. Friends at the Unitarian Universalist Congregation of Hillsborough for everlasting encouragement. Mickey Reed for bringing Shumi to chase balls outside my office window as I sweated blood over the final edits.

Kathryn Frye, an invaluable Charlotte contact, is active in preserving the history of Second Ward and Brooklyn; she introduced me to Vermelle Ely, Leon Gill, Vernon Herron, Vivian Ross Nivens, Ruth Sloane, and Robert Parks (who twice tolerated my presence at the Second Ward & West Charlotte Men's Breakfast Club). Kathryn also took me to the Charlotte Historic District Commission to meet with John Howard and Wanda Birmingham; I could not have written an accurate depiction of the old Brooklyn without their 1953 Sanborn maps.

J. R. McHone, dear friend, water brother, wherever you are now, your early encouragement enriched me. I will never not miss you.

My love and gratitude to Susan and George Devine, sister and brother-in-law, for Susie's great edits and for time-outs on Sugar Mountain. My family sustains me: Jackson Faw, Reese Faw (Chappy, Rainey, and Brian Hull), and Scott Pharr.

And, as always, Jean-Michel, husband, friend, mentor, editor, a man who knows how to make me laugh and knows intuitively when that's vital. Tu es ma lumière du soleil.

Please turn the page for a very special Q&A with Anna Jean Mayhew!

Q. What was the driving force that compelled you to write this novel?

A. I'm a native Charlottean; while I was aware that Brooklyn disappeared in the 1960s, it was decades before I realized the consequences of its destruction. (Similarly, when I was working on my first novel, *The Dry Grass of August,* things I witnessed as a teenager came to have a greater impact with time.)

As I looked into what had happened to those who lived in Brooklyn, I learned some hard facts about urban renewal. Yes, there was blight in that neighborhood. I have no way to disprove the statistics put out by the planning commission to justify destroying Brooklyn, but in numerous photos used by the commission at the time (1957–1967), I could find none depicting that it was also a thriving area of middle-class Blacks—doctors, lawyers, teachers, businesspeople. Yet such photos were available in other sources, and I relied heavily on interviews and oral histories of residents of Brooklyn.

In an exploration of the word *blight* I found two distinctly different meanings; in a 1936 edition of *Webster's Collegiate Dictionary, Fifth Edition,* the third definition is: "that which frustrates one's plans or withers one's hopes." Then, in 2017, the third definition is: "an ugly, neglected, or run-down condition of an urban area." It would seem that decades of urban renewal affected the dictionary.

Q. Was there a cemetery in Brooklyn that was demolished, with bodies dug up and moved to other graveyards?

A. No. Pinewood Cemetery for African Americans was established in 1853 near Fourth Ward in downtown (about a mile from Brooklyn); until 1969 a fence separated it from Elmwood Cemetery, which was Whites only. I found a story about a "lost" graveyard behind Myers Park Country Club in a wealthy area of Charlotte; human remains were discovered when foundations were dug for a new development in the mid-1980s, where an AME Zion church once stood. That led me to read about old graveyards—particularly those where slaves were buried—and to look into what would happen if a cemetery got in the way of urban renewal. I imagined a graveyard behind St. Timothy's, and for the purposes of the drama such a burial ground would create, I chose to fictionalize, to disregard the fact that there was no cemetery in Brooklyn.

Q. Did you know the Brooklyn neighborhood before urban renewal wiped it out?

A. Only slightly. When I was a girl, my mother took me with her when she got her shoes repaired by Reuben McKissick, whose shop was located at 419 E. Second St., where Tyler's Shoe Repair is in the novel. Mama often bought flowers from a woman who sold them in a street stall somewhere in Brooklyn. Daddy bought ice from an ice house on McDowell (the inspiration for Jackson's Ice House in *Dry Grass*), and I loved going there with him. My older sister and I went to several parades on McDowell Street. As detailed in the Brooklyn Area map at the front of the book, many places where things happen in the novel existed before urban renewal, such as Myers Street School, Queen City Pharmacy, Brevard Street Library, and the tunnel under Independence Blvd. Most of them are long gone, with notable exceptions like the Mecklenburg County Courthouse and Independence Square.

Q. Are you still in the same writing group you joined in 1987?

A. Yes, and without their support I doubt I would have finished either novel. Sometimes that support is what you'd expect, editorial, but they also give me the sort of therapy that comes with any long relationship. Recently, toward the conclusion of *Tomorrow's Bread,* I suffered a crisis of faith, a sort of "So what?" reaction whenever I thought about the book. The group didn't tell me not to feel that way; instead they reassured me that every writer—and I suppose every artist in any medium—feels that way at one time or another. My wise and wonderful colleagues saved the day again!

Q. Your first novel took eighteen years to write; how long did it take you to write this one?

A. I began working on it in about 2012 and finished in May 2017, so a little over five years. That's progress, I guess. I did find the second one to be a little easier to write.

Q. You're what, seventy-nine now? Are you working on a third novel?

A. Yes. No. Maybe.

A READING GROUP GUIDE

TOMORROW'S BREAD

Anna Jean Mayhew

ABOUT THIS GUIDE

The suggested questions are included to enhance your group's reading of Anna Jean Mayhew's *Tomorrow's Bread*!

DISCUSSION QUESTIONS

1. There are three narrative voices in *Tomorrow's Bread;* one is first person and the other two are third. Did the different narrative voices affect how you perceived the characters?
2. Many of the characters have a missing or absent parent. Why do you think the author chose such a family structure?
3. Because of laws against miscegenation, Loraylee had to conceal her relationship with Mr. Griffin, but why did she wait until Hawk was eleven to tell him about his father?
4. Senility in an aging relative is common for many of us. Was Bibi's progressive dotage accurately portrayed?
5. Which of the major characters—Loraylee, Eben, and Persy—was most important for you, and why?
6. The magnolia in the front yard of Loraylee's house on Brown Street weaves in and out of the story. What is the significance or symbolism of that tree?
7. Was it realistic for you that White patrons would have availed themselves of services like Tyler's Shoe Repair and Roberta Stokes, the seamstress?
8. When you first saw the title *Tomorrow's Bread,* what did it suggest? After reading the novel, does the title have a different meaning for you?
9. What was your favorite chapter?
10. Which character changed the most in the novel? The least?

11. If you had an opportunity to talk with one of the characters, which one would you choose?

12. Jonny No Age apparently is beaten to death because he's gay. Were you surprised that homosexuality was so disliked and feared in the 1960s? Do you think the same thing would happen today?

13. Was the conclusion of the novel believable? Satisfactory?

14. How do you imagine Loraylee and her family would be doing today, fifty-plus years later?